"What business is it of yours who I go out with? I'm thirty-two years old, Lucas, not fifteen, and you're not my father or my big brother or my boyfriend. I'm not some innocent little girl who's been locked away in a tower. I've been out with men on dates before, and yes, even men I didn't know well. Hell, I even lived with a man for two years who I'd hoped to marry until he showed me who he really was."

His face went white.

"Now I get we've been friends forever and up in each other's lives and business, but there's a line with any friendship and you're dangerously close to crossing it. I don't ask you who you're seeing or dating—"

"No one."

"—because it's none of my business. I don't know what's wrong with you, but you've been acting hinky lately, and until a minute ago, I was worried you were going through some kind of mental stress or close to a breakdown. Your father is living with you and making your life miserable; your son is caught in the crosshairs between the two of you; work stress. Whatever it is, you're not acting like yourself, and I've been worried. But right now I'm more pissed than worried, so before I say something I'm gonna regret or you say anything else that makes me even madder, I'm leaving."

Praise for Peggy Jaeger

"*DEARLY BELOVED* will take readers on a journey of a fairytale wedding, or rather a true wedding filled with family drama start to finish! Ms. Jaeger captures a beautiful sibling relationship that flourishes when the parents are not emotionally or physically available. Overall, the push and pull of the budding romance is delightfully written, and readers will enjoy this quick read that ties up with a red-bow ending!"

~*InD'Tale Magazine*

~*~

"A delightful start to what promises to be a winning series...with a myriad of moving parts...characters and their individual stories...that the author has seamlessly woven together into a story with emotions that will surely resonate with readers."

~*Netgalley*

Baked with Love

by

Peggy Jaeger

A Match Made in Heaven, Book 3

Baked with Love

Cover Art by *The Wild Rose Press, Inc.*

The Wild Rose Press, Inc.
PO Box 708
Adams Basin, NY 14410-0708
Visit us at www.thewildrosepress.com

Publishing History
First Champagne Rose Edition, 2020
Trade Paperback ISBN 978-1-5092-3419-6
Digital ISBN 978-1-5092-3420-2

A Match Made in Heaven, Book 3
Published in the United States of America

Dedication

To Erin and Mahen ~
An old Irish toast as you start your life together:

May you have warm words on a cold evening,
A full moon on a dark night,
And the road downhill all the way to your door.

Chapter 1

"Oh, my God, Maureen." My sister Colleen's voice rose a good two octaves from its normal sultry timbre. "Are those...*penis* pops?"

"Lower your voice," I told her as I continued to pipe buttercream roses on the cupcakes I'd made for tomorrow's wedding. "My entire inn doesn't need to know I've got those"—I grinned—"hardening in my kitchen."

"Why, in the name of all that's holy are there—" She counted out loud. "—seven chocolate candies in the shape of male genitalia on your counter?"

"Because your bride's maid of honor special ordered them for the attendants. I tried to talk her out of it, but she paid me triple to make them and wouldn't take no for an answer. Be happy there are only seven. She wanted one for each of the thirty females on the guest list. I was able to talk her out of it by promising to make those"—I pointed my chin toward the candy—"for the bridesmaids. She's going to present them tonight after the rehearsal. Thinks they'll be, quote, a scream, unquote."

My wedding planner and getting-bigger-by-the-second pregnant sister plopped down onto one of my kitchen chairs and sighed. Heavily.

"Oh, good Lord. Thanks for the heads-up. I'll make sure the moms are nowhere in sight when she gives

1

them out. I don't relish having to listen to one more complaint about this wedding. I've had enough for the past week to last me until Princess here"—she patted her round tummy—"is off to college."

I flicked her a glance and said, "Put your feet up, Coll. I can see how swollen they are from here."

With more effort than was probably warranted— she is after all, related to our grandmother, who corners the market on theatricality—she hefted her feet onto an opposing kitchen chair, then extended and flexed her toes a few times. This time her sigh was thick with fatigue and, if I wasn't mistaken, pain.

"I can't believe you're still wearing those ridiculous heels when you're almost nine months along," I chided. "Standing in them all day can't be good for the baby. Or your back."

"Stop scolding me." It was impossible not to miss the whine in her voice. "I refuse to take advice from someone who thinks flip-flops are the greatest invention known to the shoe-wearing population of the world. For the record, my back is fine and my feet don't hurt."

"No, they just look like flesh-colored water balloons."

"When did you turn so mean? You're usually the supportive, *quiet* sister."

In ordinary circumstances this was true. But with my ready-to-pop and three-inch-heel-wearing sister, I was more than willing to make an exception.

I piped the last rose on the final cupcake, laid my pastry bag down on the counter, and took a good look at her. Camera-ready face with her professionally polished outfit perfect and not a tendril of red hair out of place, the middle of my three sisters looked something she rarely did: tired. With her hands folded over her protruding belly, she'd dropped her chin to her chest and closed her eyes.

The snarky remark I was going to make about the benefits of wearing flats died before I gave it breath.

Since lunch service had finished a half hour ago and my serving staff was done with cleanup, Colleen and I were alone in my kitchen. I put the kettle on for tea and asked, "Did you have lunch?"

When she lifted her head, her eyes took a moment to clear before they focused on me, lending credence to the fact she was tired. And maybe more than simply tired.

"There's a salad waiting for me at the office. Charity got it for me while I was with the florist."

"Text her to put it in the fridge. I'll make you something to eat."

While she contacted her assistant, I plated the luncheon salad I'd concocted for today's menu, then put half a ham and cheese sandwich into my panini maker.

"Eat this until the sandwich is done." I handed her the salad and a bottled water.

"What is it?"

"Spinach, cranberries, walnuts, raisins, and carrots with a light pomegranate dressing and shaved Parmesan."

Colleen shoved a forkful in and groaned. "Oh. My. *God.* Honestly, Maureen, you should have your own cooking show. This is insane."

"Everything she makes is insane," a male voice said from the doorway.

3

It was a voice I knew well, since its owner was a frequent inhabitant of my dreams. Husky and deep, with a dash of just-woken gravel, it could cajole a lover into seduction or cut off a criminal at the knees.

Fortunately, I'd never been the latter. But I'd fantasized about being the former for years.

"Truth," Colleen said around a mouthful of salad. "Why are you here?" she asked Heaven's chief of police, Lucas Alexander, before I could. "Somebody call a cop?"

Lucas flicked his moss-green, heavily hooded eyes from my sister to me, one corner of his mouth tilting up. I actually had to contract my pelvic floor muscles whenever he looked at me so I wouldn't melt to the floor in a pool of want. My ninety-three-year-old grandmother, Nanny Fee, calls this *girding your loins*. As far as a descriptive phrase for the maneuver, it's a good one.

"You got a minute?" he asked me.

"A few. Then I have to get the dining room ready for tonight's rehearsal dinner." I pulled Colleen's sandwich from the press when the bell tinged. Lucas, always comfortable in my kitchen, moved to lean a hip against the counter and then halted midstride.

I knew the cause of his sudden stop and bit down on the inside of my cheek while I handed Colleen her plate. She caught my eye, and my stifled grin, and realized the cause. Her lips lifted, too.

Lucas cleared his throat. "Are those—? Wait. What, what are those? Are they…?"

"Are they what?" Colleen said, innocence dripping from her voice, at the same time I asked, "Want one?"

Lucas spun around to find the two of us staring at

4

him, our expressions blanked and waiting for him to answer.

He huffed out a breath and dragged a hand through his hair. "Never mind," he said, with a nervous shake of his head and shoulders.

Colleen glanced up at me, winked, and then took a huge bite of her panini. "Oh, good Lord, Mo."

I smiled and told her, "You're welcome," before I said to Lucas, "What's up?"

He cocked his head in a come-with-me move.

In the breezeway separating my private kitchen from the commercial one I use for the inn I own and cook in, Lucas stopped, bit down on a corner of his mouth, and twirled his hat in his hands. If I didn't know better, I'd think he was nervous, but nerves weren't an emotion common to this man. His army training had taught him how to remain calm in any crisis, cool under the most volatile of situations. I'd never even heard him raise his voice in all the years I'd known him.

I repeated my question.

"I need a favor."

I rolled my hand in a *go on* gesture.

"Cathy might have mentioned Robert's coming to spend a few weeks with me. Nora's getting remarried this weekend and then leaving on a long honeymoon."

I nodded. "I'd heard that, but not from Cathy." To the question in his eyes I said, "Nanny told me the other day when I dropped off her scone delivery at the nursing home. She heard it from Tillie Carlisle who got it from Maeve Capshaw, whose granddaughter, Olivia, told her. Nanny said Olivia was the one who introduced Nora to her intended at a divorced-and-looking event she'd hosted."

"Jesus." Lucas shook his head again. "Small towns."

I couldn't help but smile. "A curse and a blessing, as Cathy is fond of saying."

"Yeah, well, your sister is one of the smartest people I know. Anyway. Nora doesn't want to leave Robert home alone. He's too old for a babysitter, but at fifteen, still too young to be left to his own defenses. He just started driver's ed and doesn't have a valid license yet, so it was easier to take him while she's gone."

"So he's gonna stay with you and your dad until they get back?"

"Yeah."

"Why don't you sound happy? Whenever Robert's visited for school breaks before, you've always been thrilled since you don't get to see him as much since they moved."

He huffed out another breath and leaned a shoulder against the wall. My pregnant sister wasn't the only one who was tired.

"I'm not *not* happy he's coming to stay. It's more, things with Dad now aren't good, and I'm afraid he's gonna make the kid's life miserable with all his complaining and griping. Last time Robert came for a weekend, all Dad did was harp on him. Get a haircut, stand up straight, stop mumbling. Poor kid couldn't wait to get back to his mother, and that's saying something, because she's almost as bad. I don't want him to spend all his time with his grandfather while he's here, getting criticized for merely breathing."

"I'm assuming this is where the favor you need from me comes in?"

He nodded. "The kid needs something to occupy

6

him while he's here. I've gotta work, and I can't take any time off. I don't want him sitting home all day fighting with Dad or locked in his room playing video games. I want him to get out of the house. Get a job. You hire high school kids to bus tables and help serve. I'm hoping you'll take Robert on as summer crew. Then, I'll know where he is during the day, he'll earn a little money of his own, and I won't be concerned about coming home to World War III every night. Plus…"

"Plus?"

"Well, if he's with you I won't…worry about him. I know he'll be in good hands. You'll feed him and watch out for him like he was one of your own. Like you do everyone else."

To say I was thrilled by the offhand compliment was an understatement. Even if I wasn't on the lookout for extra help, I would have hired Lucas's son.

"Sure. I can always use another body, especially in the summer when I've got a full house every weekend from Colleen's wedding parties."

Lucas's shoulders dropped a couple of degrees from where they'd stationed themselves at his ears, and he let out a breath filled with relief. "Thanks, Maureen. Really."

I waved my hand at him. "Don't worry about it. When does he get here?"

"Sunday morning. Nora's dropping him off before she leaves for the airport."

I nodded. "Get him all unpacked and settled, and then you can bring him by Monday. I'll go over everything with him then, okay?"

"More than okay. Again, I can't thank you enough. You're truly a lifesaver." He took my hand and squeezed it. Lucas had done this hundreds of times over the years, and like every other time he had, the wiring in my heart went a little haywire.

And like every other time, I swallowed the temptation to tug on his hand and pull him close enough so I could kiss him.

"Any time okay?" He let my hand go.

I had to physically refrain myself from pulling it back. "After breakfast service would be good, so around ten-ish?"

He nodded. Whatever he was going to say was cut off by the beeper at his waistband blaring. "Sorry." A quick glance at it and he shoved his hat back on his head. "Duty calls." He grinned. "See you Monday."

I waited until he walked out the inn's front doors before going back to the kitchen. In all honesty, I needed a moment alone to center myself. Seeing Lucas, no matter when or where, always made my insides flutter, my toes tingle, and my heart beat faster.

From the time I was a kid, Lucas Alexander had been the only man I'd ever loved. Nine years older than me, he'd been my brother-in-law's best friend from the cradle and a part of our family since I was a baby. But the first time I'd ever spied him in his army uniform, I'd lost my heart forever. Cliché though it is, Lucas in a uniform had slayed me, even as a little girl. Twenty-plus years later, I still felt the same way whenever I saw him in his police attire.

And in his regular clothes, too.

Colleen was still in her chair, feet up, the plates in front of her now empty, and her chin kissing her chest again. I had to smile. This was the sister who defined the term *perpetual motion*. To see her actually napping during daylight hours was akin to seeing a leprechaun's pot o' gold. This pregnancy, her first at the age of thirty-seven, was weighing heavily on her and zapping the energy she was blessed with. I didn't have the heart to rouse her.

With as little noise as possible, I went about tidying the kitchen. The sharp ping of her cell phone signaling an incoming text ten minutes later called her slumber to an end.

She startled, blinked a few times, then tugged her phone from her pocket. No one I knew could type faster than my sister. A series of rapid-fire finger taps and then the *whoosh* of her text being sent filled the room.

"Did I fall asleep?" she asked, while she stretched her arms high above her head.

"Just for a few minutes. I'm betting this was the first time you've sat all day."

With another of those soul-weary sighs, she hefted her feet from the chair and stood. After a full body stretch, she said, "No rest for the wicked. Or wedding planners the day before a big wedding."

"Where are you off to now?"

"The church, the spa to check tomorrow's appointments, the printers to pick up the programs for the ceremony. Then back to the office for a conference call." She ticked each stop off on her fingers. "I can check off the rehearsal and reception right now. Everything set?"

"All taken care of. When you all get back from the rehearsal, I'll start service. Some of the non-bridal-party guests have already begun arriving. I had Janie put all the goodie-bags in their rooms this morning. The bridal suite is all set for tomorrow. I have the champagne in the cooler, and I'll put it in the room during the reception." I swiped a hand toward the cupcakes I'd been decorating when she arrived. "In lieu of the cake your bride didn't want, I've got the cupcakes she did all ready to go."

Colleen sighed and kissed my cheek. "I honestly don't know what I'd do without you."

"You'd survive, but you wouldn't get the family discount or the personal service-with-a-smile you're used to."

Her laugh warmed my heart.

"Before you go…" I moved to my industrial refrigerator, pulled out a bundle of aluminum foils, and put them in a shopping bag. "Here. Leftovers from yesterday for you and Slade. Now you don't have to cook tonight."

Colleen took the bag and then tugged me into her arms for a full body hug, not an easy accomplishment with her belly bump in the way.

"I simply adore you," she said, with another cheek kiss. "My husband does, as well. You take care of us better than anyone."

"I aim to please."

"Speaking of, what did Lucas want?"

I glared at her. "How did you take 'I am to please' and equate it with Lucas?"

"He's just another person in your realm who adores you and who you take care of."

I shook my head. "Okay, first? He adores my cooking, not me. And second? My realm? Really, Coll? You make me sound like some imperial and benevolent ruler."

"Benevolent for sure. I won't go so far as to call

you a ruler because then I'd be your subject and I'm older than you, so, no way."

Her laugh drew one from me.

"And as far as Lucas adoring your cooking and not you, they're one and the same, sis. Now, why was he here?" She held up the shopping bag. "To mooch one of these go-bags for him and his dad?"

She wasn't wrong in asking if I'd given him his own to take. More times than not, Lucas would stop by on his way home after a long day for a quick cup of coffee and a chat. He never left empty-handed if Sarah—my assistant—or I had anything to say about it.

I explained about Robert Alexander and the favor Lucas had asked me.

"Win-win for you," she said. "You get extra help, which I know you can always use, plus you get another person to take under your smother-love maternal wing and care for."

"What do you mean?"

"You know exactly what I mean, Maureen Angela Bernadette." She flapped her free hand in the air like she was waving a wand. "You may be the baby in our family, but you act more like a mother hen any day of the week. You cook for us, look out for us, heck, you even research solutions to problems like you did when Cathy's dog got sick, or when I was suffering through that awful early-stage morning sickness. Adding Lucas's son, a teenage boy who's probably got all the angst and raging emotions inherent in the breed under your wing, and I bet my secret stash of stress-candy, the kid's never gonna look at his own mother the same way again." She kissed my cheek one more time and said, "I've gotta go, so toodles. I'll see you later when I come back to escort the bridal party to the church. Thanks for lunch." She lifted the bag. "And dinner."

To her retreating back I said, "Just FYI, it's not such a secret stash. We all know where you keep it."

Her response was to toss me a backhanded wave as she went through the doors of the inn.

With my hands fisted on my hips, I shook my head.

So what if I tended to spoil the people I love? Make sure they got enough to eat? Always had a bed ready they could crash in, or a willing ear they could confide in? They deserved it. It was my humble opinion if more people showed how much they cared about one another, instead of simply tossing out an offhand *I love you* every now and again, people, in general, would be much happier.

If that was smothering, so be it.

Back in my kitchen, I washed Colleen's dishes, then reheated my cup of untouched tea. While I drank it, I planned the next few days in my head and went over the staffing I'd need for the busy weeks ahead of me. When I added Robert Alexander's name to my mental tally, it was his father's ruggedly handsome face that popped into my mind's eye.

The exhaustion I saw floating in his eyes was worrying. Having his aged and ailing father living with him was taking a toll on Lucas's mental well-being. Hogan Alexander cornered the market on the term *curmudgeon*. He'd been crabby and ill-tempered ever since I could remember. My grandmother claimed it was because his wife up and left him after sixteen years of marriage, saddling him with a teenage son Hogan didn't know how to relate to. The fact Lucas grew to such a wonderful man and upstanding citizen was one of the wonders of the modern world. Cursed with a father who doled out complaints instead of compliments and a mother who left to find herself at the age of forty, Lucas could so easily have gone to the dark side. Instead, he'd enlisted in the army with his best friend, served three tours, then come home to roost.

When his own marriage had gone south, Lucas didn't turn bitter as his father had but made every effort he could to be a good father to his son.

A quick glance at the wall clock and I stopped my woolgathering. I had to get the private dining room ready for Colleen's bride's rehearsal dinner. Before, though, I needed to wrap the chocolate pops and get them to the maid of honor. Remembering the look of confused horror on Lucas's face when he spied them brought a smile to my own.

But then, just thinking of him always did.

Chapter 2

"Almost everyone's checked out, Maureen. Want me to get the girls started on breaking down the rooms?"

I glanced up from the shopping list I was making to find Sarah, hands on her hips, peering down at me.

"That always sounds like you want to take a hammer to everything and smash it up instead of getting the sheets into the laundry and the rugs vacuumed."

My assistant grinned and shrugged.

I gave her the go-ahead to start cleaning the vacated rooms. Breakfast service had ended a few minutes ago, and my kitchen crew was busy getting everything ready for lunch. Mondays could typically be a slow day with leftover weekend guests departing and not many checking in. The first day of the workweek was also restocking day, and my shopping list was almost complete when I heard Sarah greet Lucas.

He popped into the kitchen a moment later, his son in tow.

Tall, like his father, give Robert a decade, and he'd be Lucas's clone. The same angular jaw, the identical thick eyebrows over those hooded lids and moss-at-midnight green eyes. I pitied the poor hearts of the girls in his age group when those gangly arms and shoulders filled out; he'd be a heartbreaker for sure.

"Hey," Lucas said, his typical greeting sounding a bit strained.

"Hey, back." I rose from my chair, a smile on my face as my gaze settled on Robert. The first time I'd ever seen him was the day he was baptized in our parish church. He'd been a quiet, calm baby during the ceremony, never crying when the holy oil and water had been dripped on his head. When I was a teenager, I'd babysat him on odd weekends when Lucas was home on leave from the army and he and Nora wanted a date night. He'd been an easy kid, still quiet and calm, and it took a lot of coaxing to pull a smile from him. But I always managed to.

Through the years following his parents' divorce, I'd caught glimpses of him when he'd come to visit Lucas, and he'd always treated me to one of his rare smiles.

Now, standing behind his father, his hands slung in his well-worn jeans' pockets, shoulders rounded, and his chin dropped to his chest, a curtain of thick black hair covered most of his face. I could hear Hogan Alexander's voice in my head admonishing him to get a haircut.

"Well, look at you." I scanned my gaze up and down the long and still-growing length of him. "I think you're a foot and a half taller since the last time I saw you at Christmas." Robert finally lifted his head. Those deep green eyes were tense and guarded. Maybe even a smidge wary.

I smiled and opened my arms. "Come give me a hug, Bobby-Boy." The use of the old nickname pulled his lips into a half grin that morphed to a full-fledged smile by the time he crossed the space between us and melted into my arms.

"Good lord," I said, patting his back. The top of my head grazed his chin. "You're not only a giant, you're a tank." I squeezed one of his upper arms. "Robert Langdon Alexander, you've been lifting."

A cocky grin, another feature he had in common with his father, spread across his face.

Yup, the boy was gonna fracture several hearts in the years to come.

"New gym coach. He's into weights."

His height wasn't the only change in him since the winter. His voice had taken on a decidedly deeper, masculine quality.

"Well, working for me will keep those muscles in good form," I said, letting him go. "You okay with this? Did your dad tell you what's involved?"

He shoved his hands back into his pockets, shrugged, and then gave a little head flick to swipe the hair out of his eyes after he nodded. "Grunt work."

I laughed and snuck a quick glance at Lucas. His brows were beetled, and his mouth tugged down at the corners. Before he could scold his son for his reply, I said, "Pretty much. But you get breakfast and lunch every day included, and you can be a taste tester for anything I'm baking. Still got your sweet tooth?"

His grin was fast and open, and he looked like a little boy who'd been told he was the sole owner of the keys to the candy store. "For your stuff, always."

I swatted his arm. "Flatterer. Okay, let's get you up to speed."

Lucas had watched the entire interplay between his son and me without saying a word.

"Come back by four," I told him. "We'll be done

by then."

Those deep green and heavily lashed eyes took a tiny sweep from my face down to my apron. Today's was a birthday gift from my oldest sister. Baby blue, with *My Kitchen Is My Happy Place* embroidered across the bodice.

One side of Lucas's mouth ticked up a bit when he read it. As always, whenever his attention was focused on me, a thousand butterflies flapped against my insides. My knees went a little soft, and I swear I could have stood there all day basking in his gaze.

"Well, we all know that's the truth." He lifted his chin to indicate my apron. To his son, he said, "Mind Maureen and do what she says, okay?"

The free and easy smile flew from Robert's face. He shrugged, then dropped his chin back to his chest. My heart went out to the boy.

"Can I talk to you a minute before I leave?" Lucas asked.

"There are some sugar cookies in the jar by the coffeemaker," I told Robert. "Help yourself. There's milk in the fridge. When I'm done with your dad, I'll give you a tour and get you set up, okay?"

I don't know if it was because the thought of eating my sugar cookies made him happy, or the fact his father was leaving, but the boy's smile returned.

I walked Lucas out to the front door.

"What's wrong?" I asked.

A sigh as cavernous as the Grand Canyon blew from between his lips. It took every ounce of will I could muster not to wrap my arms around him.

"Nothing, now that he's here with you. Yesterday, though, was...tough."

Peggy Jaeger

"With his mother?"

He shook his head. "Dad. Lit into the kid as soon as he was dropped off."

"About what?"

His laugh was short and caustic. "Pick a subject. Hair's too long, stand up straight, eat something, smile. Flashbacks hit me hard when I heard him. It was like I was fifteen again and having all that tossed at me instead of my son."

I was too young to remember when Lucas's mother had left, but according to things I'd heard over the years from Cathy and Nanny Fee—for whom the term *nosy parker* was invented—Hogan Alexander took her departure hard and made his son the brunt of many a tongue-lashing. The general consensus in my family was Lucas joined the army at eighteen to get out of the house and away from the verbal tirades he lived through daily.

"And I was no help cuz I got called out to a domestic disturbance and had to leave the two of them alone. Robert sequestered himself in his room until I got back, six hours later. He hadn't eaten or even come out to go to the bathroom because he didn't want to deal with his grandfather."

The worry and fatigue clouding his eyes had me wanting to give any comfort I could to shoo those clouds away.

"The old man's attitude is getting worse, and I really think it's because he's alone so much. With me at work all the time and none of his old cronies coming by to visit anymore, he's got to be lonely. He can't drive since the stroke, so he can't get out like he used to. You'd think having his one and only grandson come for

18

an extended visit would make him happy, give him something to look forward to. Unfortunately, no."

"You don't have Visiting Nurse come in anymore to help him?"

"He stopped them as soon as he was able to walk, unassisted. Told me he didn't want strangers in the house telling him what to do. It's not like I can force it on him."

"No, you can't. And I'm betting he wouldn't be willing to go live at Angelica Arms, would he?"

That acerbic laugh barked from him again. "Not in this lifetime. I've asked him a couple of times if he wanted to be admitted to the assisted living part where your grandmother is. His response is he's not gonna die in a nursing home filled with old people. The last time I broached the subject he threw a book at me. Conversation closed."

Which was a shame. If Hogan was admitted to the Arms, he'd be able to enjoy the company of people his own age, get waited on hand and foot by the staff—something Nanny loved—and Lucas wouldn't have to worry about him being left alone for so much of the day.

He glanced down at his watch. "Anyway, I've gotta go, but I wanted to tell you again how grateful I am Robert's with you." He wrapped one of his large hands around my upper arm and squeezed. Warmth seeped into my entire body. I wanted to pull his other hand around my waist and have him hold me close.

And possibly do more than just hold me.

"First time the kid's smiled since he got here was when he saw you," Lucas said, oblivious to my thoughts.

"We've always had fun together in the past. Don't worry about him," I managed to say. "I'll make sure he's okay."

"I know you will."

As if realizing for the first time where his hand was, Lucas took a quick glance at my arm, his hand around it, and then back up to my face. His head tilted a little to his left, and his brows drew together until a deep, solid line formed between them.

I held my breath while his gaze bounced between my eyes, searching for…something.

There have been so many times in my life I've regretted not telling Lucas how I felt about him. When I was a teenager, I couldn't because he was already an adult, married, and had a kid. How humiliating it would have been to divulge my crush to him then. After his divorce, years later, when I'd reached maturity and wasn't a skinny, shy, and quiet teenager anymore, it would have been easy to let him know. But I hadn't. At the time, my twin sister had been dying of breast cancer, a disease she was stricken with soon after we'd signed the ownership papers on the inn. All the times we'd been together over the years at weddings, funerals, when Nanny has needed bailing out (Don't ask. It would take too long to explain), even those times he dropped by for a chat and a cup of coffee after a long day, and I still hadn't made my feelings known.

Why? Well, that was the million-dollar question, wasn't it?

I could chock it up to opportunity lost, or my own deep-rooted anxieties about any man loving me. I was the twin sister no one noticed, the quiet one to Eileen's gregarious and outgoing personality. With her death, I was still considered the shy and retiring one, a situation I hadn't done anything to correct. I could even assign blame to the fact I thought Lucas and Cathy would get together after her husband died. They'd known each other forever and had been best friends for as long as I could remember. But my oldest sister had recently gotten engaged and her wedding was coming up in three weeks, so that excuse didn't fly anymore.

Right now, with his long, strong fingers circling my upper arm and his eyes zeroed in on mine, there were so many things I could say or do to let him know how I felt. Once again, I made the choice to do nothing.

With a curt nod, I took a step back, forcing Lucas to drop his hold.

"Well, we've both got things to do." I placed what I hoped wasn't a maniacal smile on my face. "You go keep the citizens of Heaven safe, and I'll put your son to work."

His eyebrows smashed together, the tiny wrinkles at the corners of his eyes fanning out and deepening. I understood his confusion.

"Maureen—"

I opened the door before he could say anything else. "See ya later, Lucas. Stay safe."

Talk about the bum's rush.

With one last questioning frown, he nodded, plopped his hat on his head, and left.

I took a moment to lean against the closed door and rub a hand across my midsection in a ridiculous attempt to quell those flapping butterflies.

****

"Holy crap." Robert fell into my kitchen chair, his long, lanky legs man-spread in front of him, his arms dangling, lifeless at his sides. "My entire body is sore, and I didn't even lift any weights. You work like this every day?"

I bit back a chuckle. Today's luncheon service had been a third what it usually was during a busy season like fall, or leaf-peeping season as native New Hampshirites referred to it. And since it was a Monday, I could shave even a few more guests off the list.

"Honestly, Bobby-Boy, what you just worked through was nothing. Wait until this weekend. I've got one of Colleen's weddings taking place here, and the guest list is around two hundred for the reception."

Half-dollar coins were smaller than the size his eyes widened to.

I let out the laugh I'd been holding back. "Now you understand why I feed you breakfast and lunch."

"Yeah. Gotta keep the strength up. I get it." His eyes took a slow stroll to my cookie jar.

"Go ahead and grab a few," I told him, adding, "if you can move."

Suddenly, his fatigue joined the plight of the dinosaurs and went extinct. A handful of cookies later, combined with the huge glass of milk I poured him, and the sugar rush did wonders to perk him up.

"So what do you do next?" he asked.

"I start planning and cooking for tomorrow. Sometimes I bake. Since I'm doing the cake for this weekend's wedding, I'll be starting it on Wednesday, decorating it whenever I can get some time until Friday."

"What can I do?"

"For now, why don't you come to the market with me and help me get supplies? You can be my muscle and help me carry everything, and we can talk about your hours and where you see yourself while you're with me."

"What do you mean?"

I pulled off my apron and hung it on a peg by the pantry door. "Follow me."

I told Sarah I was leaving for a bit.

"You can choose from housekeeping or staying on kitchen and serving duty, or you can work in the laundry. I need bodies in all those spots," I told him once we were in my car. "Each section has its own daily duties, and you'll report to either Sarah or me."

While I drove, I brought him up to speed on the requirements for each section of the inn.

"I have a regular staff who work year-round," I told him when he grabbed a shopping cart. "But every weekend, I bump the body count up because I'm usually full and I've got a wedding reception booked. Extra servers are always appreciated, as I'm sure your dad told you. Summer months, though, I like to have extra hands during the week as well because we tend to get a lot of vacationers stopping over for a night or two during their travels. Plus, the Chamber of Commerce has a weekly business breakfast booked at the inn, and the Rotary meets every week for lunch. A couple of local ladies' groups come in once a month for lunch in addition to the library's book club."

"I never knew you were so busy. I figured you just"—he shrugged as he followed me with the cart—"served a few meals and made the beds every day."

Nodding, I pulled out my shopping list. "There's more to running an inn than merely cooking and changing the sheets."

"No kidding," he mumbled.

My older sister, Cathleen, is fond of saying living in a small town is a blessing and a curse. A blessing because you know almost everyone you meet on the street, at church, or in the local market. And there's the curse of it too because you know *everyone* you meet on the street, at church, and in the market. A routine twenty-minute shopping trip took an entire hour because so many people stopped us to chat. Well, to chat with Robert, really. Until he'd moved with his mother to the next town over four years ago, Robert had been a fixture in the town. As the only child of the chief of police, he was as well-known to the community as Lucas himself. In every aisle, we were stopped by at least one—sometimes two or three—people who asked after his mother's health, grilled him about her new husband, questioned how he was doing in school, his plans for college, and in a few cases tossed me a nosy glare and inquired why he was with me and not his father.

Having grown up in this small, insular community with a well-known and respected father, Robert was an expert in the art of dealing with the busybodies and their intrusive questions. Not that they meant to be intrusive. No, the people of Heaven generally cared about each other and were truly invested in one another's well-being. It didn't stop gossip from rearing its ugly head at times, though, so I was quick to explain why Robert was accompanying me on my usual Monday afternoon shopping trek.

Once we'd finally gotten through the checkout line and had all the groceries I needed for the week packed in the trunk of my car, Robert let go with a laugh jumping between comic and tragic.

"I don't think I've talked to so many people or answered so many questions since before we moved."

I pulled out onto the main road. "They don't mean to be so…" I lifted a shoulder.

"Nosy? Snoopy? Gossipy?"

This time it was my laughter filling the cab. "You should be a writer. Cathy's hubby-to-be is one. I'm sure if you asked him he'd give you some advice on where to put your verbal skills."

His open smile was quick and boyish and reminded me so much of his father my hands gripped the steering wheel a little harder than was necessary.

Back at the inn, we found a visitor waiting in my kitchen, sipping tea.

"Hey." I put one of the grocery bags down on the counter and kissed my oldest sister's cheek. "I was just talking about you. What are you doing here?"

Cathleen stood and, ignoring my questions, opened her arms, a cheek-wide smile on her face.

"Hey, Aunt Cathy." Robert melted into her embrace, returning it with a full hug.

"I saw your dad in court this morning," she told him, as she kissed his cheek, "and he mentioned you were working for Mo. You getting all settled in?"

He pulled out of her arms and rocked back on his sneakered feet. With a nod he told her, "Yeah."

"How's your mom?"

They spent a few minutes chatting, with Robert giving her details about the wedding and his new stepfather, while I put my apron back on and went about storing the groceries away.

My oldest sister and Lucas had been friends since

both of them were eight and in my grandmother's Communion preparation class. Lucas had been Cathy's late husband Danny's best bud from birth, and the three of them were a unit until both Lucas and Danny enlisted in the army on the same day. Lucas had come home after three tours to live his life with his wife and baby son. Danny Mulvaney had decided to make the army his forever-life and had subsequently given his life to the job. When Robert was born, Cathy had gladly accepted the official role of godmother to him.

"Well, since you'll be here for a few weeks, I'll get to see you a lot more often than I have since you guys moved. Plus"—she ruffled his hair—"you can come to my wedding."

Robert shot me a quizzical look from under the fringe of his bangs.

"What?" Cathy squinted from him to me and back again. "You're not making him work on the day I get married, Maureen. He's my godson."

"I had no intention of doing so. I've already got a crew scheduled for your big day."

Cathy hugged Robert again. "Good. I want to dance with my favorite guy here, and I don't want him forced to wear an apron when I do."

The look of horror sailing across Robert's face had me biting back a laugh.

"Okay." Cathy let him go and focused back on me. "Second reason I'm here. Nanny's birthday party this Sunday. We all good to go?"

"All I have left to do is make the cake. She's called me every day for the past week to remind me how much she loves chocolate."

"Anyone who knows her knows that." Cathy rolled

her eyes. "Colleen will bring her since she'll be here seeing her bride and groom off before they leave for their honeymoon."

"The bride and her party should be pretty much gone by the time you guys arrive. Most of them requested early checkout. I figured we'd have the party in the morning room. It's intimate and sunny, and Nanny can hold court there easily."

"Nanny can hold court anywhere as long as someone's paying attention to her." To Robert, she said, "You, your dad, and granddad are invited, too."

He nodded and then flicked his head to swish his hair out of his eyes.

"Okay, well, I've got to get back to the office. I've got a few meetings scheduled this afternoon." She dragged Robert back into a fierce hug again. "I'm so happy you're staying for a bit."

Before she left, I handed her a shopping bag, as I had to Colleen. "Left-over fried chicken and macaroni and cheese. I know how much Mac likes them."

"Loves, not likes. You're spoiling him, Mo."

I waved a careless hand at her. Who better than to spoil but the people you loved? "And here. I made these for Georgie." I handed her a tin of organic doggie snacks from a recipe I'd pulled off Google. "Maybe she'll like these better than your shoes."

"Oh, Lord. Your mouth to God's ears."

"Who's Georgie?" Robert asked.

"My new dog-niece," I said.

"George…died. Over the winter." Cathy's expression saddened as she explained how her fifteen-year-old Labrador had finally succumbed to age and illness.

"I'm sorry," Robert told her. "George was a great dog."

Cathy nodded. "Mac and I adopted a new Lab, and we named her Georgie. She's six months old and a terror."

"And by terror," I said, "she means the puppy is into everything."

"No lie. Mac and I have taken to putting our shoes on the top shelves of all our closets. Her favorite thing in the world is chewing and eating Mac's sneakers."

"Cool. I mean, not cool about the sneakers, but cool you got a puppy. Can I come over sometime and meet her?"

"I'll talk to your dad and make a date for you guys to come for dinner soon."

With a quick kiss for him and then me, and our typical *Love you, Love you more* goodbye, she was off.

"Georgie really is adorable," I told him. "But a stint in puppy school wouldn't hurt."

"I wish we could have a dog." He slung his hands back into his jeans and rested back against the counter. "Mom is allergic, though, and Dad works so much he says he can't be responsible for one more thing."

The wistfulness in his voice, etched by sadness, tore my heart.

"Come on," I told him, pointing to a chair. "Let's get your hours and duties settled. Then you can help me figure out what to make for lunch tomorrow."

An hour later, Lucas walked into the kitchen.

"You're early."

"There was a sudden lull in criminal activity in the area."

I laughed while Robert mumbled, "Lame, Dad."

"How'd everything go?" Lucas accepted the cup of coffee I poured for him and, as his son had earlier, leaned a hip against my kitchen counter.

He'd addressed his question to me.

"Good. What do you think?" I asked Robert.

"Yeah. Cool."

"That's it? Just *cool?* Can't you elaborate a little for your old man?"

Before his father arrived, Robert had been sitting with his elbows resting on the table, going over the list I'd given him, an open, free grin on his face as he read through the kitchen duties I'd assigned him.

Now, he was tense and nervous. He was sitting up straight, had his hands folded in his lap, his face blank, his chin grazing his chest.

As Lucas drank his coffee, I noted his posture wasn't as relaxed as it came off. His shoulders were settled halfway up to his ears, and his eyes were watchful as they rested on his son, the two corners of his mouth pulling inward a bit.

Tension rose from these two like steam from a hot spring on winter's day.

It didn't take a genius to understand the cause, and my heart went out to both of them.

I caught Lucas's eye, tilted my head toward his son, and opened my eyes a little wider.

He caught my meaning and had the grace to look uncomfortable. As he cleared his throat, he moved to the table. After pulling out a chair and sitting, he lifted the list and examined it.

"You're working alongside Maureen in the kitchen?" he asked.

Robert lifted a shoulder and kept his attention on

his lap.

"That's great, son."

The teen's mouth fell open at the exuberance in Lucas's voice.

"You gonna teach him how to cook like you do?" Lucas asked me. "Cuz if she does," he said to his son before I could answer, "I'm volunteering to be your taster for life. No one cooks as good as Maureen."

Those chronic Lucas-induced butterflies were flapping so hard against my stomach I snuck a peek downward to make sure they couldn't be seen ramming against my apron.

Turning his attention back to me, Lucas asked, "Are you gonna let him bring home, like, samples of stuff you teach him to make? Or give him baking homework?"

Robert dropped his chin again and mumbled, "Geez, Dad."

"How old are you, Lucas Alexander?" I asked in a Nanny-Fee-worthy tone while I was secretly more pleased than decency warranted. "Cuz you sound like you're four."

"Old enough to know a good thing when I hear it. Or taste it." His grin turned boyish, Robert's finally following suit. A sight-impaired person would have been able to see they were related with just that smile for evidence. "Speaking of, you do any baking today?" His expression was so hopeful I was unable to pull back a laugh.

Shaking my head, I pulled the cookie tin over to the table and lifted the lid. "Yesterday's leftover cookies. Beggars can't be choosey. You'll get what I have available, and you'll be happy about it."

"I'd be happy with cookies from last week if you were the one who baked them." He snaked his hand into the jar and pulled out a good half dozen with his fist, placing them on the dish I set before him.

"Share," I commanded, thrusting my chin to his son.

"Yes, ma'am."

Lucas divided the cookies between them.

Father and son chatted while they ate, Lucas reaching into the jar several times to replenish the pile. They talked about the duties Robert would have and the schedule I'd come up with. I hadn't thought a teenage boy would want to be stuck indoors and in a kitchen with me every day of his summer vacation, and I'd wanted to build in some free time for him to do what he wanted, even if it was simply while away the hours playing video games at his dad's.

Robert, though, had another idea. He didn't mind coming to the inn every day or working wherever I needed him, not only in the kitchen. It dawned on me he was probably either lonely, missing his friends from home, or didn't want to incur the wrath of his grumpy grandfather. Maybe even a combination of all three.

"What time do you need me to drop him off in the mornings?" Lucas asked when they'd eaten and drunk their fill. Robert excused himself to use the bathroom before they left. "I know you start breakfast service pretty early. I can have him here whenever you want."

"Lunch is usually busier than breakfast because the service time is shorter, so I'm good for early shift. If you can have him here by seven or seven fifteen every day, it'd be fine. Pick him up any time after three."

Lucas nodded. "He seems pretty stoked about

working, something I'm surprised about. Glad, for sure, but surprised. I figured…" He shrugged.

"I know. I thought a fifteen-year-old boy would rather be any place than in a kitchen every day, but he actually asked to work most days during the week and on weekends for the weddings. We'll see how long this enthusiasm lasts." I grinned up at him while I towel-dried a mug.

"I don't know, Mo. If it was me, I wouldn't mind being stuck in a kitchen every day—"

"That's because you're always hungry."

"—if it was with you."

My hand stopped rubbing the porcelain.

Okay, what?

I'm usually fairly adept at not showing my feelings or have what's running through my mind cross my face. Nanny has commented many times over the years I'm the person she least likes playing poker with because she can't *read* me. The ability to hide my true feelings has gotten me through some testy times with my parents, a bad breakup with a verbally abusive boyfriend, and my twin's illness then death. Plus, for as many times as we'd been together over the years, Lucas had never once guessed how I truly felt about him.

Right now, though, I was finding it next to impossible to school my features and body into its usual calm nonchalance. I can only imagine how I must have appeared to him, standing there with the towel thrust into the mug, my hand paralyzed—my body as well— as I stared up at him, silent.

"What's wrong?" He uncrossed his arms and took a step toward me, his brows grooving toward the middle of his forehead. "Maureen?"

I blinked a few times when his hand snaked around my upper arm. A soothing, comforting warmth seeped through me from his touch. I wanted to move in closer, melt into his arms, and snuggle into all his heat. When I found myself shifting so I could, I took a step backward, mentally and physically. Lucas didn't drop his hold but kept his hand on my arm, his other one following suit.

"Nothing. Sorry. I'm fine." I shook my head a few times and planted what I hoped looked like a self-deprecating grin on my face.

"I lost you there for a second." His gaze swept across my face, searching, silently questioning.

"Sorry. I've got a lot going on up here." I pointed a finger at my head. "Thinking fifteen steps ahead about what needs to be done around this place."

He waited a beat, those intelligent, intense eyes never wavering from my own. "Why don't I believe that's all it is?"

It was no wonder he was such a good lawman. With his gaze zeroed in on me, piercing and probing, and his voice low, deep, and commanding, almost seductively sly in its cadence, I imagined people who'd broken the law were no match for him when it came to his garnering confessions.

I pulled a Colleen-worthy eye roll. "Because you're a cop and you're naturally suspicious. It's ground into your DNA. Like the green in your eyes."

One eyebrow quirked high up on his forehead. "The green in my eyes?"

His mouth stayed perfectly straight, but I got the distinct impression he was laughing at me.

"It's true. Your eyes are green, and you're

naturally nosy."

His inspection grew more intense as he dipped his chin and glared at me. The heat in his stare shot straight down to my core and exploded. I'm pretty sure I shuddered.

Lucas's fingers kneaded my arms. Every nerve ending in my body stood straight up, like I'd walked across a rug in the dead of winter and then touched something metal, sparking an electric shock. I licked lips that had suddenly gone desert-dry.

His gaze took a slow stroll down to my mouth and lingered. Enough so those butterflies finally made a break for freedom. Without any will to prevent it, my mouth fell open and I dragged in about a quart of air, my shoulders lifting, then dropping with the effort. I lost the grip on the mug and when it slipped out of my hand, Lucas let go of my arms as we both reached for it at the same time.

My reflexes are quick. Lucas's are like lightning.

Both our hands went around the cup at the same time, but in moving for it, Lucas had to bend from his substantial height. When he did, our heads connected and a resounding *thwack* echoed around us.

"*Ow.*" I let the mug go free into his hand and palmed the spot of contact on my forehead. "Your skull's made of cement."

Lucas placed the mug on the counter, then tugged my hand off my head.

I swatted him away. It was like slicing air because it had no effect on halting him from touching me.

"Let me see. Stop squirming." He cupped my chin to hold me in place.

In all honesty, I'd gone statue-still again the

moment his hand curled around my jaw. I knew Lucas's fingers were strong, an effect of being a life-long shooter. Thick-skinned, coarse, and powerful, his grip was surprising gentle though, as he held my face in one hand and pressed against the throbbing notch on my forehead with the other.

"You're gonna have a goose egg."

"And whose fault is that?" I mumbled.

"Better get some ice on it, fast."

This time when I glanced up at him, he was attempting—and failing—to hide a grin.

Through narrowed eyes, I said, "Thanks for the advice. Mind letting go of me so I can?"

Lucas glanced at the hand wrapped around my chin, frowned, then drew his attention back up to meet my eyes.

Calling them green hadn't done them a bit of justice. There are so many variations of the simple color, and none of them applied to Lucas.

They weren't the bright green of a shamrock or the metallic sheen of jade. Neither were they pale like sage nor brilliant like winking emeralds. The purest and most accurate way to describe them was they mimicked the color of fresh moss at midnight: deep and dark with shards of yellow in the mix reflected in moonlight. Long lashed with a tiny tilt at the corners and subtle lines fanning out to his temples, Lucas's eyes had always been captivating to me. Right now, with his hand holding my chin, and his body so close I could detect the brand of soap he'd used in the shower, they were mesmerizing.

The air between us changed in a finger snap. Energized. *Ignited.*

Something in Lucas changed, as well. His shoulders were drawn up almost to his ears, and his breathing went a little deeper, a little louder as we stood there. The groove between his eyebrows folded inward even more than it usually did. When his tongue flicked out and crossed over his bottom lip like mine had a few moments ago, I bit down on the need to press my own mouth to his.

I may have moaned.

The swift inhale Lucas took convinced me he'd heard the sound and recognized it for the naked desire it was. The hand at my chin tensed and drew me in closer. So close, I could count every hair of the afternoon stubble shading his etched cheeks and strong jaw.

An insane urge to run my tongue along the length of that shadow hopscotched through me. I might have succumbed to the impulse if Robert's voice hadn't spilt into the room.

"Dad?"

We both blinked at the sound.

"What's going on?"

"Maureen dropped a cup," Lucas told him after a moment, his attention never wavering from me. His voice was thick and low. "We bumped heads when we went to get it. Grab some ice from the freezer, would ya, son?"

"There's a cold pack in there," I said, stepping back when Lucas finally freed his hold on me.

He stood, immobile and silent, in front of me while his son set about his task.

I'd give anything to know what he was thinking, but his expression had gone back to its usual relaxed one. His body, though, remained stiff and tense.

Robert handed me the cold pack and said, "Here." When he glanced at my forehead, he added, "Ouch. Dad, you hurt her."

"It's nothing," I said, wrapping the pack in the dishtowel I still held in one hand. I placed it against the throbbing ache I now felt on my head and winced. "Okay, ouch is right. But it was an accident, Bobby-Boy."

I wanted to alleviate the troubled expression on his face, so I added, lifting my lips in what I hoped was a comical smirk, "Your father's got a head like a rock. No surprise, there."

My quip hit its intended mark as both of the men in my kitchen grinned. Lucas's shoulders finally relaxed, and the ghost of a sigh slid from him.

They left shortly thereafter with Lucas promising to have his son to work on time in the morning.

Chapter 3

"Do you think I could learn to do that?" Robert asked with a chin thrust to the layered cake I was putting the final touches on for the weekend's wedding.

He'd made it to Friday without any mishaps, problems, or one single complaint. I don't know who was more impressed: his father, me, or Robert himself. He'd been upbeat every day when Lucas dropped him off, worked at whatever job I assigned him, which was mostly bussing tables from breakfast, serving and then bussing at lunch, and cleaning and sweeping up after both meals, and not much more. The days had gone swiftly by, and before I could take a few minutes to give him some cooking instructions, his father showed back up to bring him home.

The awkward moment in the kitchen wasn't mentioned by either Lucas or me, although I would have given anything to know what he'd been thinking that day.

"Of course you can." I piped the final flourish on the third and top tier and said, "Help me get this into the walk-in fridge. I've got some free time until I need to start cooking for the rehearsal dinner, so I can show you a few things."

"Cool."

Back in my kitchen, I pulled out a tray of cupcakes I'd made the night before when I couldn't sleep. Baking always helped me wind down, and somewhere after the third batch was cooling on a wire rack, I'd been able to put my head back down on the pillow and catch a few hours of rest.

My piping bags were still full, so I figured we could use them.

"I need you to do something for me, first, though," I told him while he washed his hands.

" 'Kay."

"Since this kitchen is used for commercial food prep, there's a laundry list of rules I need to abide by from the state to keep my license to serve valid. One of them concerns hair."

Robert cocked his head at me, swishing his fringe out of the way when he did.

"You probably noticed Sarah, all the girls who work here, and I keep our hair pulled back in ponytails, or if it's short, like Jill's, back from their faces with a headband."

"Yeah. So?"

I reached into one of my counter drawers and pulled out a hairnet and an elastic band. I showed them to him and said, "You've got three options, one of which we can't deal with today. You'll either need to cut your hair short enough so it doesn't keep falling in your face, wear a hairnet over it when we're dealing with food, or pull it up in a bun. Up to you, but the easiest option is to cut it."

He stared at me for a few beats. In all truth, from the way his mouth fell open and then slammed shut, to the way he started blinking like he was delivering some kind of Morse code, I figured he was going to tell me to forget the whole thing. Teenaged boys are as vain about their hair as girls are. I knew he wasn't about to cut it, the thought of wearing a hairnet to keep it contained probably made him nauseous, and let's be honest, not every guy can rock a man-bun.

It was hard to hide my surprise when he tilted his head, then said, "Okay. I'll get Dad to take me to get it cut. For now"—he reached out a hand and took the elastic band I held—"I'll pull it all back. Okay?"

"Fine." I turned away so he couldn't see how he'd shocked me.

I washed my hands as he'd done and then pulled out a baking sheet and put a piece of parchment paper on it.

Handing him one of the bags, I said, "I'll teach you some simple basics first, on this. When you feel comfortable with the maneuvers, you can try them on a cupcake."

"Don't you need those for an event or something?"

I grinned at him. "Nope. These are totally for my own pleasure."

His eyes widened when they drifted over the three dozen I'd pulled from the fridge.

For the next hour, I taught him the basics: how to hold the pastry bag and the right amount of pressure to exert to get the piping perfect. He graduated from straight lines to curlicues in less than ten minutes.

"This is cool," he said at one point when he was practicing making stars. "But it's nowhere as easy as you make it look."

"She makes everything look easy," Lucas said from the doorway before I could respond.

He was leaning against the jamb, his arms crossed over his chest, one shoulder settled against the woodwork.

"How long have you been standing there?" I asked.

"Long enough for my mouth to water."

I had the wild hope he meant it as a compliment to me and not my cupcakes.

"Please tell me this is one of those times the kid gets to bring home something to work on?" he asked, coming next to us. "And by work on, I mean eat."

I couldn't have pulled back the laugh if I'd tried. Like a five-year-old standing in front of a sweets counter who'd just been told he could have one piece of everything in the candy store, his face broke out into huge, expectant grin.

"God, Dad. Lame, much?"

Lucas faced his son. His facial muscles went slack, and he tilted his head a bit to the side. "Is that a—" He circled a hand in the air. "—whatchamacallit? Ponytail?"

Robert's cheeks went ruby red in a heartbeat. He dropped his chin to his chest, and his shoulders folded in on themselves. I'm fairly astute at reading body language, a left-over side effect of being the quiet, observant one living with a gregarious, headstrong twin. Right now, I'd have bet a million dollars Robert was trying to make himself smaller, maybe even invisible, by the way he was folding in on himself.

Lucas hadn't meant to sound so judgmental, but unfortunately that's how his teenage son had taken his words and the tone slicing through them.

"The technical term is *man-bun*, and I think Robert's rocking it," I said in a voice which left no doubt of it. The boy's head shot back up to face me, his father doing the same. "Not many guys can pull their longish hair back like he has"—I pointed to Robert—"and still manage to look masculine."

I explained the need for Robert's hair to be contained while in my kitchen doing food prep work. "Since he couldn't get a haircut before we started, it was the best option. He knows if he wants to keep working in the kitchen, though, he's either gonna have to get it cut or wear it tied back like this every day."

"You wanna get it cut?" Lucas asked his son, who told him he did.

"We'll go right now."

I put the cupcakes Robert had been practicing on in a sample box.

"Please tell me we're taking those home," Lucas said.

The sound of his stomach rumbling pulled a laugh from his son and a frown from me.

"Did you have lunch?"

"Nope. Got called to a traffic accident out on Glory Road. I just finished up about ten minutes ago and figured it was easier to pick Robert up now. I'll grab something while he's at the barber's."

"Sit down." I pointed to a chair. "Robert, you go get washed up. We can continue with this next week."

"You don't have to make anything, Maureen," Lucas said after his son left the room. "I can scarf down a couple of the cupcakes on the way home."

Before I could say I had plenty of food left over from lunch, Sarah came in to the kitchen, escorting a visitor.

"Mr. Boyd is here to see you, Maureen."

Crap. I'd forgotten I'd scheduled a meeting today.

Donovan Boyd stuck out his hand. When I slipped

my own into it, his cornflower blue eyes widened and his broad smile beamed.

"Well, it's lovely to finally put a face to a voice." Ireland wrapped around his words, and it was impossible not to smile back at him. His lilting tone mimicked my grandmother's.

"Mr. Boyd, thank you so much for coming out here today. It's difficult for me to get away during the workday for meetings. I really appreciate it."

"No problem. I like gettin' outta the office when I can. And call me Van, darlin'. Mr. Boyd's me father."

I laughed. "And I'm Maureen."

"Maureen O'Dowd." He shook his head, his handsome smile twitching at the corners of his mouth. "You've a name and beautiful face telling me there's Irish blood running in your veins. Are ya sure you're not a transplant, like me?"

"Sorry. Born and bred right here in Heaven."

"Ah, well."

I glanced down to discover he still held my hand.

When a not-too-subtle throat clearing sprang from next to me, I pulled my hand back and turned. Lucas's face was filled with curiosity. Eyes pulled a little tighter in the corners, chin dropped a notch, head tilted a few degrees to one side. It was an expression I'd seen him toss my grandmother any number of times when he'd arrested her for some bit of public malfeasance.

"Lucas," I said, "This is Donovan Boyd. He's an architect with Ascension Architects. Van, Heaven's police chief, Lucas Alexander."

"Nice to meetcha, Chief." Boyd extended his hand to Lucas, his open smile still in place.

It took him a moment, but Lucas shook it. He

didn't return the smile. "I'd heard Kevin Anderson had someone new working for him."

"Aye, that'd be me. Arrived about a month ago. They're keepin' me busy, for sure."

Lucas nodded slowly, another sign he was evaluating the man in front of him.

To be honest, Donovan Boyd was a bit of a surprise. I don't know why, but when we'd spoken on the phone to set up the appointment, I'd gotten the impression he was older, maybe forties, or even early fifties. I was wrong. He was a few years older than me, but not by much. Tall and lean, he had wide shoulders that filled out the sports jacket he wore nicely. Those clear eyes occupied a pale, angular face, sharp with high cheekbones I was a little jealous of. A thick thatch of midnight hair sprinkled with thin threads of gray at the temples was a stark contrast to the light blue in his eyes.

Nanny's voice shot into my head. *He's Black Irish, Number Four. A striking combination and easy on the eyes, to be sure.*

She wasn't wrong.

"You all settled in, then?" Lucas asked.

"Aye. Got a little place over on Rapture Road." He chuckled. "Funny name for a street, eh? I keep expectin' to see angels come 'round every corner."

"All the streets have some kind of biblical tag." I grinned. "The town charter dictates it. All the businesses, too, have to abide by the rule. Hence"—I lifted a hand and swiped it around the room—"Inn Heaven and Ascension Architects."

"It's charmin' and quaint, to be sure."

"I'm curious," Lucas said, interrupting us. "What

brought you to our town? Ireland's a ways from here. You have family in the area?"

"Unfortunately, no. It's just me." His gaze slid back to me for a second. "For now."

Both men continued to stare at one another. I got the feeling there was some kind of hidden male telepathy-agenda going on between them, but for the life of me I couldn't figure out what it was.

Men were such a mystery. Growing up in an estrogen cloud with three sisters, Nanny, and my mother, I'd never learned the ins and outs of the male mind. My father tended to shut himself up in his office more times than not to avoid all the *female drama* occupying the daily lives of his girls.

The looks passing between these two were…interesting, to say the least.

"Kevin's an old friend of my former employer," Van told him. "They went to college together. When the position opened up, Liam—that's me old boss—thought it might be something of interest to me, seeing as I'd been lookin' for a change." He focused on me again. "He wasn't wrong."

"Still. You're a long way from home."

"I am, it's true. But this is a delightful town you have here. I'm finding it, and the people, most welcoming."

"Dad?" Robert came back into the kitchen, his hair back down. "I'm ready to go.

Lucas glanced at his son, then back to Boyd. "My son, Robert," he said.

With a smile and a nod for the boy, Boyd turned to me and lifted a cylindrical tube. "I brought a few preliminary sketches with me for ya to go over, based on our brief conversation last week."

"Great. We can use my office." I handed the box of cupcakes to Robert. "Don't let your father eat all of these," I told him. "You enjoy them, too, since you decorated them."

"Yes, ma'am."

"Sketches?" Lucas asked me. "Of what?"

"Nosy, much?" I fisted my hands on my hips. "Don't you have stuff to do? Barbers to visit? Criminals to apprehend?"

His brows pulled into kissing distance. "I've got a minute."

I rolled my eyes and shook my head before I opened the refrigerator. While I pulled out leftovers from lunch service, I said, "If you have to know, I'm expanding the inn. With a full house almost every weekend, I've had to turn people away more than I'd like."

Now those brows rose almost to his hairline. "I didn't know you were thinking of adding on."

"Why would you?"

He shrugged.

"I've been mulling around the idea for a while." I took a shopping bag out from the pantry closet. "Eileen had a dream to build individual guest houses out in the back of the property for families when we first bought the inn. Unfortunately, the idea got pushed to the back burner when, well…when everything happened."

I didn't need to explain the reason it had to Lucas.

He nodded.

"Now seemed like a good idea to start exploring my options. Here." I handed him the shopping bag filled with the wrapped tin-foiled leftovers. "This should be enough for the three of you for dinner."

Lucas stared down at the bag, then back to me. With his tongue pressed against the inside of his cheek and his head titled at an angle again, he looked a little confused. About what, I hadn't a clue.

"Dad? Are we going, or what?"

He pulled out of his musings and, with a deep breath, nodded. "Thanks for this."

I swiped my hand in the air. "Don't forget Nanny's party starts at twelve. Sharp," I told them. "And she hates—"

"When anyone's late," Lucas finished. "Yeah, I know. I'm always on time, so don't worry."

"Your dad's invited, too. Nanny specifically asked for you to bring him."

"Easier said than done," he mumbled.

Robert groaned. When he realized he'd been heard, a deep flush drenched his face and neck.

"I can only promise to try," Lucas said. "If he's in a mood, well…"

"Let him have one of those"—I pointed to the box of cupcakes—"tonight, and tell him I'm baking more for the party. It might persuade him to come."

His grin shot out so fast I wasn't prepared for its power over me, so I didn't have time to brace myself. Instead, my breath hissed in audibly and my neck grew hot.

"I know it would convince me to," he said, oblivious to my reaction.

With one last glance at Boyd, he tossed me a nod. "Catch you later. And thanks again." He lifted the bag of food.

Once my kitchen was empty of the Alexander men,

I took a calming breath and smiled at my guest. "Okay. I need to start cooking soon, but I'm all yours for the next thirty minutes."

The charming grin on his face widened when he said, "Now there's a proposal a man would have to be daft to refuse."

The half hour flew by as Boyd showed me the ideas he'd drawn up.

I was impressed. By both the time and effort he'd put into the drawings and layouts, and with the man himself.

The subtle mirth in his smile and the concentrated way his eyes held my own for a beat longer than was required showed me he was a bit of a flirt, not unlike my grandmother. The two of them could have been cut from the same bolt of flirt fabric, in fact. While I was used to the way my grandmother acted around any human with an X and Y chromosome, it was an unfamiliar sensation having that kind of attention focused on me.

Before he left, we made another appointment for the following week to give him enough time to draft the changes we'd discussed. Once again he agreed to come to the inn.

"I can't tell you how much I appreciate it," I said as I held the front door open for him. "Running this place takes up most of my time and leaving even for a few hours during the day can be hard at times, so thanks again."

While he shook my hand and continued to hold on to it, a tiny line sprouted between his brows. "You're busy during the day." He nodded. "But do you never take a night off, then? Just to relax and maybe pop down to the pub for a bit?"

I laughed before I could think not to.

"And that's amusin', why now?"

I shook my head. "Not amusing, sorry. This is a twenty-four-hour-a-day business. There's not a lot of room to *pop* out anywhere for a drink, a quick meal, or much of anything else."

"You've got assistants, though, haven'tcha? The lovely woman who let me in, Sarah, it is? Sure, she could spot ya a time or two?"

"I couldn't run this place without her, that's the truth. But she's got her own family to go home to every night. I live here, and truthfully the last thing I want to do after being on my feet all day is to go out, especially when I have to be up at an early hour each day to get breakfast for my guests."

He tilted his head and leaned a shoulder against the door jam, his concentration centered on me. "So if I suggested we meet at, what's it called now? The Love Shack, aye?"

I nodded.

"If I asked ya to come and join me for a pint one evening when you've an hour to spare, would you?"

I shouldn't have been surprised by the invitation. He had been, after all, giving me signals he was interested in more than just the plans while we'd gone over them. It had been years, though, since I'd been involved with a man. In any capacity, be it meeting for a quick drink, or dating. Not since I'd walked out on my last boyfriend when he'd selfishly ordered me to choose between him or my sister.

"Ah, I can see you're debating the pros and cons, as such," Van said, laughter in his voice. "You're a dying breed, Maureen, darlin'," he added, his mouth twisting into a grin.

"A dying breed?"

"Aye. A dedicated business owner who puts the needs of others ahead of her own. 'Tis charmin' and a wee bit daunting for a man."

As far as compliments go, it was a lovely one. Why, then, didn't it fill me with pleasure?

"Well, I'll be heading out, now." He lifted the cylinder. "I'll work on these and incorporate the things you want included for next time."

He stopped and turned before he was through the threshold. With a glint in his eyes, he cocked his head as he regarded me. "Let me know if you decide there's more pros than cons to my idea of sharing a pint or two of an evening."

He bent and kissed my cheek, then walked to his car, whistling as he did.

When I closed the door behind him, I leaned my head against it and dragged in a breath.

Eileen, my deceased twin, had been the sister the male population had been drawn to as naturally as hummingbirds are to nectar. Vivacious, mercurial, and an apprentice at my grandmother's knee in the coquette department, Eileen was the sister who'd never gone dateless one weekend in high school or college. She'd been Prom Queen, voted Best Liked by our graduating class, and elected Class President during our senior year. College had been no different.

My entire life I'd watched from the sidelines as she'd brought sunshine and warmth into the life of every boy she'd dated. Her breakups were never dramatic or torturous, and she was able to remain friends with all her exes.

I was labeled the quiet twin. Shy and unobtrusive. A thinker and a loner.

The descriptions were spot on. I was happy to stay in the background while Eileen shone in the foreground. Her death hadn't changed the dynamics of my personality one whit. I was still the private, silent one who spent a lot of time in her head and alone with her thoughts.

So, to have a man like Donovan Boyd show his interest in more than a professional way toward me— well, it was a little strange, a little baffling, and a whole lot of flattering.

And I had no idea how to deal with those strange emotions.

Now, if only a certain chief of police could show the same kind of interest.

Ah, well.

With a sigh, I got back to work.

Chapter 4

Nanny was, as usual, prompt for her party. More than prompt, actually, since she'd arrived with my sister Colleen and her husband Slade right after ten-thirty mass ended.

My ninety-three-year-old grandmother had been a fixture in all our lives ever since the eldest, Cathleen, was born. A professional pianist, Nanny had toured the globe performing with various symphonies until my father married my mother and they began having babies. Nanny had given up touring for several years to help raise us—in her word—*properly*. My mother and grandmother had never gotten along, each vying for the love and attention of the man of the house. Because of their barely concealed animosity, our home was many times a battle of wills between the two for household dominance.

Case in point: our names. My mother wanted to play up our Irish roots, especially when we'd all popped out with red hair, fair skin, and blue eyes, by calling us similar-sounding, traditional names. Cathleen was the eldest, next Colleen, then Eileen and me, four minutes apart. Nanny considered our names ridiculous and began calling us by our birth order ranks as a way to protest the names and, I'd always thought, annoy my mother. Cathy was referred to as Number One, Colleen was (horribly) Number Two, Eileen, Number Three, and because I was the youngest, I was christened Number Four.

In all fairness to Nanny, when our names were spoken collectively, it did sound obnoxious: Cathleen, Colleen, Eileen, Maureen. But referring to us by number was equally as unpleasant, especially for Colleen who suffered terribly as a child with the moniker. Nanny taught religious education classes for a time when we were kids, and we were all in her class at one time or another. Calling her granddaughter "Number Two" in front of a room full of childish seven- and eight-year-olds had damaged my sister in ways none of us could really relate to. To this day, her color still blanched whenever Nanny set her sights on her.

From the time she arrived at the inn, Nanny had been talking, nonstop.

"Now, Number Four, I've dropped enough hints these past few weeks about the flavor of me cake. I hope, lass, you've heard them." She took a sip of the post-church tea I'd made her.

"Loud and clear, Nanny."

"Ah. There's a good girl, you are. Now, remember: no candles. At this age there's a chance we could burn the inn down when I blow them all out."

"She ain't kidding," Colleen mumbled beside me as she helped me plate the first course.

"I heard that, Number Two."

Colleen's hands went still, and she bit her bottom lip.

"I may be ninety-four today, but I've the hearing of a bat, I do, young lady."

"Did you just call yourself an old bat?" Slade,

Colleen's husband, asked, with a cheeky grin. When Nanny shot him a squinty-eyed glare, his grin grew and he kissed her cheek.

"You're quickly losin' status as me favorite grandson-in-law."

"I'm not worried since I'm your only grandson-in-law," he told her, then bent and took a sip of her tea as way to divert her attention away from Colleen. The way he always protected my sister warmed my heart no small amount.

"Hey!" Nanny cried.

Into this, Lucas and Robert walked.

"Ah, here's the law now," Nanny declared. "First time you've ever shown up when I needed ya. Officer Alexander, I've been mugged."

"It's chief, not officer," Lucas said, as he bent to kiss her cheek as well. "And what do you mean you've been mugged?"

"Slade took a sip of her tea," I told him. "She calls it being mugged because"—I pointed to the cup now in Nanny's hand and lifted my eyebrows—"mug. Get it?"

My insides went into convulsions when his thick lips pressed tightly together. I nearly melted to the floor in a heap of lust when he lost the battle on his control and burst out laughing. And when those tiny laugh lines creased from the corners of his eyes to his temples, I had to physically restrain myself from grabbing his face and planting a kiss across his mouth.

"There's never a dull moment when you're around, Fiona." He bent and kissed her other cheek. "Happy twenty-first birthday. *Again.*"

Nanny doesn't get flustered easily. Her lifelong habit of being the one in the room who always said something outrageous to get a reaction was well known by everyone in her realm. So when the tops of her cheeks turned ripe cherry red I wanted to high-five Lucas.

Nanny's recovery was quick, though, when she spied Robert, hands slung in his pockets, standing behind his father.

"Well now, lad, look at you. You've grown a foot since last I saw ya, and you're more handsome than ever. Come and give us a kiss, Bobby-Boy." She lifted her arms to him.

With a shy smile, he did, allowing himself to be pulled into a hug.

"Ah, there's a good lad. How's your mother? Got married recently, I heard."

I kept plating while Lucas came to stand next to me.

"Hey."

"Hey. Where's your father?" I asked softly, after peeking first at Nanny to make sure she didn't overhear.

Lucas sighed audibly. "Couldn't convince him to come, no matter how hard I tried." He shook his head, and for the first time I noticed the shadows playing under his eyes. I'd thought him tired a few days ago, and here was physical proof of it. "Even the knowledge you'd be the one cooking and baking, and he still said no."

He shook his head. "He's getting worse, Mo. Harps on Robert all the time, and when I defend the kid, he starts on me. I can take it since I've been hearing the same crap all my life. It's not fair to my son, though. I can't thank you enough for giving him a place to go every day so they don't have to be alone together. I'm not sure one night I wouldn't come home to a crime scene if they were left to their own defenses every day."

I wanted to tell him he was being dramatic, but one look at the defeated expression crossing his face and I knew he wasn't.

"Anyway." He shrugged. "At least your grandmother is being sweet to him. I don't want him to think all older folks are mean and grumpy like his grandfather."

"Don't let her hear you call her old. You may not get out of here alive."

The melancholy cast in his eyes eased, and those thick, perfect lips curled into a sinful grin that made my heart rate quicken and my hands tremble.

"I'm not worried," he said, a cocky smirk on his face. "I'm the one in the room with a gun."

I snorted and then immediately felt heat run up my cheeks from my neck.

In a feeble attempt to hide my embarrassment, I grabbed a few plates of salad and carried them out to my dayroom where we were due to celebrate.

I was surprised when Lucas tagged after me, holding two plates in his own hands.

"What are you doing?" I asked.

"Helping. What does it look like I'm doing?"

"Lucas, you're a guest. You don't need to help. Go back and visit, I've got this."

He laid the plates at two table settings, then fisted his hands on his hips as he regarded me. Brows grooved, chin dropped a few notches, and his head cocked at a bit of an angle, his expression seemed...vexed.

"What?" I asked.

"Guest?"

I nodded.

His eyes narrowed.

"You're here to help celebrate Nanny's birthday so, *duh*"—I lifted my hands from my sides—"that makes you a guest."

He took a step closer, the intensity in his gaze, alien to me.

"What's the matter? You're looking at me like I have three heads."

Another step and he was right in front of me. I had to lift my chin to keep his face in focus.

"That's really how you see me? As a simple guest?" He wrapped one of his hands around my upper arm and gently squeezed, all the while his gaze lasered on mine, the expression drifting across his eyes questioning.

"Of-of course you're not *simply* a guest." I amazed myself I was able to get that much out. The heat from his hand was as hot as a branding iron. It was a wonder my skin wasn't smoking. "You're a-a friend, too. Good golly, you're practically family."

"A friend?"

I nodded. "A good one."

I didn't have a clue what was behind his head tilt, but it was no wonder Lucas was so good at his job. I can imagine all kinds of criminals vomited up confessions when he trained his heated, pointed, and spill-your-guts glare at them.

"That's what I am, Maureen? A good...friend?"

I swallowed, the sound cutting through the tension between us.

Why did he make it sound like an accusation and

not a fact? He *was* a friend.

"Aren't you?" I asked, my voice now a whisper.

We stood so close I could discern the palette of individual greens in his eyes. So close it would take nothing to lift up on my toes and press my mouth to his like I'd dreamt of doing for most of my life.

"Is that what you want me to be?" he asked.

In truth, no, it wasn't. Not even close.

I could never say those words out loud, though, no matter how much I ached to.

But dear God, I wanted to. So much.

Fear was the reason I didn't now, and never had, told him what I really wanted of him, how I felt about him. Lucas was too important to me, too much a fixture in my life. Confessing I loved him, and not in a good friend kind of way, was something I feared would change our relationship forever, and possibly not for the better.

I swallowed again to buy precious time to answer.

Cathy's voice stopped me from doing so when she entered the room.

"Hey," she said from the doorway, peering at the both of us. "What's going on?"

I would have jerked out of his grip, but Lucas held me in place for a beat, as if knowing my intent.

"I'm helping Mo set up," Lucas told her with his trademark calm when he finally let go of my arm. I put as much distance as I could between us. He turned to her, a smile on his face. "Hey. Just get here?"

She nodded.

"Where's Mac?"

Her head ping-ponged from him, to me, then back to him again, her left eyebrow lifting high on her forehead. "In the kitchen, flirting with Nanny. Why?"

"Good. I need to talk to him about his bachelor party. I've got a couple ideas I want to run by him."

"Oh, good Lord." Cathy shook her head. "Please tell me it doesn't involve strippers or anything illegal."

He kissed her cheek and grinned. "I'm the chief of police, Counselor. I'd never condone illegal activity of any kind."

"I didn't hear you deny anything about strippers," she said to his retreating back.

His deep laugh echoed in the breezeway.

Slowly, she zeroed her attention in on me, folded her arms across her chest, and pulled her face into what Colleen calls *Cathy's killer lawyer stare.*

Just like Lucas, Cathy is exceptionally good at her job. But in my sister's case, I was immune to her penetrating, tell-me-all-your-secrets expression. I'd had a lifetime living as her baby sister, and I'd apprenticed at her knee when she'd dealt with our grandmother by using diversionary tactics.

"So." She ambled toward me. "Lucas."

I blanked my face. "So Lucas, what?"

She took a beat, then said, "Lucas and…you?"

I kept my eyes steady on hers, knowing if I glanced away she'd take it as an affirmation of her unsaid suspicions. Or worse, weakness. Like I said, I'd watched her my entire life and knew exactly how effective she could be when she wanted information someone was unwilling to give. She was a master of the silent wait-out, an interrogation technique she used frequently when she was in court and questioning a witness. Nine times out of ten, her silence would get to the person and they'd blurt things they'd sworn to keep hidden.

But we weren't in the courtroom today, on Cathy's turf. We were in my inn, on mine. And if I knew how to do anything, it was keep my own counsel.

After several moments of noiseless staring, Cathy grinned at me. "You're like a locked vault with a missing key. Not opening for anyone."

Since it wasn't a question, I didn't feel the need to answer her.

Nanny's voice rang out from the kitchen.

"That doesn't sound good," I said.

"She's just sparring with my man as usual," Cathy countered. "Come on. Baby is hungry." She rubbed a hand over her tiny belly bump. "And so am I."

Back in my kitchen we found Cathy's fiancé, Mac, holding Nanny's hand, a devilish grin on his face.

"Number One," she said as soon as she spied us, "tell this young man o' yours it's rude to tease an old lady, especially on her birthday."

"You're the youngest person in this room," Mac said in reply. He lifted her gnarled hand and kissed the back of it. "The youngest and the most beautiful, to be sure," he added, mimicking her brogue to perfection.

Nanny's periwinkle-blue eyes softened. She clicked her tongue, then batted the hand he held with her free one. "Don't be thinking ya can charm me now, Mac Frayne. Better than you have tried and failed. It's ninety-four I am today and still as sharp as I was in me twenties."

"As sharp as a stiletto," Lucas whispered close to my ear. While I'd begun plating more salad, he'd come to stand behind me. "And equally as deadly."

As I bit back a giggle, he reached around me and

took the two plates I'd prepared, his hand brushing against mine. The snigger died in my throat, and I had to tell myself to breathe.

"Robert, help Maureen. Take these inside."

I was all set to tell him not to because he was a guest today and not a worker, when I caught the challenging look Lucas tossed me. I bit back my knee-jerk response.

"Thanks," I said to the boy.

"Why won't ya tell me?" Nanny asked Mac. " 'Tisn't a state secret, after all, is it?"

"Cathy and I agreed we want to go old school with this and not find out the sex of the baby. I'm not keeping any secrets; we simply don't know and"—he pointed at her—"we're not going to find out until the baby's born, so there's no use asking."

"Colleen and Slade know they're having a girl," Nanny stated, her lips pulled into a pout a teenager would have been jealous of. "Makes it so much easier to buy a baby present, knowing the sex."

"I wanted to know so we could paint the nursery, Nanny," Colleen said from her chair. Her feet were elevated on the one opposite her and, for once, she'd worn flats.

Slade rubbed her shoulders. "You know how obsessive Colleen is about things," he told my grandmother.

"I don't think it's obsessive to want everything ready when the time comes," Colleen countered. "It makes sense from a time-management perspective. And from a health one, too. I don't want paint fumes in the house with a brand-new baby."

"We all know time management is your middle

name, babe." Slade kissed the top of her head.

"Well, whatever the reason, knowing the sex, I can shop effectively," Nanny said. She nodded at Cathy. "I don't want to give me great-grandchild a generic-colored gift." Her beautiful blue eyes narrowed, and I could almost see the gears grinding in her head. "You know, I could die before your babe arrives, Cathleen Anne. It's not young I am any more. Could go in a blink, just like such." She snapped two of her fingers together.

"You're gonna outlive us all," Cathy said, while Lucas once again whispered from next to me, "Promises, promises."

This time my giggle blew forth. I shifted to find him staring at me, his eyes crinkled in the corners, his lips twitching.

God, he was gorgeous.

"Stop," I mouthed.

His grin grew.

"Come on, everyone. Let's get this party started," I said to the room.

"Fiona, I'd be delighted to escort you to your party." Lucas extended his arm to her.

"Delighted, are ya?" she asked, slipping her hand into the crook in his elbow. "Not worried I'm gonna slice ya to bits, seeing as how I'm sharp as a, what did ya call it, now? A stiletto?"

Lucas had the grace to look sheepish, despite the cheeky grin on his face.

"Deadly instruments, they are," Nanny told him, "so you'd better mind yourself."

An hour later, after a lunch of salad, cold salmon (Nanny's favorite), asparagus, and more laughter than my dayroom had seen in a while, it was time for presents and cake.

I cocked my head at Robert, and he followed me into my kitchen.

"Want to help me bring the cake out?" I asked. "You did, after all, help decorate it."

"Sure."

He went to the sink and washed his hands without being prompted.

"Your hair looks great," I said as I joined him. "How do you feel with it shorter?"

"Lighter, like I've lost weight."

I laughed and bumped him with my hip while I dried my hands on a dishtowel. The local barber was known for his love of military crew cuts, and I'd been worried Robert would wind up looking as if he was off to boot camp. But he still had some length on the top and sides, even though a large volume of it had been sheared.

"Well, now I won't be pestering you to pull it back when we do food prep. Plus, I have to imagine it dries quicker when you get out of the shower."

"In, like, no time flat," he answered.

We lifted the three-tiered cake he'd helped decorate from my walk-in fridge and placed it on a serving tray.

I lit the two numerical candles, a nine and a four, I'd bought knowing Nanny's words were true: ninety-four candles all lit at the same time were a fire waiting to happen. I placed a single birthday candle next.

"For luck," I told Robert.

We walked the cake into the dayroom.

"Okay, everyone. Time to sing."

While we serenaded her, Nanny beamed from her seat. She loved being the center of attention and always had.

"Make a wish, Nanny," Cathy said when we were done. "And don't waste it on wanting to know my baby's gender."

When the laughter died down, Nanny's gaze ran from Cathleen, to Colleen, and then settled on me. With a twitch of her lips and a twinkle in those wise eyes, she winked at me and then blew the candles out.

"There now, I think that's grand," she said, smiling at us all.

After the cake was cut and served, Nanny took a bite of the rich, dark chocolate sponge I'd made, filled with chocolate buttercream and a thimbleful of Bailey's.

"Magnificent as always, darlin' girl," Nanny said.

I smiled while I went around the table refilling teacups.

"Why three tiers, lass?" Nanny asked as she lifted her cup to me. "Looks like a wedding cake, and I've no one on me man-dar right now I'm looking to get hitched to."

From where I stood, I spotted Colleen's face blanch and her eyes go wide. Her hand flew to her belly, and she started blowing out breaths through lips she'd pursed together.

While I filled Nanny's cup, I kept my attention on my older sister. Slade began rubbing her shoulders and caught me staring. A subtle headshake told me everything was okay. I wasn't one hundred percent sure it was but kept my worry to myself.

"I figured you could take the bottom tier back to

the Arms and share it with your friends after dinner."

"Ah, now, you're a thoughtful lass, you are, Maureen. They'll love it. But then, they love everything you bake. Spoiled, they are, with your generosity."

The room slammed still. To hear our grandmother call us by our Christian names was tantamount to finding a leprechaun, and yet she'd referred to each of us that way over the past hour.

I was all set to ask her if she was feeling okay when Colleen moaned, then cursed. The quiet room exploded with a deafening silence again as everyone's attention settled on her. My heart stuttered a bit as worry shot through me. Colleen had another few weeks to go in her pregnancy and shouldn't be having contractions.

"Sorry, Nanny," she said, the pallor in her cheeks highlighted with the instant raspberry color of her blush. "These dam—er, darn Braxton Hicks contractions are driving me crazy today."

"False labor pains?" Cathy asked. It didn't escape my notice she placed a hand over her own belly. "I read about those in the prenatal book Olivia gave me."

"Yeah. They started fast and furious a few days ago," Colleen said.

"The doctor says not to worry about them," Slade told us as he continued to massage his wife's shoulders. "It's just her body getting itself ready for our special delivery."

"Which can't come soon enough," Colleen murmured. "Feels like snail mail, and I want overnight express."

Her cracking a joke went a long way in calming my anxiety. Since Colleen was the first of us to have a baby, with Cathy right on her heels, I'd done a huge internet search about pregnancy and all the complications that can go along with it, including at delivery time. I didn't sleep for three nights after reading over three hundred thousand women still die in childbirth every year, worldwide. The implications of the statistic, especially when my sister was having her first baby at what was called the advanced maternal age of thirty-seven, had rendered me unable to sleep. I wound up baking eight dozen cookies, six loaves of bread, and three dozen muffins during those midnight hours.

My guests had been delighted with the wealth of sugary carbs my insomnia rendered.

Nanny reached over and grabbed Colleen's hand. "Ah, darlin', I wish I could take the pain for ya. I know how it feels. Your father was a real in pain in me uterus and va-jay-jay when me time neared. I couldn't hardly sit without him banging his head against me girly bits to get out, and me thighs never touched from the sixth month on. Very impatient he was, even before his craggy face made an appearance into the world."

The heavy silence in the room was broken when Mac let out a belly laugh that had the chandelier chains trembling. Slade came next, a choked guffaw bursting through his lips, followed by Lucas who outright barked with laughter, his eyes almost closing with the effort. Cathy stared over at her fiancé and shook her head, a smirk pulling at her lips, while Colleen alternated between grinning and grimacing when the muscle cramps hit.

I glanced over at Robert who stared at my grandmother as if she were an alien life form who'd just landed from a distant planet. Jaw slack with his mouth dropped open; eyes wide and filled with astonishment. His cheeks were fever-red, the tips of his ears crimson. The poor kid was probably horrified at hearing an elderly woman talk about her private body parts in such an offhand, easy fashion. I couldn't blame him. While we were all used to Nanny's outlandishness, Robert wasn't.

Nanny's gaze touched each of us as she ran it around the table. An almost invisible twitching of her lips was all the evidence I needed she'd said what she had for the effect it would cause to lighten the mood and my sister's predicament.

I simply adored this woman.

"Well, now..." She folded her hands in her lap. Moral indignation laced her brogue when she said, "You're all laughing like hyenas, when the poor lass here is suffering. Ya should be ashamed a' yorselves, you should. 'Tisn't an easy thing to bring a new life into the world."

She reached over and squeezed Colleen's hand again. "These'll pass soon, lass. No worries. And you'll have the gift of a beautiful baby girl when it does."

Tears glinted in my sister's eyes. "Thanks, Nanny."

When her eyes narrowed Cathy's way, I felt a come-to-Jesus lecture about to be unleashed. To avoid it, I brought the remainder of the cake back to the kitchen to remove the bottom tier and box it up for Nanny to take back to the nursing home.

As I walked from the room, she said, "At least I know one great-grandchild is a girl. Little solace it does me, though."

"Your grandmother is the only person I know who

can compliment and censure in the same breath," Lucas said as he followed me into the kitchen.

" 'Tis a gift, to be sure," I said, channeling the woman in question.

"You do that well."

I lifted a shoulder. "Lifetime of practice."

He carried a few stacked plates in one hand and my teakettle in the other. "This is empty," he told me, lifting the kettle.

"Put it on the stove and give me those." I stretched out my arms for the dishes. Lucas shifted away from me to prevent me from taking them.

"I've got it. You want them in the dishwasher?"

"I need to rinse them first. Put them down on the counter, and I'll do it after everyone leaves."

He ignored me and proceeded to rinse, then stack, the dishes into the dishwasher.

"Really, Lucas. You don't need to do that."

With a side-glance first, he said, "What phrase does Father Duncan love to quote? Many hands make light work?"

I hadn't crossed a church door since Colleen had gotten married and hadn't for two years prior to that, so I kept my mouth shut and let him work.

Robert brought more things in from the table, Mac helping while I went back to boxing Nanny's cake.

"I can't believe you left Cathy to deal with Nanny's wrath," I told my soon-to-be brother-in-law.

"Your sister can hold her own against Fiona any day of the week." He put the plates down on the counter and slapped Lucas on the back. "Saturday works," he said. "Slade's free, too."

"Unless Colleen's labor changes to real from

false," the man said, as he appeared, he too carrying dishes and flatware. "Otherwise, I'm in."

Lucas continued rinsing and loading.

I have to admit, having so much testosterone in the form of three gorgeous men and one gangly teenager in my usually female-laced kitchen was a little unusual and whole lot of exciting. Especially since one of those men starred in the lion's share of my dreams every night.

And the fact they were all doing kitchen chores was even more amazing.

My sisters had each hit the partner-for-life jackpot with the men who'd claimed their hearts. Slade and Mac resembled one another enough they could have been cousins with their lean, runner's bodies and handsome faces. While Slade was fair-haired, Mac's thick black mane was threaded with gray. Ex-corporate executive and now full-time law professor, Slade oozed alpha from every pore, while Mac was the quiet writer and beta all the way. Both were, though, whole-heartedly in love with my sisters and had proven their devotion in so many ways. I could love them simply for the fact they loved my sisters, but it was more. They had each changed their lives to be with the women they loved. Slade had transferred his from the chaos of New York, as had Mac, both claiming they could work anywhere as long as they had the women they adored by their sides.

Cathy and Colleen were lucky women, indeed.

How would it feel for a man to change his entire life because he loved me and didn't want to lose me and what we had together? It was an unknown concept for me. The one man I'd ever considered a future with had grown jealous of the bond between my twin and me and had given me an ultimatum: choose. He hadn't even put up a fight when I'd picked Eileen.

In all honesty, I wouldn't have chosen him even if he had fought for me. No man who professes to love you should ever make you choose him over everything and everyone else.

"What were the three of you talking about?" I asked Lucas once the others left the kitchen.

Before answering me, he closed the dishwasher and wiped his hands on a dishtowel.

He leaned back across the sink ledge and crossed his arms over his chest. The material on his dress shirt pulled against the bulk of his biceps, and my mouth went dry as unprocessed baking flour.

"Mac's bachelor party. Cathy said she's busy next weekend finalizing some wedding stuff with Colleen, so they're both free. We're gonna do something Saturday night."

"What? Heaven's not exactly the place where three guys can run amuck as a last hurrah to bachelorhood. Not that you'd ever run amuck, but still."

His right eyebrow rose on his forehead. "Run amuck?"

I shrugged. "You know what I mean."

When he dropped his chin to his chest, I got the distinct impression he was laughing at me and didn't want me to see. When he shook his head, I was certain of it.

"I should pay you to help Robert with his SAT prep. Amuck. Good word."

"And accurate. So, what are your plans? Getting out of town for the night? Driving into Concord or

Manchester? Hitting a few bars and drinking your weight in beer?"

He angled his head to one side as he regarded me through half-closed eyes. His entire stance as he leaned against the sink, arms folded, ankles crossed and pushed out in front of him, radiated a calm, cool, and disinterested façade. I knew he was anything but. Lucas Alexander was never so focused, so intense, or so stealthy as when he appeared exactly the opposite.

His ability to remain calm and unreadable was another facet of his personality I loved.

"Why do you want to know?" he asked me. "What are you worried about?"

"I'm not worried."

"You say one thing, but your body language says another."

I rolled my eyes. "My body language says nothing. There's no reason for me to be worried about anything since Slade and Mac are going to be with you, Lucas. Whatever you wind up doing, I know they'll be safe. I'm asking because, like my sisters are fond of saying, I inherited Nanny's nosy gene."

His brows pulled together between his eyes and that head tilt shifted.

"What do you mean you're not worried because they'll be with me? And what did that crack about me never running amuck mean? *Jesus.*" He unfurled his arms and swiped his hands through his hair at the temples. "I've said *amuck* more times than I've ever said it in my life."

"That's a dumb question, since you're the chief of police." I held my hands up at my sides. "You're the most responsible and trustworthy human being I know.

You don't do anything that crosses a line either morally, ethically, or legally. I've seen you drunk once in your life after Danny's funeral, and you deserved to be since you'd just lost your best friend. You're dependable, Lucas. Completely."

It was a wonder he didn't get a headache from the way the skin over his forehead puckered inward.

"Dependable and trustworthy? You make me sound like a cub scout, or an unemotional robot with a stick up his ass. Dull and boring. Like I don't know how to have a good time and never do."

"I'm sure you do, but I'm also sure since you became chief, you're more aware than ever of the small minds and big mouths living in this town. You can't be seen doing anything"—I shook my head again—"questionable or *unseemly,* like getting drunk in public at a bachelor party. You need to be on the safe side of gossip at all times. And you are. It's what makes you such a good leader."

"Unseemly? Lord, Maureen. Now you're making me sound like a modern version of Josiah Heaven. You gonna accuse me of having a God complex next?"

How the heck had this conversation veered into him thinking I was comparing him to our town founder?

"What?" I fisted my hands on my hips, well and truly confused and getting irritated by the second. "Weren't you the one who told my sister in that very breezeway"—I pointed behind me—"not more than two hours ago you weren't going to condone anything illegal because, quote, you're the chief of police, unquote? I don't think I imagined it, Lucas."

It was as if he hadn't heard me.

"I'm not old and tired and worn out yet, you know." He started pacing back and forth, his hands slung in his trouser pockets.

"I never said you were. I—"

"I've got responsibilities to this town and its citizens, Maureen. I'm on call twenty-four hours a day for the city. Never a day to myself, never a night to call my own. *Christ.* I had to promise Pete Bergeron three weekends in a row off in order to be free Saturday night."

"Lucas, what—"

"I haven't had a vacation in six years. In addition, I take care of a man who wants nothing more than to die and finds it amusing to take pot shots at my son."

For the first time in my memory, Lucas's voice rose. He was always the proverbial calm during a crisis, the one everyone gravitated to for guidance, the man people regarded as a natural leader.

It dawned on me he wasn't simply tired, but exhausted. And not only physically. The weight of all the responsibilities he carried on those strong, broad shoulders was taking its toll, and he had no one in his life to help shoulder them.

Placing myself straight in front of him, I barred his pacing. I reached out, wrapped a hand around his forearm, and pressed, forcing him to pay attention to me.

He blinked hard a few times, as if coming awake after a deep sleep. The confusion in his eyes worried me.

"Lucas. Stop."

He focused in on me, then to where I held his arm. When he lifted his gaze back to me, his forehead was furrowed. "Maureen?"

I squeezed his arm again. "Are you okay?"

He tilted his head to one side while he continued to stare at me for a few beats.

"I'm worried about you," I told him.

"Worried?"

"Yes. You're being"—I shrugged then shook my head—"weird. And you're scaring me."

He blinked a few times. "You're worried about me?"

"Yes, dammit." I stamped my foot, frustrated and getting mad, now. "I care about you, and I'm worried because you're acting so out of character. What about that is so hard to comprehend?"

I removed my hand from his arm, only to have him grab it back with his own.

"Let go of m—" I stopped dead. One look at the expression on his face and any and all words were forgotten. The confusion reeling in his eyes shifted, cleared, then flew completely to be replaced by a piercing, all consuming...*hunger*.

As surprised as I'd been when his voice rose and as frustrated with his repeating everything back to me, the intensity swimming in his eyes was staggering, especially since it was focused entirely on me.

Lucas licked his lips, then repeated my name in a voice as far from a shout as possible. Quiet; controlled; seductive. This time there was no mistaking his tone for confusion.

With his free hand, he covered the one he held and pulled me in, until our torsos touched, his intent clear.

Crystal clear.

He was going to kiss me.

Kiss me.

In my kitchen with a room full of people we both loved a few feet away. Mesmerized is the only word I can find to describe why I didn't try to put a halt to his intention. Well, that, and the fact I'd wanted him to kiss me forever. The idea my fantasy was about to become a reality rendered me unable to run away.

I lifted my chin, and I stretched up to meet him halfway, instead.

Our bodies touched from chest to knees. The warmth of his breath caressed me as his lips hovered over mine. His lids dropped partway, but he held my gaze captive as if he were openly gaping at me. In truth, I didn't want to look away, couldn't. As our lips were a whisper from touching and I'd finally know what it felt like to be kissed by this man, his pager went off.

Lucas's head jerked back, his eyes blinking in a rapid tattoo as he clamped his lips together and shook his head with a jagged shudder. For my part, my heart slammed against my rib cage so hard I swear my blouse moved with the motion. The pager's blare was shrill and piercing, the noise exploding in the room. Lucas pulled away from me, shot a hand to his hip to silence it, then backed away and reached with his other hand for his cell phone. All the while he kept his eyes trained on me.

His breathing was loud and coarse as he snuck a peek at the pager's screen, then tapped on his cell phone. As he was speaking, Robert came back into the room carrying a few teacups. He glanced at his father, then at me, a question crossing his face.

My lungs were working overtime. I tried to slow my breathing by taking a deep breath in, holding it for a few beats, then letting it out.

It didn't work. Robert's concerned perusal verified it.

"Your dad got paged," I told him, silently cursing the strain in my voice. "Here, let me have those."

He ignored my command as his father had, holding them fast. "Your grandmother told me to wash these by hand because they can't go in the dishwasher. Something about fine china and etch marks." He lifted a shoulder and placed the items into the sink.

"I've got to go," Lucas said in a voice as tense as mine had been. "Pete and one of my deputies are at a domestic disturbance, and they need backup." He turned to his son, his brows drawing over his eyes. "I need to drop you home, first."

"Robert can stay here with us."

"I don't know how long this is gonna take, Maureen. It could be fast or it could be a while."

"Then I'll bring him home if you're going to be stuck. He can help me get ready for tomorrow once everyone leaves. No worries."

His shoulders relaxed as relief darted across his face. "Thanks. I'll call you when I know what's what, time wise."

He went to Robert. "Sorry, son."

Robert gave him a one-armed shrug. " 'Sokay."

"Mind Maureen."

The boy nodded.

Lucas came to me and said, "Say my goodbyes to your grandmother."

"Stay safe," I told him after assuring him I would.

He stared hard at me for a moment before he squeezed my upper arm, flicked a look at his son, then left.

"Come on," I told Robert a moment later when I was sure my voice wouldn't betray my anxiety. "Let's grab some more desserts from the fridge. Nanny's probably ready for her second round of sweets by now."

"How many rounds does she do?" Robert asked as he followed me.

"As many as I provide," I said with a laugh.

While he helped me plate the chocolate cookies I'd made during my most recent bout of insomnia, I did something to ease my mind: I sent a silent plea up to my twin to watch over Lucas and help keep him safe.

I may not attend church or practice the religion I grew up with any longer, but I still considered my sister one of Heaven's—the celestial one—angels, challenged with watching over us all. There had been many days and circumstances where I'd silently pleaded for her watchful eye on a family concern. Since Lucas was as close as family, those requests included him, as well.

Chapter 5

"I'm meeting with the architect I told you about again this afternoon," I said, as I swiped a speck of dirt from the base of the marble. "Donovan Boyd. What a name, right? Midthirties, cute. He flirts as much as Nanny does." I laughed and stretched my legs out on the blanket. "In fact, I should introduce them. He's a bit young for her, and she told us on Sunday she's not on the lookout for anyone to marry right now, but you never know. She'll charm the pants off him like she does every male she comes in contact with."

I took a sip from the water bottle I'd brought with me and winked an eye up at the sun. The day was bright and beautiful, the humidity low, and the sky clear. The tall trees surrounding this quiet space were lushly leaved, the grass freshly groomed and pungent. Overall, a perfect Wednesday in Heaven.

"I'm thinking of adding five cottages with enough room for families of four or five in each, depending on the ages of the kids. Two bedrooms in each, two bathrooms, and a sitting room. They could also be used as overflow for Colleen's wedding parties. Four adults could easily stay in one, or the bridesmaids. Whatever."

I glanced down at my watch to make sure I wasn't running late. I'd left the inn right after lunch service was finished, telling Robert I had an errand to run. When he offered to come with me, I begged off and told him it was something personal. Teenage boys act exactly the same as grown men when you tell them this. The idea it could be something *female* related, and they stop asking to accompany you, lickety-split. Robert's face had gone as red as a maraschino cherry, and he'd avoided my eyes until I left.

"Anyway, since the place is doing so well and I'm booked fifty-one out of fifty-two weekends a year and most weekdays as well, now looks like the best time to expand. Since that was your dream and I'm in such a good financial spot right now, I thought, why not."

I sighed and closed my eyes. When I opened them again, I stared straight at the marble slab in front of me with my sister's name engraved across the face. Under the lettering were the dates of our shared birthday and the date she'd finally succumbed to the horrible breast cancer that took her from us.

"I can't believe it's almost three years, Ei. Cathy's wedding is coming up and then your…anniversary. Although calling the day you died an anniversary sounds weird."

I adjusted the sunflowers I'd brought—Eileen's favorite—in the vase in front of the headstone. I tried to come and visit her here at least once a month. It was difficult during the winter because the grounds weren't always maintained due to the copious and often record-breaking snowfalls we were plagued with. But during the other seasons I never missed a month. She'd been on my mind constantly of late, more so than usual. With Colleen's wedding behind us and her baby's imminent arrival, plus Cathy's wedding and pregnant state, I'd been thinking of how much Eileen was missing in our lives. She would have made a fabulous aunt and mother, had she been given the chance.

Thinking of my sisters had me remembering the last time we'd all been together on Sunday at Nanny's birthday luncheon. After Lucas had left to answer the domestic disturbance call, Robert and I had gone back to the dayroom. Soon after, Nanny yawned, and we all took it as a sign she'd had enough. Even though she's as spry and sharp as she was in her heyday, she was still ninety-four. Cathy and Mac drove her back to the nursing home, armed with the cake I'd boxed. I'd waved off the offer of help to clean up from Colleen and Slade. My sister was about as done in as I'd ever seen her, so I shooed them both home. With just Robert and me left, we spent a few hours baking for the next morning's breakfast offerings and practicing his decorating skills.

Lucas swung by around six to pick him up after notifying me he was on his way. One look at his face when he came into my kitchen and I knew better than to ask him how it had gone. I sent them home with a bag filled with leftovers.

Lucas mentioned nothing about the almost-kiss, and I hadn't asked him about it. But that didn't mean I didn't think about it. Or wonder what would have happened if his pager hadn't interrupted us.

Since then, he'd dropped Robert off in the mornings without coming in and picked him up in the afternoons after texting him he was on his way.

"Did I tell you I'm Cathy's maid of honor? Since Colleen had the honor at Cathy's first wedding, it made sense it's me for this one. Besides, Colleen is so big she can barely move three steps without needing to sit down. If I didn't know better, I'd think she was carrying twins. As it is, her baby's bound to be a ten-pounder."

"Good thing your sister's not around to hear you call her huge."

I lifted my head to find Lucas standing behind me dressed in his uniform, his cap on his head shading his face from the sun. He held a bouquet of sunflowers in his hand.

"I never said she was huge, just big."

"There's a difference?"

"A…huge one. What are you doing here?"

My pun hit its mark because he tossed me a grin as he moved past me and placed a hand on top of the headstone. "Hey, Lean Bean." The nickname he'd called her when she was a kid made my heart sigh. His grin morphed to a smile when he glanced over his shoulder at me and said, "Great minds."

He crouched down and added his own flowers next to mine.

"Mind if I sit?" It was his turn to sigh. "It's been a morning."

I scooted over on the blanket, and he plopped down, resting on an elbow and facing the headstone as I was, his long legs stretched out in front of him, crossed at the ankles.

"Thanks. To answer your question, I saw Sarah coming out of the market when I was downtown and asked why you and Robert weren't doing the shopping. Robert told me about last week when he went with you and everyone stopped to chat."

"It was like old home week and an FBI interrogation rolled into one. I felt bad for him, being the object of so much scrutiny and nosiness."

He shook his head and clicked his tongue. "Small towns. Anyway, she told me you'd taken an hour personal time. I figured I'd find you out here, visiting."

"How did you interpret I needed an hour's personal time to mean I was at my sister's grave?"

He shrugged and lifted his face to the sky. When he closed his eyes, I was able to stare at his profile without his knowledge.

"I know you come out here once a month to visit. Figured an hour of personal time was code for it."

"Code?"

"You know what I mean. You're a creature of habit, Maureen Angela."

I was, and since he was right, I wasn't upset with him saying it. "That's why they pay you the big bucks, I guess. Your unmatched detecting skills."

"Must be." A tiny grin split his lips.

"Thanks for bringing flowers for Eileen."

"No thanks necessary. I know they were her faves, like I know yours are lilacs."

"More ace detecting?"

"Good memory skills more than anything. I've known you since you were born, Mo. You've never passed a lilac bush you haven't stopped at and sniffed. I've seen you do it more times than I can remember, and Eileen never missed an opportunity to pluck a bunch of sunflowers and then eat up all the seeds."

"Lord, she loved those things. I could never understand why. I hated them then and still do. But she'd spend every last dime of her allowance to buy bags of them to snack on."

He winked an eye at me and cocked his head. "Remember what happened when she snuck into Mrs.

Blaylock's garden?"

On a groan I said, "How could I forget? Eileen was grounded for a month, and so was I even though I didn't do anything. In my father's eyes, because I was her twin, I was guilty by association. *Always.* So unfair." I grimaced and glanced at him. "I can't believe you even know about that much less remember it."

"Cathy laughed like a hyena when she told me and Danny Eileen got caught red-handed ripping old lady Blaylock's prize-winning sunflowers from her garden because she wanted the seeds and had already spent all her allowance money for the week. The way she described how your sister had been dragged straight to your father's office, all the while stuffing the seeds into her mouth to get rid of the evidence, still makes me laugh when I think about it."

"Eileen wasn't laughing when she barfed the 'evidence' up on Daddy's carpet. My hands were raw for a week after he made us scrub the darn thing clean."

"Your sister sure had an easy time finding trouble, didn't she? She gets it from Fiona for sure."

"No lie," I said, shaking my head.

"Good thing I wasn't police chief when you two were kids. I've had enough on my plate with your grandmother."

"Let's just be clear on this again, Chief." I placed extra emphasis on his title. "I wasn't the one getting into trouble and running wild. My only crime was being born four minutes after my recalcitrant sister."

Lucas chuckled again. "Duly noted."

We were silent for a few moments, as we both stared at my sister's headstone.

"The anniversary's coming up soon," he said,

breaking the quiet.

"Before you got here, I was thinking it's hard to believe three years have passed already. So much has happened she's missed out on. Colleen getting married. Danny dying and Cathy about to get hitched again. Both of them having babies a few months apart. Life-changing stuff she'll never get to be a part of. Eileen would have made a terrific aunt."

"As will you."

"But Ei would have been the fearless, daredevil aunt, you know? The one the kids would always want to do scary stuff with, always be up for an adventure with, like riding rollercoasters, rolling down hills, following into the deep end of the pool. There was a reason she was the known as the fun twin, you know, while I was always referred to as the quiet and boring one."

Lucas cocked his head again at me, a quizzical line forming between his brows. "I don't think I've ever heard anyone call you boring."

"That's because you didn't go to school with us. Every boy we went to middle and high school with called me boring." I immediately bit my tongue as an inferno of heat flew up from my neck at the declaration. The words pathetic and loser jumped in there to add to boring. "Eileen was the sparkly one, the one who had an entourage. Both boys and girls. She was the one people gravitated to. The one who could charm the socks off anyone if she put her mind to it." I rolled my eyes again. "She obviously got the lion's share of Nanny's flirty DNA."

"Well, you're still quiet, that's the truth. Except with family and close friends. Cathy always says she thinks your brain works twenty-four seven, but you only give a voice to about one-one-hundredth of the stuff you think about. Still waters and all. I don't think she's wrong."

"She's not. My brain never shuts down." Hence, my chronic insomnia.

"But you've never been boring."

"Like I said, you didn't go to school with us. Trust me."

"Kids can be mean," he said, with a shoulder lift. "And high school boys, I'll admit, are the worst. Believe me, I know since I was one, once upon a time."

"Robert's not."

"No, and thank goodness he isn't. I don't know who he takes after, but I'm glad he's such a good kid. And"—he nailed me with an intense glare—"don't sell yourself short in the aunt department. You may not like to ride rollercoasters or do daredevil stuff that could give a mother nightmares, but you've got the caring and loving disposition down in spades, which means a lot more than who likes to do death-defying stunts. Plus"—he slanted a side glance at me, the corners of his delectable mouth tugging up—"your nieces and nephews are gonna know how to bake and cook like no one's business. I foresee future chefs in your family line and young adults with food-prep skills that will do them well in life. That's a big plus nowadays."

The heat rushing up my neck grew hotter.

"Those scones you sent Robert home with last night, by the way, are a prime example of those baking skills and were a big hit. And not only with me. My dad had two of them this morning. When Robert told him he helped make them, the old man was impressed.

Well, as much as he showed, anyway. He's not known for giving praise, but any time he's not belittling the kid is a plus in my book."

"Why does he do that?" I asked, ignoring the compliment. "You'd think as his only grandkid, Hogan would be happy to have Robert visiting for the summer and be all over him like white on rice, like Nanny is with the three of us. And she sees us every day of her life."

Lucas blew out a long breath and lay down, his head cradled in his bent arm, his eyes closed again. "The easiest answer is because he's my son. Every time Dad looks at Robert he sees me at the same age, the age when my mother…left."

"Which isn't Robert's fault, just like it wasn't yours."

"Not in Hogan Alexander's mind."

"Okay, that's plain wrong. And sad. For you, but for Robert most of all."

"It is what it is. He's a bitter old man, and he was a bitter middle-aged man. I don't remember him ever smiling or joking when I was a kid, either. Which is probably why my mother left in the first place."

Lucas had been sixteen when he'd woken one day and found his mother gone. She hadn't left a letter for him, and he'd never had a word from her since. Not that I knew of anyway, and I'm sure I would have heard to the contrary. Cathy was his best friend, and he would have told her if his mother had reached out at any time over the years. It had been him and his dad ever since. As soon as Lucas's eighteenth birthday came, he'd enlisted as a way to get out from under his father's depressing, combative, miserable thumb.

"Luckily"—he winked an eye open at me— "Robert's got you to go to every day. He doesn't have to sit around and be browbeaten. You take care of him, treat him like one of your own, and pull him out of his adolescent shell." He smiled when he added, "And Fiona paying him so much attention at her party really made an impact on him. On the way home, he couldn't stop talking about her. About how interesting her life has been and how nice and welcoming she is with everyone. He figures it's the reason you and your sisters are so nice, to use his word. You get it from your grandmother."

I rolled my eyes and shook my head. "So he's like every other male on the planet and has a crush on a ninety-four-year-old, eyelash-batting flirt with a brogue."

His laugh warmed my insides.

"Honestly, I wish I could bottle her charm and sell it on the open market. We'd all be gazillionaires," I said.

"I didn't have the heart to tell him your grandmother's not my biggest fan."

"You know it's only because you've arrested her more times than any of the other police chiefs have. She has to keep up a good front of moral indignation and give you her rebellious face because you represent the 'establishment.' " I put air quotes around the word. "Truthfully, she adores you. Always has ever since she had you in her Communion class with Cathy and Danny."

He sat up and wrapped his arms around his knees. "Maybe. She certainly didn't give me such a stink eye before I was elected."

"Again, it's because you've hauled her in so many times. You haven't let her get away with anything like chiefs Palmer and Brady did. You call her on her crap, don't give her an inch of wiggle room, and she can't charm you like she can every other walking Y chromosome. She's not used to a man treating her that way, and it's frustrating for her."

"Yeah, that's obvious. She hasn't gotten into any trouble since she was admitted to the Arms, though. I haven't had to bring her down to the station once. That's a good thing."

I nodded. "For all of us, Cathy most of all, since she's Nanny's lawyer and de facto one call. Cathy's not biting her nails as much now or having her stomach knotted with worry that she's gonna get a call in the middle of the day about some new act of civil disobedience Nanny's been accused of. She can concentrate on the wedding, Mac, and the baby."

Mentioning my sister's upcoming nuptials put her fiancé's bachelor party back into my head, which had me then remembering the almost kiss with the man seated next to me.

And the behavior leading up to it. If I asked him about why he'd been so upset in my kitchen, I risked bringing up the kiss-that-almost-happened incident and I was hesitant to do so. Even though, for whatever reason, he'd been avoiding me the past few days, things appeared to be back on an even keel right now and I was reluctant to disturb the balance. I'd missed Lucas during his absence.

"Speaking of your older sister, you're her— *whatchamacallit*? Matron of honor, right?"

"Maid, not matron." I pointed to my chest. "Not

married, so maid."

His gaze flicked to where I'd pointed, dead center between my breasts. His perusal, however innocent it was, caused my nipples to tighten and pull inside my bra. I didn't need to look down to know they were balled into two points, their shape visible where they pressed against my blouse. When the tops of Lucas's ears pinked and he pressed his lips together, the notion his thoughts were anything but chaste drove through me.

"Right. Maid." He brought his attention back to my face.

"Why?"

"Why what?"

"Why do you ask?"

Confusion drifted across his features as he swallowed and blinked a few times. "Um, because Mac asked Slade to be his best man."

"I know. They've gotten close these past few months, which is really nice."

"Yeah, but Slade told him no because he wants to stick by Colleen's side in case she goes into labor. I'm Mac's backup choice."

"So you're his best man now?"

"Yeah."

"Does it feel weird? I mean, since you were Danny's best man, too?"

"I'm thinking it should, but it doesn't. It's not like they were divorced and I had to choose whose side I was gonna take. Danny died. Cathy is lucky she's getting another chance at happiness with a guy who loves her as much as Danny did."

I kept silent on that statement. A few months ago,

Cathy had revealed to Colleen and me that when he was home from his last tour, her soldier husband had told her he'd fallen out of love with her. He'd had multiple affairs while away on duty and wouldn't stand in her way if she wanted to divorce him. When she'd finally made the decision to file, army representatives had shown up at her door informing her Danny had been killed by an insurgent while he'd been on patrol. All thoughts of divorce had been forgotten. When Cathy tearfully revealed the story to us, I'd asked if Lucas had known about his best friend's behavior. Cathy hadn't wanted to ask him, knowing it would put a wedge in their friendship if he had, and didn't want to besmirch her husband's name to his best friend if he hadn't.

Lucas's words about Mac loving my sister as much as her first husband had proved to me he hadn't been privy to Danny's army behavior. I wasn't about to tell him the truth.

"Your sisters are making me rent a tux." The eye roll he tossed me coupled with the way his lips pulled down on one side told me what he thought about that. "Cathy won't let me wear a suit."

The picture forming in my mind of this delicious man in formal wear had my toes tingling and those damn nipples pulling tighter.

"She wants the wedding to be 'elegant.' " He cupped the back of his neck. "That's Colleen's influence for sure. If it was up to Cathy, I don't think it would be so formal."

"Don't bet on it. She's had more time to plan this wedding than the first time around. She's not eighteen this time and wants this ceremony to be different from the last one where you and Danny were in your dress uniforms and she was stuck wearing our mother's dress. There was no time to really plan a wedding before you both went off to boot camp. Thankfully she's got Colleen to run the show, so everything should be perfect."

"Yeah, I get that, but I wish I could wear something where I won't feel like I'm bound and tied. Whoever invented the bow tie should be horsewhipped."

"Don't say that to Cathy. You'll upset her."

"I won't, but I need a favor."

"I'm not talking her out of you wearing a tuxedo."

"No, I know. I'd never ask you to. Slade's got one he says I can borrow, but we're not built the same way."

That was the God's truth. Both were tall, but Slade was lithe, like the runner he was. Lucas was built like the linebacker he'd been in high school: broad shoulders, thick neck, and biceps like he lifted two-hundred-pound weights before breakfast. There wasn't an ounce of fat on him anywhere the eye could see.

I wished I knew what my eyes couldn't see, namely, what was housed under his shirt and jeans.

"When I tried on the jacket, I could barely move my arms," he said, pulling me out of the fantasy of Lucas in his birthday suit. "I need to run up to Concord to rent one because no place in town has one I can fit into."

"You're not leaving yourself a whole lot of time. The wedding's a week from Saturday."

"I know, which is why I'm asking for the favor. Cathy's tied up in court for the next few days, and Slade isn't letting Colleen travel anywhere outside of town in case, God forbid, she goes into labor. Mac's in New York doing promo for his book release. I wondered if you had some free time to go with me and give me some advice in picking the damn thing out. You know what your sister is looking for, plus you've got a great eye when it comes to visual things. I don't want to rent something Cathy'll hate."

The fact he was asking me to go somewhere with him should have filled me with joy. But in all honesty, I didn't have a moment I could think of to spare. I had a full house as usual, meetings scheduled with my architect, plus a wedding of Colleen's this Friday evening, the last one she was scheduled to be in charge of until after the baby was born. In addition to the other ninety things that came up hourly in my life, I really didn't have any free time at all.

One look at his face, though, and I knew I could never tell him that.

"When were you thinking of going?"

"I can swing it so I have tomorrow afternoon off. Pete said he'd cover for me for a few hours. I know you've got a wedding this weekend, so I won't ask if you can do Friday or Saturday, and the rental shops are all closed on Sunday, so tomorrow afternoon is it. Are you free? Or I guess the better question is, can you be?"

I did a quick calculation in my head. If I started decorating the wedding cake tonight and got some of the food prepared ahead of time for the reception, I might be able to pull it off.

Hell, I wasn't sleeping more than two hours at a clip these days, anyway.

I told him I could swing a few hours.

His face beamed like a lighted Christmas tree when

he thanked me.

"I'm not really doing it for you, you know," I lied. "I want this wedding to be as perfect and as stress-free as possible for Cathy, and if it means helping you pick out the right tux, so be it."

"It will be. Perfect, I mean. Especially since you're doing the food. If I have to wear a monkey suit, at least I know I'll get some great chow out of it."

Again, the compliment made my insides go all squishy. I glanced down at my watch so he wouldn't notice my face heat.

"I've gotta get back." I stood. Lucas did too and helped me fold the blanket I'd brought to sit on. "I have an appointment at the inn in a half hour, and I want to make sure everything's going okay before it. I don't anticipate any problems, but you never know."

I placed a hand on top of the marble and patted it. "Bye, Ei. Miss you. Love you."

Lucas mimicked my gesture, offered his own goodbye, and put his hat on.

As we walked back toward the parking lot together I said, "I wish I could hear her say, 'Love you more,' one more time."

"Cancer sucks."

"You won't get an argument from me."

Our cars were the only ones in the lot. Lucas had parked his squad in the spot right next to mine.

"You had this whole big lot of empty spaces and you're squeezed in next to me?" I shook my head.

He shrugged. "Efficiency. Who are you meeting with?" he asked as I stowed the blanket in the back of my car.

"Donovan Boyd. He's coming over again to show

me the plans for the bungalows he's drawn up since we met last week."

"You're not meeting at his office?"

"It's easier for him to come to me." I let out a breath. "Visiting Eileen took up all the free time I could squeeze in today."

From the way his eyes narrowed, I could tell he was thinking hard about something.

"I know that look. It usually precedes a grilling worthy of CIA operatives."

A smirk tugged at the corners of his mouth. "And here I assumed I had a great poker face."

"You do. I'm just really good at reading…people. Comes from being the quiet, observant, and boring twin."

Lucas shook his head. "We're not having that discussion again."

"So what's with the look?

With his arms crossed over his chest, Lucas leaned back against the squad.

His face was blanked, but since I'd made a second career of memorizing every facet of his personality, I knew something was cooking in his head. It was my turn to mimic him as I settled back against my car and crossed my own arms over my chest. "What?"

He took his time answering, but after a few beats in which his gaze dragged across my face as if he was searching for something, he said, "You work harder than anyone I know."

"Says the man who hasn't had a vacation in six years."

"That's different. I serve at the pleasure of the public, and crime never takes a holiday. You own your own business. You can take time off if you want to, and no one will be mad at you or call for your resignation or claim you aren't living up to the duties of the job."

"Spoken like a man who's never run his own business." I shook my head. And one who sounded like he was questioning his career choice.

"You never get"—he shrugged—"I don't know…Tired of it all? Constantly being at the beck and call of the guests? Cooking for people who don't appreciate it like they should?"

I squinted across at him. "My guests appreciate everything I do for them."

"Yeah, but it's not like they're family or friends. They're paying you for the privilege. You're just providing a service to them."

A tiny spark of anger wormed its way through me. "That's insulting."

"I don't mean it to be." He shook his head. "I'm sorry if it sounded that way." He raked his fingers down his face and blew out a breath. "Just…ignore me."

Not in this lifetime or any other.

"I don't know what's wrong with me today. Like I said, it's been a morning."

"Look," I said, the anger dissipating, "I love my inn. Love running it and catering to my guests. And yes, every now and again I get an obnoxious one I can't please for trying. But every other time I get real joy in doing what I do. When Eileen first came up with the idea for us to own and operate the inn, I'll admit, I was scared. But her fearlessness, her absolute belief it was the perfect thing for us convinced me it was. And I've never regretted my decision."

He nodded.

"Even this expansion was something she'd planned before she got sick. She knew in her heart the inn was going to be a success, and she had big ideas to make it grander." I snuck another look at my watch. "And on that note, I've gotta go. I don't want to keep Boyd waiting, especially since he's charging me by the hour." I opened the car door.

Before I could get in, Lucas grabbed my arm. "Mo, wait."

I stayed standing, my free hand resting on the door ledge. The difference in our height was never so profound as when we stood close together. I barely came to his shoulders, and since I never wore heels, I was forced to crane my neck to keep looking at his face. "What's wrong?"

"What do you know about this guy?"

Puzzled by the question, I said, "Other than the fact he comes highly recommended as a commercial architect, you mean?"

"Yeah."

I shrugged. "He arrived a few months ago, he's single, seems like he knows what he's doing design-wise, and he sounds like he and Nanny came from the same hometown in Ireland when he opens his mouth. Other than that, not much. Why?"

"He seemed pretty…interested, in you last week."

I rolled my eyes. "He's interested in my bungalows. It's a big project for him, and I imagine he wants it to go well."

"Not buying it, Mo. Guy looked like he was dying for a drink and you were a long, tall glass of ice-cold water. He wanted to slake his thirst with you."

I laughed loud and freely right at his face.

A face that went through a jumble of expressions when I did. From cocky, to confused, to finally settling on borderline annoyed. "What's so funny?"

"I don't think I've ever been referred to as thirst quenching before. I can't decide if I hate it or like it."

"You know what I'm saying, Maureen."

"No, I really don't." I tried to pull out of his hold.

He held on fast. "I watched his face when he was with you. The guy is into *you,* not your bungalow project."

I shrugged. "Okay. So what if he is?"

"What do mean, so? Did he ask you out?"

"What if he did?"

"And are you going?"

I wasn't, but he didn't need to know that. "What business is it of yours if I do?"

"You've just admitted you really don't know anything about him."

"Which is the purpose of going on a date with someone. To get to know them."

"So you are gonna go out with him." It sounded like an accusation.

"Again, so what if I do? What are you so concerned about?"

"So many things it would make your head spin, but first and foremost, he's a stranger."

"So is every guest who stays at my inn when they check in."

"That's different."

"I can't see it is."

"You don't make a habit of dating your guests."

He had me there. "But he's not a guest, so your point is moot."

He leveled that piercing glare at me I knew made people squirm in their seats. Chin dropped, head cocked, eyes focused and dripping with power and intent. If I didn't know him, I'd probably pee in my pants if he trained it on me.

But I did know him, and I was confused about what was going on.

"You might want to consider the fact that he's got no family here, no one to vouch for him except his boss. He's from another country."

"So was Nanny when she first got here."

"Yeah, a hundred years ago—"

"Don't ever let her hear you say that."

"—not a few months ago. He could have a criminal record or be a serial murderer for all you know, with a wake of dead women in his past."

I stood, rooted, gaping at him. "Oh, my God, listen to yourself. You realize you sound nuts, right?"

"What I sound is concerned for your welfare, Maureen. I care about you and don't want to see anything happen to you. You don't know what this guy's motives or intentions are."

"His *intention* is to design the bungalows I asked for, Lucas. That's it."

"Maybe that's his in."

"His what? You're making absolutely no sense. What the hell is an 'in'?"

"I'm making perfect sense only you're not seeing it. You're a woman living all alone in a big house—"

"I don't live in a house all alone. You make it sound like I'm in a shack in the middle of the woods with no one within five miles to hear me if I scream. I live in an inn, surrounded by people all the time. People who work and sleep there. What is wrong with you?"

"Nothing is wrong with me, and you still haven't answered my question—"

"I don't even know what it was anymore because you've gone off the rails talking about serial murderers."

The deep, jagged breath he pulled in was all the indication I needed to know about his level of frustration. Through lips barely parted, he ground out, "I want to know. Are. You. Going. To. Go. Out. With. Him?"

For the second time in my life, I was witness to Lucas raising his voice. The first time I'd been concerned. This time, though, concern gave way to aggravation. I tugged on my arm harder, jerking it back until he let it go. "And I want to know what business is it of yours who I go out with? I'm thirty-two years old Lucas, not fifteen, and you're not my father or my big brother or my boyfriend. I'm not some innocent little girl who's been locked away in a tower. I've been out with men on dates before, and yes, even men I didn't know well. Hell, I even lived with a man for two years who I'd hoped to marry until he showed me who he really was."

His face went white.

"Now I get we've been friends forever and up in each other's lives and business, but there's a line with any friendship and you're dangerously close to crossing it. I don't ask you who you're seeing or dating—"

"No one."

"—because it's none of my business. I don't know what's wrong with you, but you've been acting hinky lately, and until a minute ago, I was worried you were going through some kind of mental stress or close to a breakdown. Your father is living with you and making your life miserable; your son is caught in the crosshairs between the two of you; work stress. Whatever it is, you're not acting like yourself, and I've been worried. But right now I'm more pissed than worried, so before I say something I'm gonna regret or you say anything else that makes me even madder, I'm leaving." Before I slammed the car door behind me once I was seated, I added, "I'll see you when you pick up Robert."

I snapped into my seatbelt, put the car in gear, and took one last look at him.

He was still standing next to his squad car with his hands balled at his sides, and the shocked expression on his wide-eyed face would have struck me as comical if I wasn't so angry.

I backed up and pulled out of the parking lot.

Lucas never moved from his spot.

Chapter 6

Speeding when you're late for an appointment is one thing. Putting the pedal to the metal when you're pissed off is quite another, so when I almost blew the same stop sign my grandmother had a few months back, ending in her T-boning another car, I took a deep breath, relaxed my shoulders, and eased up on the gas.

What the actual hell?

Never once in all the years I'd known Lucas Alexander had he acted or spoken the way he just had. Domineering; overbearing; *crazy.*

I could count on the fingers of one hand the times I'd actually been mad at him and still have fingers left over.

It wasn't any of his business if I went out for drinks or dinner or anything else with Donovan Boyd or any other man. In the truest sense of the phrase, I was a free agent. And likely to remain that way since the man I was currently furious with was the one who held my heart and didn't even know it.

As I stopped at a traffic light, I took another deep breath. Two things Lucas had said kept repeating in my head. One, he'd stated he cared about me and didn't want to see me get hurt. As a longtime friend, I knew his statement was true on face value. How I wish it went deeper though and he'd been admitting he cared about me in more than a friendly fashion.

The second thing was he'd said he wasn't seeing or dating anyone.

Even though I found it hard to imagine, it thrilled me he wasn't involved. In my own warped way, the old "if I couldn't have him, no one could" declaration shot through me.

After his divorce, gossip had run rampant among the town busybodies the reason for the split had been infidelity on Lucas's part. While the cause of the breakup had been cheating, it hadn't been Lucas who'd broken his wedding vows. Being chief of police was a taxing, never-ending job, and Nora Alexander had made known her displeasure about all the time she spent with only their son for company. Often and loudly to anyone who would listen. She'd threatened she was going to leave him several times if he didn't resign and get a "normal job" where they could spend time together as a couple and a family.

A moral obligation gene ran deep through Lucas, though, and he'd made a promise to the community he'd been raised in to do the job to his utmost.

Nora had no such gene floating in her DNA, and when Lucas had refused to quit, she finally made good on her warning and had taken a lover.

And then another.

After two years of trying to avoid the whispers about his wife's extramarital activities, Lucas had finally had enough. He'd filed for divorce, and she'd gladly signed the papers. Due to his erratic hours, Nora had been given sole custody of eleven-year-old Robert, but in one moment of genuine goodness, she'd declined it, opting instead for shared custody.

Once he was a free man, the single women in the

area had descended on Lucas, to hear Cathy tell the tale. Olivia Joyner, the town matchmaker, had even tried to fix him up with one of her single-and-lookings. There had never been a hint of scandal or gossip about anyone else in his life, but I never imagined it meant he was sitting home alone at night. I'd figured after the public shame he'd already suffered from his wife, he'd taken steps to ensure whoever he was dating was kept under wraps.

I couldn't blame him. Wagging tongues, judgmental rumors, and nasty gossip was the life's blood of a small town. I know, since I've lived here my entire life and have heard more of it than I ever care to hear again, so I'd assumed Lucas kept the women he'd dated out of the spotlight.

When he'd said, without hesitation, he wasn't dating anyone, I admit, I was shocked. Pleased more than I should be, but surprised nonetheless.

Why wasn't he? I was dying to know the answer, but the only person I could ask who might have an inkling was my oldest sister. I was loath to bring up the subject of Lucas's love life with her because I knew without a doubt she'd read into—correctly—why I wanted to know. My feelings for Lucas had been speculated upon by my sisters more than once over the years.

When I was a teenager, they'd teased me about how I went uber quiet whenever he was around and snuck worshipful glances—Colleen's description—at him. Even before Robert had started working for me, my sisters had commented on the number of times Lucas dropped by the inn to grab a quick dinner of leftovers or have a cup of coffee before he headed home. I'd never given them any reason to suspect how deeply I was in love with him, but they were both extremely astute women.

When I pulled into the inn, I spotted a familiar car in one of the private spaces I kept for family. The sound of laughter rang out from my kitchen.

"How come I didn't know we were having a party?" I said when I came into the room.

My sisters were sitting at my table, each with a cup in front of them, the tin of insomnia cookies opened and on the table between them. Robert was at the sink, washing dishes, as Sarah pulled something from the oven.

"Where have you been?" Cathy had one of Colleen's swollen feet in her lap and was massaging it.

"I had an errand to run," I said, sneaking a side-glance at Robert's back. "Why are you two here?"

"I wanted to check to see if everything was set for Friday's event," Colleen said.

"You couldn't just call? Or send Charity? Slade specifically said he doesn't want you driving alone at this phase."

"He's not the boss of me." She pouted, then reached into the jar and brought out two more cookies. "He's treating me like I'm the first woman ever to have a baby. I'm pregnant, not infirm or useless. And I've got a business to run."

"He's worried about you, sis. This is your first baby. His too. He gets to be overprotective if he wants."

"Says who? I'm the one carrying around a basketball the size of Montana in my body, not him."

"It says so in the marriage rules," I told her. "First-time fathers are allowed to be a little overbearing and

104

overprotective of their pregnant spouses."

The pout morphed to a tiny grin. "I must have missed that chapter."

"Most likely wasn't listed in your Cliff Notes edition."

"Must be. Besides, Cathy drove. I merely thumbed a ride and rode shotgun when she said she was headed here."

I drew my attention to my oldest sister, lifted my eyebrows, and tilted my head. "Any reason in particular? Or were you just craving cookies?" I asked when she pulled a handful from the jar as Colleen had and put them on her plate.

"Don't chide me. I'm stress-eating," she mumbled around the cookie. "There are a million details running through my brain, and I'm petrified I'm gonna forget something. Between work, this wedding, and getting everything settled for the two weeks we'll be gone, I'm going crazy. I don't remember being so stressed and nervous the first time I got married," she added after swallowing.

"You were a kid then, Cath. Nothing stressed you." I glanced up at the wall clock.

"And Mom and Nanny were in charge of all the details," Colleen said, licking her fingers. "All you had to do was show up at the church looking young and virginal."

Robert dropped a dish in the sink, the sound shattering through the room.

"Sorry," he muttered over his shoulder to me. "Nothing broke." The skin around his neck was cherry-red, his ears an even deeper shade.

I tossed him a smile. "No worries." To my sisters, I

opened my eyes wide and pulled a "tone it down, there's a kid present" face.

They got the hint and nodded.

Sarah patted him on the back and said, "Finish up, and we can go check the last load of sheets. They'll be dried by now."

He wiped his wet hands on a towel.

"I just left your dad, so he's probably gonna be here soon to pick you up. Everything going okay?"

He nodded, flicked a glance over to my sisters, then followed Sarah out.

"Where did you see Lucas?" Cathy asked, popping another cookie in her mouth.

"At the cemetery."

"That was your 'errand'?" Cathy air quoted the word.

"Yeah."

"And Lucas was there, too?"

"He had something to ask me and needed a quick answer."

"What?"

"Nosy much, Cathleen Anne?"

She narrowed her eyes at me.

"The anniversary's coming up," Colleen said as she rubbed circles over her protruding abdomen. "We should do something."

"Let's get Cathy married and your baby here, first," I said, "before we make any decisions. Those two events are enough to get through."

Cathy was giving me her lawyer death stare, and I could sense more of an inquisition coming about Lucas. If I've learned anything from my oldest sister in my thirty-two years, it's how effective diversionary tactics can prove. Before she could lay into me, I jumped in.

"When is Mac due back?" I asked her as I tossed on my apron. Today's had been a Christmas present from Nanny and read *Be nice to me or I'll poison your food* on the bodice.

Not exactly a reassuring phrase for a cook, but Nanny's sense of humor has always been a little warped and a lot of wicked.

"Not until Friday night."

"I think it's the reason you're stressing out so much," Colleen told her. "You're missing your man. Whenever Slade's gone to the city for foundation business and I can't go because I've got a wedding, I don't sleep a wink. I'm so used to him being right next to me in bed every night that when he's not, I can't settle down. Something seems"—she shrugged—"off. Not right. You know?"

"Yup. I haven't slept more than an hour a night since Mac left. The bed feels empty. Georgie sleeps at my feet, but even she's been hard to settle down. I think she misses him, too."

Cathy and Mac's black Lab puppy was difficult to settle at the best of times.

"There ya go." Colleen pointed a pregnancy-puffy finger at her. "You should call him before you climb into bed and have a little hot phone sex before you go to sleep. It'll calm you down."

"Or it'll ramp her up even more," I said.

Colleen shook her head. "Nope. It does wonders for relieving stress."

"First-hand experience?" Cathy asked.

"How do you think I've been surviving the last two months? Junior here doesn't allow for a lot of personal interaction between Slade and me which creates a bunch of frustration."

"And talking dirty to your husband helps?"

"More than you can possibly know. In fact—"

"Excuse me, ladies."

All three of us turned to that lilting cadence. Donovan Boyd stood in my kitchen doorway, a long cylindrical tube on one hand, the other stuffed into his pants pocket, and a look of wry amusement traipsing across his face.

To me, he said, "Forgive me, Maureen darlin'. I don't mean to intrude on your…conversation, but your assistant said to come on back."

"You're not intruding at all," I said, coming to him and shaking his hand. I introduced him to my sisters, both of whom stared at him with open and obvious interest.

"Well now," Donovan said to them with a devilish smile, "you three are making me homesick for Ireland, y'are. All that glorious red hair and those sparklin' blue eyes. Beauty certainly runs in your family."

Since we'd all grown up at Nanny's knee, witness to her never-ending coquettish ways, you'd think we'd be immune to his blatant flirtatiousness.

I, in truth, was. Not so my older sisters. Colleen actually blushed, something I hadn't seen her do in years, when she smiled across the table at him. Cathleen swiped the cookie remnants from her mouth with a flick of her pinky finger, then ran her tongue around her teeth to remove any tell-tale chocolate before she sat up as straight as our mother had taught us to and graced him with a beguiling grin.

"I've got those revised plans we discussed last

time," Donovan told me. "I think you're gonna be pleased."

"What plans?" Colleen asked.

I explained about the expansion.

"I knew you'd been thinking about expanding," she said, "but I didn't know you'd actually hired an architect."

"Can we see them, too?" Cathy asked.

Boyd looked to me for approval. I gave it.

After I removed the dishes and cookies from the table and wiped it down, he placed the new plans on top of it. Robert and Sarah returned, and soon my kitchen was filled with several pair of eyes perusing the sketches he'd made.

I have to admit I was thrilled by what he'd drawn. Boyd explained how he'd modified the plans after our last visit, the space he'd added to each cottage, and the differing layouts we could incorporate into each if I was so inclined. He stood close at my side, his hand brushing my arm several times as he reached to indicate something on the drawings.

"You've more than enough space to add a second level on a few, should ya wish," Boyd said.

"I hadn't considered a second level, but it makes sense and adds even more sleeping space."

"They'd be like little efficiency cottages," Cathy said. "For families who have kids."

"Or for bridal suites," Colleen added. "All the attendants could stay together, for instance."

I nodded. "That was my original thought. It would be easier for parties to be together than spaced out around the inn. Bachelorette parties could all stay in one place, too."

"You wouldn't have to do every one the same." Boyd leaned over me again, this time resting his hand on my shoulder. "You could do every other one, or put the second levels on the ones in the center of the group."

"Oh, my God, I love this!" Colleen grinned from ear to ear. In the next second, her smile flew. Her shoulders folded in on themselves as she placed her hands, open palmed, across her bulging belly. "Okay, *ow*. Lighten up, kid."

The room went silent, all eyes on my sister.

Cathy latched onto her upper arm as I came around the table and crouched down in front of her.

I laid my hands on her knees and asked, "Are they the same as you've been having? The Braxton Hicks, not the real ones? They don't feel different, do they?"

She didn't respond while she held her breath. A fine sheen of perspiration popped out over her eyebrows and top of her mouth.

"Do you want us to call Slade?"

"Or take you the hospital?" Cathy asked, her face gone white, "just in case...you know? The baby really is coming?"

Colleen managed to shake her head, but there was no mistaking the fear breaking through the pain in her expression.

"Hey. What's going on?"

I looked over my shoulder to find Lucas ambling through the doorway. He held his hat in his hand, his gaze targeted in on me. A wave of profound relief broke through me. Lucas was the calm in any storm. Despite being miffed at him, he was a blessing to see.

"Colleen's having contractions," I told him.

"We're worried."

He made a motion for me to move out of the way.

I stood tall so he could take my place beside my sister. He slipped one of her hands off her belly and cupped it between both of his.

"Coll, look at me." With wide, unfocused eyes, she did. Lucas, a tiny tilt to his head, his expression soft and kind with the ghost of grin crossing his lips, said, "Ya gotta breathe, kiddo. Come on. Let it out, then take a breath in, slow and steady now, okay. Do it with me."

Calmly, he guided her through it, breathing along with him to his commands. After a few moments, her shoulders relaxed and she let her eyes drift close, one final, deep breath following through.

The mood in the room collectively calmed. For the first time since she'd grabbed her belly, I was finally able to take my own full breath.

When she opened her eyes again, I slid by Boyd, who'd been watching silently from next to Sarah, and handed her a napkin to wipe her sweating brow and lip. She stared across at Lucas. "If I didn't love my husband with everything in me, I swear, Lucas Alexander, I would marry you in a heartbeat. Thank you."

The tips of his ears went pink. "Real or fake?" he asked.

"Fake."

"You want me to drive you to the doctor's office to make sure?"

"No. No, I'm sure. This is the way they've been. A quick punch lasting about a minute or two, and then it eases."

"No regularity to them?"

"No, none, which is why the doctor isn't

concerned. Since this is my first pregnancy and I'm over thirty-five, these are more common. He said I can start to worry when they occur a little more like clockwork. For now, it's only been one or two a day."

Lucas glanced up at his son, then back to my sister. "Nora went through this, too. Scared the bejesus out of us at first. Most important thing to do is time them and breathe through them."

"That's what the doc told us."

"You sure you don't want me to take you in to be checked out as a precaution? Or I could take you home. I've got the squad right outside. It's no bother." A corner of his mouth lifted. "I'll even let you play with the siren if you want."

Right there was the reason I could never stay mad at this man and why I loved him with every ounce of my soul.

Gentle laughter bounded around the room.

"I think I'll take you up on that. Slade should be there about now, so I won't be alone."

"Let me call him first, to be sure." Cathy pulled her phone from her pocket.

"You okay to stand?"

"Like I told these two and my husband"—she cocked her head at me and Cathy—"I'm pregnant, not infirm."

"Yeah, but your center of gravity's a little off, so it's no shame to ask for help, especially when changing positions."

"You should mention that to Slade. If he keeps trying to haul me out of a chair, I'm afraid we'll both wind up in the hospital. Me in labor, him in traction."

He slid an arm around her back and kept hold of

her hand while she hoisted herself from the chair. Boyd moved to take her other arm.

"Okay?" Lucas asked.

She nodded.

While both men helped her and Cathy gave Slade a rundown over the phone, I packed up a go-bag of leftover lunch items.

"Here." I handed it to Lucas once Colleen was upright. "Carry this for her." To Colleen I said, "It's quiche Lorraine, a few slices of whole wheat bread for dinner, and some cookies for dessert. Let Slade deal with it so you won't have to cook, and you can sit with your feet up, rest, and be catered to."

"I won't say no because Slade loves your cooking." She gave me a side hug while Lucas held her by the other arm. Boyd stepped back to his spot by the sink. "And you know I never miss the chance to be pampered and catered to."

"Remember Nanny's motto," I told her. "Never stand if you can sit, and never sit if you can lie down. She may be a bit much at times, but that philosophy is what's gotten her to ninety-four years old."

"God's truth," my sister said.

"Call us later, okay?" Cathy told her, bussing her cheek. "Let us know how you're feeling and if we can do anything."

"Will do."

"I'll come back for you after I get her settled, okay?" Lucas asked his son. "Unless you're done now and want to come with us."

Robert shook his head. "I've got a few things left to do."

Lucas shot a glance at me, then back to Robert.

"Okay. See you in a bit."

"Well, that's more excitement than we've seen in a while," Cathy said once they'd gone. She reached over to the counter and grabbed the insomnia cookie jar again. "I need these right now to calm me down. Who else wants?" She lifted the open jar to the others.

Boyd was the only taker.

"It's a wonder you're not getting a sugar high."

"I'll crash later," she said around a cookie.

A moan flew through the room, ringed with a loud sigh of pleasure. "Well, now, these are the best t'ings I've ate in a while. Don't tell me ya made these yourself?" Boyd addressed me. "Taste like nectar, they do. Can't have been made by a mere mortal." The moisture in his eyes twinkled as he trailed his tongue across his bottom lip and pulled in a bit of cookie crumb, his gaze never moving from mine.

The man was a shameless flirt, and while I was pleased with the compliment, it was a bit overboard and dramatic for a cookie. I mentally ticked off another thing he had in common with Nanny.

Robert beat me to an answer, the hard tone in his voice unusual. He sounded an awful lot like his father when he said, "She bakes everything herself. And everything she makes tastes great, not just the cookies."

I smiled across the room at him. The scowl pulling his brows over his eyes and the downturn of his mouth told me he didn't like Boyd's response to my cookies.

"That's the gospel truth," Cathy said, finishing off her final cookie. "Of the three of us, Maureen got the majority of the cooking DNA." She placed the jar back on top of the refrigerator and turned to me, a winsome expression flashing in her gaze. "I don't suppose you have any more quiche you want to get rid of, do you? I don't have anything good at home for dinner. I haven't gone shopping since Mac's been gone." She widened her eyes and bit down on her bottom lip. I wasn't fooled for a moment with her pathetic pout. I'd seen her use it one too many times on our parents when we were kids as a way of getting out of a punishment or a scolding. It worked on them every single time.

It didn't on me.

"Did you give it all to Coll?" she asked.

Without a word, I wrapped up a half tin of the leftover lunch. "You're on your own for bread, though, since I gave her the last of it."

Her expression changed from downtrodden to bright and airy in a millisecond. "I'm better off not having any bread anyway. Those cookies were all the carbs I need for the next week, or I won't be able to fit into my dress come wedding day."

While I bagged the quiche, she told Boyd, "I love your plans, Mr. Boyd, and I think adding the second levels is a great idea."

"Well now, I'm glad for you saying so, but it's ultimately up to your sister whether or not she wants them. And please—Mr. Boyd's me father. Call me Van, darlin'."

"Either way, it's going to be great, Van." She shook his hand, then accepted the shopping bag from me. I'd tossed in a cupcake when she wasn't looking. "Walk me out," she told me before she pulled Robert into a hug.

"Don't let my sister work you to the bone," she said in a stage whisper. "Have some fun while you're here, too."

His response was to kiss her cheek and nod.

I excused myself and followed her through the breezeway to the outside hall.

"Oh my God, Mo," she whispered after a quick glance over her shoulder.

"What?"

"What do you mean *what*? Donovan Boyd is one serious piece of gorgeous, and he can't keep his eyes off you."

I lifted a shoulder.

"Don't tell me you haven't noticed, because I know for a fact you're not blind. He's seriously into you. Has he asked you out?"

First Lucas and now Cathy. Why was everyone so concerned about my social life all of a sudden?

I ignored the question. "I'm not blind, nor deaf, Cathleen Anne," I said.

"What?"

"The man is a little too charming for his own good. Works that Irish lilt as much as another shameless flirt we happen to know."

She flicked her hand at me in a dismissive fashion. "An old woman who flirts is nothing compared to a hot guy who does. Nanny does it for attention and nine times out of ten to get a rise out of people. For the shock value. A man like Boyd does it to let you know he's interested and wants to get to know you better. You didn't see him watching your face when he was showing us those plans."

"Probably because he was gauging my reaction to what he'd drawn up. He wants to make sure I like it so I'll approve the project. It's a big one, and I suspect landing it will be a feather in his cap at the firm."

Cathy was tailor-made to be a lawyer. Our father, after all, had groomed her to follow in his footsteps since her birth. The way she dropped her chin a millimeter, slanted her head to one side, and peered at me through eyes that had gone just a little closed, was a look I knew was meant to elicit information. From a witness on the stand sworn to tell the truth, it worked.

But once again, we were in my home, not a courtroom, and I wasn't putting my hand on any Bibles.

I glared right back at her and kept silent, something I know frustrated her to no end.

With a dramatic sigh, she finally capitulated. "It's amazing you never studied law or went into law enforcement. You'd have made a kick-ass FBI agent, you know."

"Two lawyers in the family and having Lucas around is all I need to know I could never make it as a cop. Now, go home, play with your puppy, and eat dinner. And take Colleen's advice and call Mac before you go to bed. I've got an inn to run."

I leaned in to kiss her cheek, but she pulled back. "Maureen."

I could feel a lecture coming on and wanted no part of it. "Cathy, really. Go home."

This time she let me kiss her. With a shake of her head, she finally left.

Back in my kitchen, Sarah was speaking to Boyd, who had a mug in his hand, while Robert was silently removing dishes from the dishwasher.

"Ah, there she is," Boyd said with a smile when I entered. "The lovely innkeeper."

Honestly, the man really could have apprenticed at Nanny's knee. The sound of a cup meeting a saucer banged through the room.

"Sorry," Robert mumbled as he snuck a side eye at me.

"Why don't we go into my office and go over these plans in more detail," I said to Boyd.

"Brilliant. Thank you for the tea, Sarah, darlin'," he told her. "Tastes as wonderful as if my sainted mother brewed it herself."

Boyd's charm may have been wasted on me, but not so my fiftyish assistant. A red flush streaked up her chubby cheeks as she graced him with a shy smile.

Boyd must have gotten the hint I wasn't interested in his flirting, because once we were in my office with the drawings open and laid out on my desk, he was all business, something I was happy for.

After about fifteen minutes, a knock came on my open door. Robert peeked his head through and said, "Sorry. Dad's here."

"That's fine. We're finished, anyway," I told him.

Boyd rolled up the designs, and I went back to my kitchen. Lucas had the tin of insomnia cookies in one hand, his other buried inside it. He grabbed a handful and caught my eye as I came into the room.

A grin as boyish and infinitesimally more charming than anything Boyd could conjure bloomed across his face. I could live the rest of my life on just that look and never grow hungry or weary.

Of course I couldn't let him know that, though. With my arms crossed over my chest and a lift of an eyebrow, I peered at him like a mother would a naughty child.

"I didn't think you'd mind if I swiped a few," Lucas said. "No time for lunch. I got...busy."

Some of his busy time had been spent sparring with me at the cemetery. Shaking my head, I strode past him, pointed to the table, and said, "Sit."

He did as I commanded without a word, taking the cookies with him.

"You, too, Bobby-Boy."

From the refrigerator, I pulled out slices of ham from yesterday's lunch, bread, mayonnaise, and mustard.

"Colleen okay?" I asked as I put together some sandwiches.

"Yeah. Slade was there, got her all settled on the couch with her feet up." The smile I'd heard in his voice changed. The reason for his sudden mood shift was explained when Boyd strode back into the room.

"Chief," he said, bobbing his head Lucas's way.

It took Lucas a moment before he said, "Boyd."

It didn't escape me neither of them attempted to put out a hand.

"I'll contact ya in a few days with the next round of designs, darlin'. I think you're makin' the right decision addin' on the second levels. 'Twill give ya a lot more room."

"I agree. It's the right way to go."

He smiled, then snuck a glance at Lucas, who was eyeing him like a hunter with Boyd caught in his crosshairs.

"I can see m'self out." He gave me a wink and pressed my shoulder.

I swear I heard Lucas growl.

"Chief. Young man." A moment later he was gone.

I plated the sandwiches and handed Robert two glasses. "Pour some milk."

"That guy's pretty touchy," he said as he lifted the carton.

"What do you mean?" Lucas asked.

He hitched a shoulder and snuck a glance at me. "He kept touching Maureen while he was showing us those drawings. Like, on purpose."

"I don't think it was on purpose," I told him, waving it off. "We were pretty crowded around the table, which is why I wanted to look at the plans in my office, so we could spread them out and not be bumping into one other."

Robert shook his head. "I don't think it was by mistake. I thought we weren't supposed to touch people without their permission. I mean"—he tossed a quick glance at his father—"we get talked at about personal space and crap all the time in school. Mom's forever grilling it into me, too."

"Was he handsy?" Lucas asked me. "Did he make you feel uncomfortable?"

I rolled my eyes. Lord, protect me from alpha males and their cubs.

"Honestly, no." I shrugged. "He's a harmless flirt, like my grandmother. And—" I pointed a finger at Lucas before he could ask another question. He closed his mouth. "—before you tell me it's not the same, don't. Now eat, then get on home, the both of you. I've got work to do."

"Maureen—"

"Don't, Lucas. We already discussed this once today, and you know how it ended. I don't want to go over it all again."

His lips tightened, but he didn't argue with me this time. If Robert hadn't been sitting across from him, he might have, but he let it go, for which I was thankful.

I had no personal interest in Donovan Boyd and certainly didn't want to discuss him with the man whom I did.

I went to speak with one of the guests who had a question and left them to finish their snack.

"Robert wants to come with us tomorrow. I mean, if you're still willing to go shopping," Lucas said when I came back. "When I told him about you helping me pick out a tux, I realized he didn't have any dress clothes with him. I want to get him something appropriate to wear to Cathy's wedding. Okay with you? Can you spare him? I don't want to leave you shorthanded."

I grinned over at the boy in question. "I think the inn will survive without the both of us for a few hours, don't you?"

One corner of his lips lifted. A tiny milk mustache lined his upper lip, and he was so adorable I wanted to hug him. I loved this boy as much as if he were my own.

My heart pinged as I thought for the first time what it would be like if he were. Or if I had one of my own children to love and cherish. It was a dream I hadn't allowed myself in several years.

Since Eileen's diagnosis and subsequent death, I'd tossed out all thoughts of having my own family. The reason, to my mind, was a valid one. As twins we shared everything, the most important of which was our DNA. Eileen's cancer had been rare, but as her genetic clone, the fear the same cancer was somewhere looming about in me waiting to break free was always on my mind.

After Eileen's diagnosis, Cathy and Colleen had been tested to see if they carried the same rare genetic trait for the breast cancer she'd been afflicted with. Thankfully, they were both clear of it. I'd told them, when asked, I'd been tested too, which was a bold-faced lie, because I hadn't.

The reason why was easy: I was terrified of the results.

I knew in my head I should get tested to alleviate the worry of not knowing. I even suspected that dread was the basis for all my sleepless nights. But the fear the test would confirm I was actually a carrier of the gene was so overpowering, every time I made an appointment to get tested, I canceled it.

By not knowing for certain whether or not I was afflicted, I was able to convince myself all was well. By getting tested and possibly confirming the diagnosis, I was committing myself to a death sentence.

I'd argued with myself time after time if the disease were going to rear its head, it would have done so already, since everything else in our lives had coincided. We'd gotten our first tooth within days of one another, taken our first steps the same morning. We liked and disliked most of the same foods, and each of us had an allergy to pineapple. My period had started three hours after Eileen's. I'd been born four minutes after her, but my life had run along the same course as hers. Why wouldn't the cancer do the same if it were, in fact, part of me? Eileen had been dead three years, and if the cancer were going to develop, conventional wisdom stated it would have by now.

And even knowing that, I still didn't have the courage to be tested.

So many nights I'd stood in my kitchen, trying to bake away the anxiety. It was one of the main reasons I'd never told Lucas how I felt about him. It wasn't fair to either of us for me to confess my love. I couldn't start a romantic relationship with him, no matter how much I wanted to, for fear it would be ruined with a cancer potentiality.

The logical portion of my brain called me an idiot more times than I could remember, but I was leading with my heart here and making most of my decisions based on emotions and not logic. I didn't feel it was fair to Lucas or any man to face a lover's illness and death. It was the same reason I'd opted out of ever having children. It wasn't right to leave them without a mother.

So I'd kept my feelings to myself, content with having him in my life as a friend. Well, maybe content wasn't the correct word. Satisfied didn't seem appropriate, either, when I thought about it.

Lucas rose and brought his plate and glass to the sink, his son, doing the same. "That'll get me through the rest of my shift."

"Do you have stuff for dinner?"

"Yeah, don't worry. We won't starve."

"Never thought you would."

His expression told me he wanted to say something else, but when his gaze flicked to Robert, who stood next to the counter with his hands slung in his pockets, I guess he thought better of it.

"I should be able to come free about one tomorrow. You never answered me. Are you still willing to go shopping?"

I told him I was while I mentally rearranged the staffing for lunch service so Robert and I would be able to leave without any concerns.

"Okay, well, then, we'll see you in the morning."

I walked them to the front door and then watched as they drove off in Lucas's squad car.

Hours later when the inn was quiet for the night, my guests were all snuggled down, and I'd put the finishing touches on the wedding cake for Friday's event, my phone pinged with an incoming message from Cathy.

—*You up?*—

I replied back I was. Two seconds later, my phone rang.

"It's almost one a.m.," I said without preamble. "Why are you still awake? Don't you have court in the morning?"

"I do, and I'm going to be a basket case, I know. But my mind won't calm down."

"What's the matter?" I sat down at my kitchen table and lifted my feet to the opposite chair.

"I need you to talk me off a ledge."

"About what?"

"Pick a topic. The wedding. The baby. Mom and Dad. Work. Everything that could possibly go wrong next Saturday has been pounding through me for hours. I'm worried Colleen's gonna go into labor right in the middle of the ceremony. I'm stressing Mom and Dad won't come and Mac will leave me at the altar, realizing he doesn't really want to be married to me. I had a dream last night Father Duncan died during the ceremony, and we never got the chance to say our I do's. Mac used it for his get-out-of-jail-free card."

She dragged in a deep breath, and right then I realized how close to the proverbial ledge she was. This wasn't my sister, not in any way, shape, or form. Cathleen Anne O'Dowd Mulvaney was the most logical, unemotional sister of us all. Nothing usually fazed her.

She was a great deal like Lucas in that regard.

"I feel like I'm going insane," she said, "and can't stop it."

"Okay, first of all, you're not going insane. You're the most sane human being I've ever known. What you're experiencing is normal nerves, Cathy, something alien to you so you don't know how to handle them."

"If this is simple nerves, then I'm a porn star."

"Okay, why that analogy popped into your head I do not want to know. But"—I took my own breath—"Mom and Dad are definitely coming. They asked me to keep a room open for them, and I have. They'll be here the night before the wedding, so stop worrying." Before she could steamroll over me, which she had a habit of doing, I continued. "Colleen going into labor is a possibility, and if it happens, we'll deal with it. Or rather, Slade will. I'm your maid of honor, not her. I will be there to support you whether she's in the hospital or not."

I heard her sigh through the receiver.

"The baby is fine. You had a checkup the other day, and the doctor told you all was well. You're pushing your concerns about Colleen and all this Braxton Hicks crap onto yourself. Stop. And for the love of Mike, Mac Frayne loves you more than any man ever has, including your late husband. His face lights up the moment he sees you come into a room. He follows you everywhere like your new puppy, with the same goofy expression on his face the pup has. The only difference is Mac keeps his tongue in his mouth, unlike Georgie."

A strangled laugh sailed through the line.

"Complete adoration and love is what the man has for you. He's not gonna realize he made a mistake, because he knows he hasn't. God, Cath, he loves you for being who you are." I shook my head, my own sigh blowing through my lips. "Now stop all this nonsense and unnecessary falderal and go to bed."

She sniffed, then blew her nose. "When did you start using words like *falderal*?"

"It was today's entry on my word-of-the-day calendar."

Her laugh came fast. "Sounds like something Nanny would say if she were scolding us."

"I'm sure it's in her never-ending and always-expanding lexicon."

Another sigh met my ears. "I'm sorry."

"For what?"

"Being this way. It's ridiculous, I know, but I'm so jumpy and I can't figure out why."

"One word, sister dear: cookies."

She laughed again. "That cupcake you sneaked into my go-bag didn't help, you know. I ate it first."

"Your body is on such a sugar high right now, it's no wonder your brain can't calm down. Go downstairs and make yourself a cup of chamomile tea, bring it into bed along with one of those dry legal journals you're always reading, and I'm sure you'll fall asleep from boredom in no time. And stop fixating on all the things that might go wrong on your wedding day and start thinking about all the wonderful things that are going to happen, instead. You're marrying one of the best men

I've ever known, Cath, and he adores you. I know you realize how lucky you are."

"I do. Ha-ha. You got me to practice for my vows."

With a shake of my head, I blew her a raspberry. "Go to bed, Cathleen Anne."

"Who died and made you the older, bossier sister?"

"It was a coup. I'm hanging up now."

"Okay, I get it. Thanks for being my ledge-talker-off-er. Love you."

"Love you more."

I put my phone down on the table and rubbed my eyes with the pads of my fingers. I knew exactly what Cathy was experiencing, because my mind, like hers was tonight, never settled down. Hence, the baking insomnia.

In an effort to conquer it, I shut the lights and made my way up the stairs to my apartment at the back end of the inn, after first making my own cup of chamomile tea to bring with me.

Chapter 7

"Dad, this is the third place." Robert groaned. "I'm tired, and I'm hungry."

I flicked a glance at Lucas's face. His frustration at not finding a store that could accommodate him for the short-notice tux rental was evident in his tired eyes and downturned mouth. His son's whining wasn't helping the situation.

"Let's see what their turn-around time is, Bobby-Boy. Then we can take a break. Okay?"

His answer was a typical teen's: he shrugged and slammed his hands into his jeans' pockets.

"Come on." I walked into the store with the two of them behind me.

I'd spent years following in Eileen's wake whenever the shopping bug hit her. She would flit from store to store, pick out a bunch of items, try them on and evaluate how she looked, and then we'd move on to the next store until she found exactly what she wanted. Since she never knew what it was until she found it, I was familiar with the shopping frustration both these men were suffering through.

I went up to the cashier's desk and asked if they would be able to have a tuxedo ready in the time frame we needed and was told it wouldn't be a problem. When I pointed to Lucas, the cashier repeated his statement.

"We get last-minute rental requests all the time and for all body types," he told us, waving a hand in the air as if it weren't an issue at all. For the first time in an hour, Lucas's shoulders relaxed.

The cashier brought us to a fitter who asked about the type of suit and cut we were looking for. Lucas deferred to me on this, thankfully, because I didn't think his "something that won't make me feel like a sausage" was the description they were looking for.

The fitter escorted Lucas into a room to take his measurements, and Robert followed me while I browsed around the store.

"Your dad wants you to get a suit for Cathy's wedding," I said while I rifled through the hundreds of choices on the retail racks. "Do you have any idea what you want? Dark colored? Light? Patterned?"

His answer was another shrug.

"What's wrong?" I asked.

He shook his head and glanced down at his sneakered feet.

It was obvious Robert had no siblings, and sisters most of all, because if he had he would have known it wasn't in our makeup to let a crappy mood go by unchecked. I'd dealt with all kinds of temperaments and grumpiness from my own sisters my entire life. A cranky fifteen-year-old was nothing.

Ignoring his noncommunicativeness, I pulled jackets in various cuts and colors from the rack, chatting nonstop as I did. I'd ask him a question, then answer it myself. After I held up a series of jackets against his torso, he finally snapped out of his petulance and started voicing his opinions on what I'd shown him. I gave myself a mental high five when we found a suit in his size we both liked.

"Go try it on," I told him.

Just as he was about to enter the fitting room, his father emerged.

Lucas Alexander was a man born to wear a uniform. He'd filled out his army fatigues and dress uniforms to perfection, every inch of broad shoulder and narrow waist outlined. Each time I saw him in his police uniform my knees grew soft. But bedecked in a midnight black, double-breasted tuxedo waistcoat with a starched white shirt under it, a black bow tie, and straight-edged trousers with a front pleat so defined and sharp you could slice a piece of cheese on them, the man could have stepped off a bridal-fashion-show runway.

Those shoulders spanning a yard from pad to pad were held snug and drew over bulging biceps to taper to his trim waist.

My vision narrowed and tunneled so all I could see was him. I think I gasped, audibly, because both father and son gaped at me, questions on their faces.

"What do you think?" Lucas asked me as he glanced from me to his son and back again. "Is this what Cathy's looking for?"

"You look good, Dad."

He thanked his son, but his attention remained on me. "Maureen? What do you think?"

There was no way I could answer truthfully and not make a total fool of myself. I wanted to tell him he was the handsomest man I'd ever seen, that I wished the tux was for our wedding instead of my sister's, and I wanted nothing more than to rip it off him and jump into his arms.

Yeah, I can imagine what would have happened if I'd said all this, and not one scenario ended without me being sent to a psychiatric ward for observation.

So, I kept my truths to myself and told him, "I agree with Robert. It looks good. Exactly what Cathy is going for."

The fact my voice shook and sounded as if I needed an inhaler I hoped would go unnoticed.

"You sure?" Lucas cocked one eyebrow to his hairline.

"Yes. It's formal enough for her idea of the wedding without being over the top. Mac has a waistcoat, too, so I think this choice is the best."

"Okay. If you're sure."

Father and son disappeared into their prospective dressing rooms. Alone now, I fell into a cushioned chair and fanned myself. Thank God I'd seen Lucas in his tux before the wedding. I was going to be nervous enough as it was on the big day. If I'd gotten my first gander at him looking like an old-fashioned movie star from the 1930s come to life right before walking down the center of the church, I can be sure I would have tripped going up the aisle, my focus and every thought centered on the man.

Robert emerged from the dressing room first. He'd donned the trousers with his beat-up sneakers still on, and the jacket over his T-shirt. If the look he was going for was baby-rock-star wannabe, he'd met the requirements. I wanted to tell him how adorable he was but knew I'd embarrass him if I did.

"How does the fit feel?" I asked when he went to stand in front of the tri-mirror. "Not too tight? Not too loose anywhere?"

"It feels good. Like it fits, you know? Does it look okay?"

"It looks great, and you look good in it."

Lucas walked out of the dressing room in time to hear me.

"Maureen's right," he said, going to stand behind his son so they both faced the mirror. "The pants need to be hemmed a bit, but it looks good on you. Do you like it?"

He shrugged as an answer. I called a fitter over, and he checked the fit personally, agreeing the pants needed to be shortened.

"They're working on my tux now and said it would be ready in about an hour. Can you do the same for the pants so we can take both home with us?" Lucas asked.

He was told it was no problem. While Robert went to change, Lucas went to pay.

Once we were all done, Robert asked again about getting something to eat. "There's a food court here," he said. "We could grab something fast."

"I don't feel like fast food," Lucas told him.

Robert went into hangry-teen mood again. I was all set to say it didn't matter to me where we ate, but Lucas rolled over me.

"I don't think you're gonna die from hunger if we skip the food court and go someplace where we can sit down for a bit," Lucas said, "and eat something a little more nutritious than chicken nuggets. Besides, Maureen did us a big favor by coming to help and offering her advice, so I'd like to treat her to someplace nicer than a fast-food taco stand."

I started to say it wasn't necessary, but Lucas shot me his penetrating glare, and I bit back the words.

"Agreed?" he asked, turning back to his son, when I kept silent.

The boy's mood changed on a dime. He shot me a quick look, perked up a bit, and nodded. "Yeah. You're right. Sorry."

"Come on, then. Let's go look for a sit-down place," Lucas said.

For a late afternoon on a Thursday, the mall was packed, and we were forced to bob and weave between the crowds until we found a nice family-style restaurant. A smiling maître d' escorted us to a table, gave us menus, and told us our server would be with us shortly.

As it happened, I sat between father and son, Lucas on my right, Robert across from him on my left.

"I'm starving," Robert mumbled when he opened his menu.

I bumped his shoulder with my own. "You're always starving," I said, with a smile. "Just like your father. A walking appetite."

"What does Fiona always say?" Lucas asked. "Apples and trees?"

I laughed. "That, and a million other things that hit it right on the head."

After our middle-aged waitress arrived and took our orders, Lucas leaned forward and rested his elbows on the table.

"Thank you again for coming and helping us out," he said. "I haven't worn a tux since prom." He chuckled. "The cut and the price have changed dramatically since then, that's for sure."

Robert snorted at his father's words, then flushed scarlet.

"What's so funny?" I asked.

He lifted his head, glanced once at this father and then me, then dipped his chin again. "Nothing."

"Oh, I think it was something." I snuck a side eye at Lucas and grinned. "You're trying to imagine your father at prom, aren't you, and can't quite picture it, can you, Bobby-Boy?"

Little grin lines popped up on his cheeks as he tried not to smile back.

"I'll have you know I looked pretty damn good at my senior prom," Lucas said, mild pique slipping through his tone. "I was even voted Prom King."

"Dad." Robert shook his head. "That's so lame."

I was barely able to keep my laugh at bay. "Chief of Police Lucas Alexander at eighteen. You should have seen him, Robert. Decked out in a blue velvet tux with a frilly baby-blue shirt and bow tie, his long hair slicked back like he jumped off a 1950s teen idol magazine, a pint of dime store cologne wafting from him."

I lost the small thread of control I still had when Robert burst out laughing.

Lucas's feeble "Hey!" of indignation made us laugh harder.

Our drinks arrived and while the waitress handed them out, Robert and I tried to control ourselves.

We did a pretty poor job of it.

"You didn't really wear a velvet tux, did you?" Robert asked his father.

"I think I can hunt up Cathy's prom pictures as proof. Colleen probably has them in the family albums at the house. I'll ask her tomorrow."

"Yes, I did, Robert, and you should know I rocked

it. Why do you think the whole class voted me king?"

"Because everyone felt sorry for you, showing up in a velvet tux?"

Robert had taken a sip through his straw and, at my words, laughed so hard he choked, then spit out his soda when it went up his nose, the moisture raining down all over the table.

Unfortunately, this only made me laugh harder. I don't know who Lucas gave the more stern warning glare to: his son or me.

"What did Mom wear?" Robert asked when he finally composed himself.

Lucas winced.

I answered for him. "He and your mom had broken up, so he took Shelly Bookerman, the biggest flirt in the class." I rolled my eyes and shook my head. "Shelly had a huge crush on your dad and had been after him for all of high school to pay attention to her. Followed him whenever he was in the halls, always tried to sit near him in the lunchroom. Went to all the football games, home and away, to cheer him on. She must have thought she'd died and gone to Heaven—the real one—when you finally asked her out," I added, addressing Lucas.

"Dad."

Lord, was there anything worse than hearing a teenager's voice filled with censure? Or funnier?

Lucas hadn't heard him. Or if he had, he chose to ignore it, his attention focused solely on me.

"First of all, how do you even know that? You were, what? Ten, when I was a senior?"

"Nine, and how do you think I know? Cathy, of course."

"I can't see her discussing me with you when you were a kid."

"She didn't, not exactly. But she and Danny did all the time. You were the topic of their couch conversation on more than one occasion."

"And you, what? Just happened to overhear them?"

"To be truthful, it was more Eileen than me. She was a major eavesdropper, especially with anything Cathy-related. But she always shared what she overhead."

I grinned and took a long pull of my water. "Your dating life was a wicked hot topic to twin nine-year-old girls living in a house of women. Daddy didn't count because he was at work so much. You and Danny were the brothers we didn't have but so desperately wanted."

"Brothers?" The same tone he'd used in my dayroom laced the word. I couldn't tell if he was amused, annoyed, or just trying to imagine what having bothersome little sisters would have been like. Either way, the heat blasting my way was incredibly arousing. I lifted a shoulder and took another sip of my drink in a feeble attempt to cool down my raging insides.

"So you and Mom fought even back then?" Robert asked, shifting Lucas's attention.

A weary breath blew from between his lips. "We were kids, son. We didn't have a lot of control over our emotions. Neither one of us had ever been away from Heaven, and we imagined the world revolved around each of us. You know your mom. She gets…upset. Easily, about stuff."

"What did you do to make her so upset she broke up with you before prom?"

He shook his head. "In all honesty, I don't even

remember."

"He enlisted," I said, "just a few weeks before prom and graduation."

His eyes narrowed at me. To the question in them, I explained, "Remember? Both you and Danny signed up on the same day. Cathy cried but realized it was what Danny wanted. What he'd always dreamed of. Nora"—I flicked a glance at Robert than back to his father—"didn't."

Lucas closed his eyes for a moment and shook his head. To Robert he said, "She hated that I'd joined the army. Told me if I wanted to go halfway around the world just to get myself blown up she didn't want to see me anymore. Since I'd already bought the tickets..." He lifted his shoulder.

"Shelly Bookerman swooped in." I chuckled at the expression on Lucas's face. It didn't take someone attuned to the nuances of facial tics to know he was remembering how she'd followed him from homeroom the morning after the news spread about him and Nora. Cathy, via Eileen, had laughed with Danny over how Shelly had been sympathetic about their parting of ways, and then said how much it would be a shame if Lucas went stag, or worse, not at all. Before he knew it, she'd invited herself to go along as his date.

"But you and Mom got back together eventually," Robert said. "I mean, obviously. You must have realized how much you loved each other."

I didn't think Robert knew the real reason his parents had married, and I wasn't about to elucidate him on the circumstances. It wasn't my place, nor was it something I think Lucas realized I knew.

It had been Eileen, the master of snoopiness and

font of overheard conversations, who'd told me, after listening to a phone call between Danny and Cathy. On home for a few weeks at Christmas one year, Lucas, Danny, and Cathy had gone bar hopping. Since this was Heaven, a town that only boasted three places you could actually call a bar, it hadn't been unusual to run into several of their old friends.

Nora had been among them.

Whether alcohol-infused or simply one more time for old times' sake before he shipped back out, Lucas and Nora had gone home to her apartment. Three months later, Lucas came back to town and the two of them were married at City Hall. Robert was born at the end of the summer.

Telling your teenaged son you'd done the honorable thing by marrying the high school sweetheart you'd impregnated wasn't something, I felt, suitable for dinner conversation.

Lucas must have agreed, because to answer his son, he said, "I always loved your mom. Even with all the craziness and breakups we went through. I always will, because we got you out of the bargain. You were the best thing to come of our being married."

"Dad." Robert hung his head again and shook it, his neck flushing.

"Whatever happened between your mom and me, Rob, happened. Just know how much I love you."

I swallowed and concentrated on my soda glass when tears threatened. Luckily, our food arrived and conversation suspended while it did.

While I cut my burger in half, Robert remained silent and motionless, his hands resting on the table on either side of his plate. Nanny is the queen at changing the temperature in awkward and emotional moments by inserting a humorous quip or making a bizarre statement to jolt people out of the moment.

I channeled her when I said, "Let this be a cautionary tale, Bobby-Boy, against renting a blue velvet tux for your own prom. Basic black is the way to go every time. Women drool over a man in a black, well-cut tuxedo. Trust me on this."

When Robert lifted his head, a smile so like his father's whipping across his face, I sent up a silent thank-you to Nanny. One glance at Lucas and my own smile wobbled.

His eyes had narrowed and gone half closed again, his head tilted a hair to the left and his mouth—dear God, his mouth! The seductive and secretive smirk pulling at his lips was almost my undoing. I stopped cutting my burger, the knife dropping from my hand to the plate with a resounding *clang*. My right leg began to bob under the table, a nervous tic from childhood whenever I knew I was about to be scolded, rearing itself.

"What?" I asked him.

He blinked, once, slowly and purposefully, those tiny dimples at the corner of his mouth deepening as his smirk grew to a one-sided grin. "Nothing. Eat, before that gets cold." He pointed at my plate with his knife.

The rest of the meal moved smoothly with Lucas asking his son about his plans for his junior year in high school and regaling us with funny tales about some of the strangest arrests he'd made in our little town. When the waitress brought his receipt back after he'd paid, she smiled, thanked him for the tip, and as we got up to leave, said, "It's so nice to see teenagers still go out to eat with their parents." She laughed and added, "Mine didn't want to have anything to do with me and my hubby once they turned fourteen. You have a lovely family. Enjoy the rest of your night."

One glance at Robert and I could tell by the way he hung his head again, his shoulders drooping, he hadn't been happy with the declaration. I didn't dare look at Lucas as we walked, single file, out of the restaurant. My mind was a jumble of thoughts, my body thrumming with emotions. I kept them to myself as we walked back to the rental store.

While both men went to try on their altered items one more time to ensure everything was to specifications, I ambled about the store, lost in my thoughts, imagining a life where Lucas and I were married and Robert was truly my son.

And imagining was all I was ever going to do about it, I knew. Lucas may have loved me like a good friend, but there was nothing romantic about our relationship and never would be. I'd resigned myself to it long ago.

Back in the car with the garment bags stowed in the back, the three of us were fairly silent on the drive home. Even though I wanted to make light of what the waitress had said, I was nervous bringing the subject up. I didn't want to cause Robert and Lucas any embarrassment. I wasn't a wife, nor a mother, and certainly neither to these two.

It was almost seven thirty when Lucas pulled into the inn's circular driveway.

"Well, that was a productive afternoon," I said as I unbuckled my belt and forced a smile.

"I'll walk you in." Lucas put the car in park.

"There's no need. I'm a big girl. I'll see you both tomorrow."

Sometimes I forget how stubborn this man is.

"Sit tight," he told his son. His long legs beat me to the front door, which he pushed open and held for me.

Even though it was still early, the inn was quiet. I made my way back to the empty kitchen to find a note on the table from Sarah informing me all had gone well during the afternoon.

"Well, that's good. No catastrophes while I was away."

"Just proves what I was saying yesterday. You can take some time for yourself now and then, and the walls won't come tumbling down if you do."

I rolled my eyes and moved away from him. Before I could get far, he wove a hand around my arm and pulled me back.

"What? What's wrong?" I asked.

"Why do you always ask that?" The hint of irritation in his voice showed in the lines furrowing his forehead.

"You mean aside from the fact you're scowling at me right now?"

His skin instantly smoothed, and a calming breath blew through his lips.

Holding my gaze, he took a step closer and dropped his hand.

"Nothing is wrong," he said, each word emphasized. "I wanted to thank you again for coming with me today. I know you had to rearrange a bunch of stuff to do so."

I shrugged and tried to take a step back. When Lucas was this close, I had a difficult time keeping my emotions from galloping across my face. But the magnetic pull of his eyes held me in place.

"And you can't know how much I appreciate it. Or how much I appreciate what you've done for Robert. The kid is so different whenever he's around you. Less moody, more talkative. Today was the most I've heard him laugh since he got here. And it's because of you. You make him...feel happy."

My heart skipped in my chest.

"He laughed so much because he was picturing you in a velvet tuxedo," I said to mask my pleasure at his words. I grinned up at him and added, "I'm gonna call Colleen tomorrow to see if she can hunt up those pictures so I can show him."

He squinted down at me, and my knees got all kinds of wobbly.

"You're not the only one around here who remembers proms gone by, you know."

"What does that mean?"

He took a step closer, and I swear my body temperature went up a good ten degrees from sharing his natural heat.

"I have a vivid memory of you at seventeen wearing an extremely revealing dress resembling a slip more than a prom gown."

A flash of the dress in question crossed the front of my mind. "At least it wasn't a velvet tuxedo."

He ignored the jibe. "I'd stopped by the house to speak to your sister, and you came down the stairs, all ready to be picked up by your date."

"Tick Jones." So named because he was the most annoying boy in our class, and when anyone even so much as glanced at him, he stuck like glue, happy to have a friend. Even if they were a friend in his mind only. I'd agreed to go with him because he was the only boy who asked me. Eileen, of course, had gotten several requests.

Lucas nodded. "You were wearing a pale purple dress with the thinnest of straps and a slit up the side almost to your ass. I told Cathy I was surprised your father was letting you out of the house in it. You didn't look anywhere near seventeen."

I'd loved the dress the minute I saw it in a store in Concord. Eileen had as well.

"My sister was wearing the same dress, you know. Hers was pink. Did you complain about how inappropriate you thought hers was to Cathy, too?"

He shook his head. "I never even noticed your sister. All I could see was...you."

His voice dropped on the last word, and a hot bullet of desire dropped along my insides.

He cocked his head and asked, "Did Jones ever tell you what I said to him before you all left?"

"Said? N-no. I didn't even know you'd spoken to him."

"You went upstairs to grab your bag or something you'd forgotten. I cornered Jones and told him I remembered what it was like being a seventeen-year-old boy on prom night. Sneaking liquor or beers around the back of the high school gym. Maybe passing around a little weed. Some guys even have certain expectations of how the evening is gonna end. The expense of the tux rental, the limo, the corsage. It puts ideas into their head that's cause, maybe even justification, for some kind of...payback from their date."

I knew exactly what kind of payback he was

143

referring to.

"Oh, good Lord, tell me you didn't."

His eyes went to half-mast, his lips curling at the corners in a predatory smirk. "Oh, I did. And I added if he didn't return you to your house on time for the curfew your parents set, looking and *smelling* exactly the way you had when you left with him, he was gonna answer to me come the morning."

Why I wasn't angry at this Neanderthal behavior surprised me because I should have been. Lucas had been almost twenty-six then, had already completed two tours in the army, married Nora, and Robert was on the way. He was miles ahead of the boys in my high school in world experience.

And as a man now of the world, he'd felt it was his duty to protect someone he regarded as a little sister. I couldn't be mad at him, but it did, however, explain certain things about prom night I'd mulled over afterward. Like how Tick, whose real name was John Alan, had his eyes glued to his watch all night long. In an era before cell phones were as common as colds, we'd never known the time without one. Tick had checked his watch from the moment we arrived at the gym and had rechecked it every few minutes thereafter. He'd stayed, as his horrible nickname implied, stuck to my side the entire night. He hadn't even left me alone when I'd snuck off to the bathroom. He'd followed behind and waited for me outside the door. He'd neither interacted nor spoke to anyone else at our table, including my sister who could make an igneous rock talk back to her if she put her mind to it.

When the dance ended, a few people stated they were driving up to Eagle Rock to have an after party, drink, spend the night, and watch the sun rise. Tick had grabbed my hand and escorted me to the limo he'd rented. Eileen's date wanted to go with the throng, but even though she was a rebel in many ways, she never blatantly disobeyed an edict from our father and ditched the after-party idea, hopping into my limo. Her date had gone on with the others.

Tick walked us both to the door, and after Eileen disappeared inside, I waited to see if he'd kiss me goodnight. He hadn't, tossing me a quick "Thanks for going with me" over his shoulder while he ran back to the car.

Monday, and for the rest of high school, he'd look away whenever he saw me coming down the hallways.

"That poor boy." I shook my head. "You put the fear of God into him for no reason. He was totally harmless."

"Oh, there was plenty of reason, Maureen. Like I said, I remember what it was like being a seventeen-year-old. Raging hormones and sense of entitlement run rampant. Plus…"

"Plus what? You just wanted to act like a big, badass army ranger in front of a pitiful teenager? Assert your macho manliness? God, Lucas, I can't believe you. John Alan Jones was never a threat to me or any teenage girl. He was *gay*. Everyone knew it, but since he wasn't out yet, we all left it unsaid."

He had the grace to look slightly abashed. In a heartbeat, that changed. "I didn't do it for the reasons you think I did, Maureen."

"Why then? Why torture a poor boy and make me feel even more inadequate? More lacking?"

"What the hell are you talking about?"

"Tick was the only boy to ask me to prom. Remember the conversation we had yesterday about me being the boring twin? Well, despite what you think, I was. Eileen had guys falling over themselves to take her. I didn't. Just when it looked like I'd have to either go alone and be mortified at being dateless or stay home, John Allan asked me. Do you have any idea how pathetic and unworthy I felt at seventeen? How I felt"—I flapped my hands in the air—"less than my sister or any of my friends?"

"Maureen—"

"No, Lucas, you had no right to say those things to him. I was more safe with John Allan Jones than I'd have been with any other boy in my class. It wasn't your responsibility to make sure I was. I wasn't your younger sister or a little girl or anything else you can dream up to justify needing your he-man protection. I'm still not."

The silence following my angry tirade was thunderous.

My chest heaved, banging against my ribcage with every jagged breath I hauled in. The pulse at Lucas's neck visibly slammed against his skin with the rapid beat of his heart, our gazes locked and holding. I couldn't decide if he was angry and pissed off because I'd called him out on his overprotective, unnecessary behavior, or mad at himself for what he'd done.

"No, you're not," he whispered, darkly. "You're certainly not my sister, and you're not a little girl anymore. If you were, I couldn't do this."

Before I could ask what he meant, he cupped my cheeks in his palms and tilted my head upward. With his hot gaze locked onto mine, I knew he meant to kiss

146

me.

Part of my brain screamed for him not to, arguing if he did it would change everything between us. I couldn't allow this, had to fight it.

The other part commanded I shut the hell up and kiss him back like I'd been wanting to for a lifetime.

Funny—that voice sounded an awful lot like Nanny's.

My pulse drummed in my ears and my vision tunneled in on his mouth right before he touched his lips to mine.

Lucas's kiss was everything I'd always fantasized it would be: hard and commanding, yet silky smooth and seductive.

Any protests the logical part of my brain continued to bellow I simply disregarded. Powerless against the rush of emotions surging through me, I simply gave in and let Lucas take control.

The pads of his thumbs caressed my jaw as his mouth moved across mine, learning the contours, memorizing the feel. Tiny tingles, like champagne bubbles popping, burst over my mouth. A subtle shift and he tilted my head back. With a gentle swipe of his tongue, he slipped through my lips and mated with mine. Each intimate tug caused a raging river of erotic sensations to flow through me from head to curling toes. My panties grew tight, my lower body swelling against them, begging for relief, clamoring for it.

I slid my palms up the boulder hardness of his chest to curl around his neck and thread into the coarse, thick pelt of his hair. I stretched up on my toes, barely touching the ground with the tips while I pressed in tight against his body. A body thrumming with desire.

147

It was impossible to think. Impossible to move. I'd waited a lifetime to discover this man's touch, yearned for it when I knew I shouldn't.

His hands roamed down to cup my butt, palmed it through my jeans, and molded me even more against him. His chest wasn't the only thing hard or throbbing.

The simple notion this man wanted me was overpowering, and I couldn't prevent the moan of pleasure that broke from within me.

At the sound, Lucas stilled. The drum of both our hearts beating was audible in the quiet surrounding us.

Then, with torturous slowness, he moved back from the kiss, deliberately waiting to slide his hands from my backside until I stood surefooted.

Our gazes locked, held. There was an unfathomable question crossing his eyes.

His mouth was swollen and wet from kissing me, and when he swiped his tongue across his bottom lip, my eyes went wide. I dragged my fingers across my own lips, still able to taste him.

I backed away from him, stopping only when my hip hit the counter edge, still staring at him.

Lucas took a step toward me. "Maure—"

"Dad?"

He spun around to face Robert. The boy stood in the doorway, staring at the two of us, a look of bewilderment on his face.

"You coming, or what? I've been waiting, like, forever."

"Yeah, son. Yeah." He shook his head like a dog shucking water. "I was just talking to Maureen about…something." He turned back to me. Swallowed. "We should go."

I summoned up a smile for Robert, hoping it appeared natural.

"See you tomorrow morning, Bobby-Boy."

He tossed me a quizzical eye flick and a nod.

With one last head bob at me, Lucas placed a hand on his son's shoulder and walked him out.

It was as if he'd taken all the air, all the energy in the room, and me, with him.

When I was finally alone in my kitchen, I let out a slow, deep breath and slid down into one of my chairs, my legs finally giving out.

I dropped my head down onto the table and closed my eyes.

Chapter 8

"I think I'm bigger today than I was yesterday and even the day before," Colleen said, from her perch on her couch. "Do I look like I am?"

Cathy threw me a warning glare over our sister's head, a silent message to hold my tongue.

While Colleen did look a little larger than when I'd seen her on Wednesday, I wanted to chalk it up to the cavernous dress she was garbed in. It had no shape at all, something my always fashion-conscious sister didn't usually wear.

"It's because you're sitting down with your feet up," I said. "Everyone looks bigger that way."

"So I do look bigger?"

Answering her question was a no-win situation, so I handed her a teacup filled with decaf tea and shook my head. "You're almost due, Coll. What you look is pregnant and ready to deliver."

"You have no idea how ready I am," she said, squirming. Cathy reached behind her and adjusted the slipping pillow at her back. "I swear this kid is gonna come out walking."

"Let's hope not," I said. "Although Nanny would probably be delighted because then she could buy shoes for her."

One of their cellphones pinged.

"That's mine," Colleen said. "Can you get it for

me, Mo? I can't reach."

I glanced at the face. "It's Slade. Again."

"Honestly, the man is supposed to be out enjoying himself," Cathy said, hands fisted on her hips. "That's the third time he's texted in the past hour."

"He's worried I'm gonna go into labor when he's not around," Colleen told her, "and he's afraid I won't get to the hospital in time."

"Doesn't he trust us to get you there? We're the ones"—she pointed to me and then at herself—"who've been driving these roads since we were teenagers. The both of us know every twist and turn and shortcut this town has to offer. I'd bet money either of us could get you there faster than he could."

"Don't tell him that, or he'll ask you to start sleeping here so if I go in the middle of the night, you'll be Janey-on-the-spot." She read through the text. "They're at the Love Shack. Slade says to call if he's needed."

"Text him back to enjoy himself and not worry. We've got you covered, and nothing's gonna happen. I want Mac to enjoy himself tonight, have a few beers, and relax. This book tour has been exhausting for him."

"At least now he's off for the next month," I said. "You two can get married, go on your honeymoon, and relax together."

"I can't wait."

My sister got the dreamy, faraway look in her eyes usually accompanied by a sappy grin whenever she thought about her fiancé.

A heartbeat later, the grin showed up.

"Uh-oh." Colleen glanced up from texting when she heard me.

"There she goes. The girl with the stars in her eyes," Colleen said with a smile. "Can I tell you how much *I love* how much *you love* your man?"

"I truthfully never thought I could feel like this." Cathy shook her head and drank some of her tea. "It's a little…scary."

"And all kinds of wonderful, too, right?" Colleen asked.

"Yeah."

I'm not an envious person, not usually, but right then that emotion shifted through me. Both my sisters had what they'd always dreamed of, always wanted. They each had a man who adored them and had changed their lives just to be with them, and the bonus of babies on board made their lives so much sweeter. Why wouldn't I be a little jealous?

Colleen's smile drifted toward me, Cathy's following.

"What?" I asked, although from their inquiring gazes I could guess what they both were thinking.

"I saw Lucas in court yesterday," Cathy said.

With a simple shrug, I replied, "Not an unusual occurrence."

"He told me you went shopping with him and Robert."

Another shrug, different shoulder this time. "Because you asked him to wear a tuxedo, and he wasn't certain what kind. Colleen's on a no-travel ban from Slade, you were tied up with work, and time was running out for him to rent one. And speaking of tuxedos—" Cathy pulled back whatever she was going to say. "Where are the old family albums?"

I explained about Robert and the blue velvet tux.

Colleen directed me to one of the hall closets, and I found the large plastic container my mother had stored the albums in.

"Ooo, let's go through these," Cathy said when I dragged it into the living room. "We haven't looked at pictures in forever."

I handed each of them an album and then flipped through a few to find Cathy's prom photos.

"Oh, my God. Here's my high school graduation." Cathy held the album up, face out, so we could see. "Look at the outfit on Nanny."

True to form, our grandmother, who was close to seventy at the time, was decked out in a body-hugging cherry red suit with a skirt ending above her knees and a jacket so tight the indentations from her bra straps were visibly pushing against the fabric.

"Danny and you look cute," Colleen said. "I can't believe a week after this was taken you got married."

"Here's her wedding album," I said, holding it up.

"Let me see."

I handed it to her, and she started flipping through the pages.

"We were so stinkin' young, and I was so stupid," she said after a few minutes. "It still boggles my mind Mom and Daddy didn't try to talk me out of getting married at barely eighteen."

"You weren't stupid." Colleen reached out and rubbed Cathy's arm. "Young, yes, but you'd known Danny practically since birth. Everyone who knew the two of you knew you were going to get married someday. And we all loved Danny. He was perfect for you."

"Not everyone," I said, flipping through another

album. "Eileen didn't like Dan and never had, even when we were little."

"What! Why not?" Cathy asked.

I put the album down and took another out of the container. "You know Eileen. She was a natural bullshit detector. Inherited the trait from Nanny."

"Truth," Colleen said, then sipped her tea.

"She told me she didn't think Danny was the wonderful guy he seemed and he wasn't being totally truthful, maybe even lying to you about something. She never told me what it was, but she believed it right up until he died."

"How come you never told me this?"

"Why would I? From the outside, you two appeared happy, and you never gave any indication you weren't. Neither Coll nor I knew anything to the contrary until you confessed what had been going on in your marriage."

"Eileen was always a little fey, as Nanny would call it," Colleen said. "Sensitive to what was going on around her." She flipped through the album in her hand.

I nodded.

"Hey, found your picture," Colleen said a moment later. "Good gravy, I forgot all about Lucas's hideous tuxedo."

"Let's see." Cathy stretched out her hand for the book.

There were about a half dozen pictures of Cathy and Danny, then a few of Lucas, taken in the same living room we were all currently sprawled in.

Cathy laughed as she flipped a page and found a photo of Lucas and Eileen and me. He was dressed to attend prom, that dumb tuxedo shining back from the camera flash, while we were in our pajamas. "I remember when this was taken. Eileen dragged you down the staircase screaming she wanted a picture of the three of you. What were you guys, ten?"

"Nine," Colleen said.

Lucas had picked us up and settled us each on a hip. Eileen was smiling like she'd just won the lottery, while I was staring at Lucas.

"She loved him so much," Cathy said, a mote of wistfulness in her voice. "Followed him around every time he was here, wanting to sit in his lap, show him some new gymnastics move she'd learned in class."

"He was always so patient with her, too," Colleen said. "With the two of you, really. He never got annoyed about all the oxygen Eileen sucked out of a room whenever she was in one."

"Lucas never got annoyed at anything," I said, staring at the picture. "Still doesn't."

Cathy peered over the album at me, her head at an angle and a question in her eyes.

"Eileen wasn't the only twin who thought Lucas hung the moon," she said, pointedly.

When I didn't respond to her baited statement, she held the album up. "Look at this picture."

I did. "Okay. So?"

"You're the only one not staring at the camera. All your attention is focused on Lucas, like you can't take your eyes off him."

"In these pictures, too," Colleen said, flipping through Cathy's wedding and graduation album. "There isn't one time you're not staring at him."

I'd never noticed it before, but they were right. We'd had hundreds of pictures taken over the years before camera phones became a thing, and in almost every one where Lucas was present while I was, I was looking at him.

"And now he looks at you whenever you're in a room together," Cathy said with a smug smirk gliding across her mouth.

I rolled my eyes and took a sip from my teacup.

"She's not wrong," Colleen added.

I shrugged and flipped through the album in my hands.

"I find it interesting she isn't arguing with us on this," Cathy said to Colleen.

"Hmm. Makes you wonder why not."

"Oh, I know why she isn't. You do, too. I just wonder if she realizes we know."

I tossed the album down onto the cocktail table and stared at both of them. "You know, that crap didn't work when I was a kid. It certainly isn't going to now."

"What crap? We were simply discussing something."

"Save the innocent, wide-eyed look for your husband, Coll. He's still getting used to you, while I know all your info-gathering tactics."

"That's insulting," she said, looking anything but offended.

"It's the truth." I turned my attention to my oldest sister. "Now, can we please finish with the menu for your wedding? I have a business to run and need to get back to it, and I'd like this to be finalized before I go."

"Tell me one thing first," she said.

"Oh, for the love of Mike, what?"

"Did you have a crush on Lucas when you were a kid?"

"Of course I did. Eileen did, too. He was the only guy who ever paid us any attention. Danny never did because he was always too busy trying to make out with you without Mom or Dad catching him."

"That's true." Colleen drew tiny circles over her belly.

Cathy ignored her. "Do you still?" she asked me.

I knew what she was asking but wouldn't—couldn't—answer her. Not if I wanted to retain any of my dignity. Really, how pathetic would it sound if I admitted I'd been in love with him for most of my life?

"Do I still what?"

"Have a crush on Lucas Alexander."

Technically, what I had wasn't a crush, so I answered her truthfully. "No."

"You didn't ask the right question," Colleen said to her, cutting a squinty glare toward me. "The real question is, do you love him?"

Again, the truth works best.

"Of course I love him." When they both gaped at me, I mentally crossed my fingers and added, "Like the big brother we were cheated out of having."

While they both continued to stare at me, openmouthed, I repeated my previous request. "Now I've answered your one question, Cathleen. Can we please finish this menu before it really is your wedding day and I have no food to feed your guests?"

I could tell neither of them was happy with my response. Too bad. My feelings for Lucas were going to remain mine until the day I died. If there was anyone who deserved to know, it was the man himself, and there was no way on this good earth he was ever going to hear the words *I love you* from my lips. That was a weight too heavy to share.

A half hour later, the sound of male voices came through the kitchen door.

"Where are you all?" Slade called out.

"In the living room," his wife answered.

"Why are you home so early?" Cathy asked Mac when he came into the room flanking Slade.

He grinned and hauled her up from the carpet and into a hug. "Lucas got called to an accident out on the highway at about the same time papa-bear-to-be here"—he thrust his chin at Slade—"said he wanted to go home to make sure the wife and baby were okay."

Slade plopped down next to Colleen and tossed one arm around her shoulder, the other over the hand still on her belly.

"We're fine," she told him, shaking her head. "Honestly, you'd think I was the first woman ever to have a baby."

"You're the first woman ever to have *my* baby," Slade told her, dropping a kiss to her crinkled nose.

"Our baby," she told him.

"I feel like you got cheated out of a bachelor party," Cathy said to her fiancé.

"I don't." He mimicked Slade's movement and kissed Cathy's forehead. "In all honesty, I'm beat and just want to go home and get into bed."

From the way Cathy blushed, I knew she was thinking sleep wasn't going to be on the agenda.

"On that note." I rose and gathered up the now-empty tray of sandwiches and muffins I'd brought with me. "I'll head back to the inn so you"—I nodded at Slade—"can fret over your family and you"—I turned to Mac—"can…rest."

The grin he shot me told me he was thinking along the same lines I assumed my sister was.

A few minutes later, I pulled into the inn. A note from Sarah told me all was well. The guests were all checked in, no problems had popped up, and the breakfast room was laid for the morning. Sunday mornings were typically a busy time with most of my guests checking out and taking their last advantage of a meal before getting on the road.

This morning's wedding breakfast had gone off without an issue, and I didn't have another to worry about until the following Saturday when Cathy and Mac would say their vows.

I slipped into my office and began writing the shopping list for my sister's wedding.

"I think this may be the first time I've ever come here and found you sitting down," Lucas said from the doorway a few hours later. "You're usually all over the place."

He wasn't in his uniform, but his gun was holstered on his hip and he was wearing his badge. I hadn't set eyes on him since he'd left my kitchen Thursday evening after the unexpected and world-stopping kiss.

"I'm taking advantage of the quiet to get some work done," I told him, proud I was able to keep my voice even and controlled when my insides were shaking at earthquake levels. "What are you doing here? Mac said you got called to an accident, effectively ending the bachelor bash."

He leaned a shoulder against the doorjamb. Fatigue and weariness lined his face.

"It was bad," I said.

A thick breath seeped from between his lips. "Two

fatalities. Three, if you include the buck they hit. Couple of high school kids on their way to a movie."

"Oh, good Lord. What happened?"

"The buck bolted into the road, must have gotten caught in the headlights. Speed was probably involved too, because the skid marks were short. Didn't look like the kid had a lot of reaction time, and there was too much damage to the car for the driver to have been ambling along."

He swiped his hands through the hair at his temples and dragged in a breath deep with grief.

"The state guys took control of the scene, but since the kids were Heaven's own, I was asked to do the death notifications. I just came from the second one. Parents are…destroyed. I called Father Duncan because they're members of the parish. He's with them right now."

I'd never known the emotional toll being the chief of police in our tiny town had on Lucas until right then. Hauling drunks in to sleep off their night or getting in between family disputes were common. But having to tell someone a loved one had been killed was horrible, and I'd never realized it was part of Lucas's role. Beyond the exhaustion glassing over in his eyes was something that tore at my heart: sadness. Deep, deep sadness.

My heart ached for the heavy burden he bore. Because I couldn't bear seeing anyone I loved in pain and hurting, I wanted to comfort him in any way I could, so I rose from my chair and crossed the room.

"I'm so sorry," I said as I wrapped my arms around his waist, laid my head on his chest, and hugged him as hard as I could.

His hands took their time to weave around my back and hold on to me.

"I can't imagine how awful it is to tell a parent their child is dead. Or to tell anyone someone they love is gone."

His voice was thick and strained when he said, "It's the only part of the job I hate."

I hugged him harder.

"All I keep thinking is those kids were a little older than Robert. I've been worried, like any parent, since he's gonna be driving now and the chance something could happen while he is…is huge. The two tonight weren't on drugs, or drinking, or doing anything they shouldn't have. They were simply on their way to a fun evening, and now they're dead. Gone in a heartbeat. They'll never grow old, go to college, get married. Do anything with their lives."

His voice broke, and I had to bite back tears. I had no words of wisdom, nothing I could say to ease the pain flowing through him, so I simply held on as hard as I could.

The beat of Lucas's heart, slow and steady against my ear, went a long way in calming my own nerves. In all the years we'd known one another, we'd never embraced in this manner before. Sure, Lucas had hugged me and tried to offer comfort when Danny, then Eileen, had died. But then it had been in a shared grief way, both of us raw and hurting from the loss of someone we loved. Over the years, at family functions or social events, we'd greet each other with a quick side hug and head nod. Never full body contact like now.

His chest expanded as he pulled in a full breath while his long fingers trailed up and down my back.

"As soon as I was done with the second notification, I got back in my car and just sat there for a while, trying to figure out why stuff like this happens," he said. "Why innocent lives have to be lost. There's no reason for it, no logic."

"Nanny always claims it's God's plan, and we shouldn't question it. She said that more times than I care to remember when Eileen died. She truly believes God takes people from us and has some reason known only to him, for doing so. I can't accept that. I don't think I ever will."

"Father Duncan told the same thing to the parents tonight. I don't know what to believe. It seems cruel to take a child so tragically from its parents. If anything happened to Robert, I don't know what I'd do, how I'd be able to go on. I'd be as shattered as the parents I spoke to tonight."

We both stood there for a few moments, lost.

"I've got a half dozen reports to fill out, a few phone calls I need to make," he said at length, his voice sounding as tired as he looked. "Plus I need to get on home and make sure World War III hasn't broken out in my absence. But sitting in the car, I realized I didn't want to go back to the station or head home. I couldn't." He pulled back and stared down at me. There was so much emotion filling his eyes, I found my breath catching.

He pulled his hands from around my waist and cupped my face between them. I simply got lost in the dark green and gold flecks in his irises that reminded me so much of a moonlit glen.

"I put the car in gear and aimed it right for here. Right to you. I needed to see you, Maureen. Talk to you. Just…" He shook his head and closed his eyes. When he opened them again, he said, "Knowing you'd be here to listen about the miserable night I've had, probably want to make me something eat"—my heart lifted at that—"made me feel…better somehow."

His shoulder hitched. "I'm not doing a good job of explaining this." He lifted my chin in his hands so I was forced to stare up at him. In all honesty, I couldn't have looked away if I wanted to.

"Maureen." His thumbs caressed my cheeks as his eyes gave voice to what he couldn't say with words. He shook his head, one corner of his mouth ticking upward. "When I'm with you, all the bad stuff going on around me fades away. No matter what kind of day I've had with Dad or the thousand little annoying things that come up on the job, stopping by here to see you, have a cup of coffee, or even beg a few cookies helps me keep going. Makes it easier to get through the day."

"I'm glad I can help."

"You do more than help. It sounds corny, but whenever I'm around you, I feel like I can take a full breath and just…be. It's been that way for a long while now. Why do you think I stop by so often when I have no reason to?"

I gave him a shrug now. "I figured it was because you're always hungry and you know what a soft touch I am when it comes to my family and friends."

The other corner of his mouth joined in and a small grin lifted his lips. "That's one of the perks of coming here, but not the reason." His voice lowered, deepened. "Not the real reason."

He sucked in a breath, then let it go slow and steady, his eyes focused on mine the entire time.

"What do you mean, not the real reason?"

One of his hands slipped to the back of my neck and cradled it. He ran his other thumb along the seam in my lips. A thousand heated flares ignited at his touch. My heart jackhammered inside my chest, and there was no conceivable way he couldn't hear it.

The emotions darting across his eyes changed. Desire replaced the sorrow, heat cleared away the fatigue like the sun burning off morning fog. As he bent his head down, I instinctively went up on my toes. With my arms still woven around his waist, I grabbed on to the back of his shirt so I wouldn't collapse in a puddle on the floor. When he'd kissed me before, it had been a surprise I hadn't been prepared for.

But now I knew his intent—and more: I knew what his touch could do to me, how it could make me forget all the self-imposed rules I had against telling him how I felt, how much I loved him.

"When I kissed you the other night, I never got the chance to tell you something before Robert interrupted us." He swiped his finger across my bottom lip again, tightened his hold on my neck.

"Wh-what?"

"That I don't want to be just your friend anymore, Maureen."

"You don't?"

"I haven't for a while. A long while." He hissed out a breath as he glanced down at my mouth, then back up to my eyes again. "A damn long while. I want more than the simple, easy friendship we have between us. I think, at least I *hope*, you do, too. I can't believe you'd have kissed me the way you did if you didn't want the same thing."

He had me there. Before my old self-preservation habits could kick in and explain to him why a relationship other than friendship between us wasn't good, he kissed me.

Any notion this wasn't a good idea flew from my brain like dust in the wind.

I let out the breath I'd been holding in a long whoosh and shot my hands up his chest to grip his shoulders for dear life. Forget about my knees turning into a puddle; my entire body dissolved into liquid when he slid his tongue alongside mine and tugged.

"Please tell me you want this too, Maureen." He lifted his head and peered down at me, uncertainty in his eyes.

The knowledge he was unsure of my response went a long way in proving how well I'd hid my true feelings for him.

I swallowed and traced my finger across his bottom lip. "This is a...surprise."

"I don't know how it can be."

"Lucas, you've never said or done anything to indicate you wanted me to be anything other than a friend. A close friend, for sure, but never like a, well, a *girlfriend.*"

The deep groove that so rarely appeared popped up between his eyebrows. "Don't we always have fun when we're together?"

"Of course we do."

He nodded. "And didn't you enjoy yourself the other night when we were out to dinner?"

"You know I did. But I never in a million years thought of it as a date. It was simply a friend helping a friend."

The groove deepened to a crevasse. "I'm really starting to dislike that word."

"Friend?"

"Yeah, and what it implies." He tightened his hold on me. "Maybe I haven't made what I feel, what I've wanted, clear to you in the past. But I'm saying it now. I want to be with you, Maureen, and just so there's no misunderstanding on this, not in a friend way."

The implications of that declaration were huge.

"Are you sure?"

"I've never been so sure of anything in my life." The furrow finally smoothed. "I've been trying for months to figure out a way to tell you how I feel without scaring you."

Months? Good gravy! Lucas's capacity to keep his feelings hidden rivaled mine.

"Why did you think I'd be scared?"

He shrugged, then pulled me back to rest on his chest and dropped his chin down on the top of my head. "I've known you since you were a kid. Watched you grow up. And I've always felt you thought of me like a big brother."

"You certainly acted like an obnoxious one at times. Tick Jones as a case in point."

The quiet drum of his low laugh reverberated against my cheek. "I'm not gonna apologize for looking out for your best interests."

"Keep telling yourself that."

He shifted until we were eye to eye again. "What I feel when I think about you, Maureen, is nothing like a brother feels for a sister. It's all pure male want for a woman. Believe me." The truth was written on his face. "The other day in the cemetery I almost came unglued when you said you were meeting Boyd. I realized then I had to tell you before it was too late and you got involved with him."

"Honestly, Donovan Boyd was never a consideration, and I told you that. Pointedly."

He shook his head. "I know guys like him, though. The more you say no, the more persistent they become. When Robert told me how handsy he was, I knew I was right. I wanted to wipe that smug grin off his face when I saw him here."

"And this would be you not acting like a big brother, would it?" I rolled my eyes.

"Believe me there was nothing sibling-like about what I was feeling." He hauled in a breath. "I was worried to tell you how I felt, Maureen, because I know you. I know how you think and knew you'd be frightened it would change how we are together. You'd fuss about what would happen if it didn't work out, or if we didn't suit. Or what people might say about us."

Or if you realized too late I wasn't what you really wanted.

"Those are valid concerns, you know," I said aloud. "We both have reputations in this town to uphold, and you know how negative gossip can destroy people. I wouldn't want to ruin anything between us. You're a part of my life, Lucas. An important part. I would hate if we did something to wreck it."

"I get that." His arms tightened around me. "Adult relationships are hard, I know. My marriage proved it to me. And if we do this, if we start dating, if we get involved well, romantically, things *will* change between us. But for the better. I believe that, Maureen. Can you?"

The logical part of my brain screamed a flat out *no* to his question. I had too many fears, too many secrets I'd kept from everyone I loved. I was still convinced a long life wasn't in the cards for me, and if I gave in to this desire, I knew Lucas would be hurt in the end.

But standing in my office with this man's arms around me, a man whom I'd loved every day of my memory, the emotional side of my brain kicked the smart side to the proverbial curb.

"I can," I heard myself say.

Lucas's face lit up like a Christmas tree. The sorrow flew from his eyes, and his shoulders relaxed to their normal, calm attitude.

"I can't tell you how happy I am to hear you say that." He kissed me, quick and hard, then slow and soft.

"But—"

"No buts."

"Yes, there's a but. An important one."

After a moment's consideration, he bobbed his head, once. "Okay. Tell me."

I licked my lips, and Lucas sucked in all the air around me, his gaze dropping down to my mouth. "You're practically family, Lucas. You're Cathy's best friend and Nanny's, for lack of a better word, nemesis."

"That sounds like the right word to me," he said with a nod.

"If we start dating, they're bound to have something to say about it."

"And you're worried they won't, what? Approve of us being together."

It was my turn to nod. "I know it sounds dumb, but…" I lifted a shoulder.

"Why don't we wait to deal with it? I'm not

entirely convinced either of them will have a problem with it, but if you want, we can keep what we're doing to ourselves for a while. Not tell anyone in your family. Sound fair?"

Relief flowed through me. "Yes. Thank you."

The grandfather clock in the hallway chimed the midnight hour.

"I need to go." Lucas touched his forehead to mine and sighed. "I don't want to, but I need to. There's a bunch of stuff I need to get done before I can head home. Then I'm right back on duty at eight tomorrow morning."

I pulled out of his arms, and we walked back into my kitchen. "Did you eat anything at the Love Shack before you got called away?"

"Some wings. By the time we were ready to order dinner, I got paged. Slade was starting to get antsy about Colleen, and Mac was trying to hide the fact he was yawning. As far as a bachelor party went, it was a pretty piss-poor one."

I put together a tin of leftover muffins and sandwiches from earlier. "Take these. It's not the most nutritious thing in the world, but it'll fuel you up for a while, at least until you can get home and get to sleep."

He took the bag in one hand, the other snaking around my back and pulling me to him.

"Like I said before"—he kissed my nose—"one of the perks of coming here. But not the main one."

"You're a typical man, and you like someone to cook for you. You just happen to like my cooking and baking."

"I like a whole lot more than that about you, Maureen. A whole lot more."

This time when he dragged me back into his arms and kissed me, I didn't even consider this was something I shouldn't be doing.

He sighed again. "I really do need to go."

He kissed me one last time, lingering enough for my vision to go blurry when I opened my eyes.

"After the wedding is over," he said, "and things calm down again, I want to take you out. Dinner. Maybe a movie. Something where it's only the two of us. No family around, no worries about the job or my father or Robert. Just us. Okay?"

I nodded.

I watched as he drove away, then closed and locked the door and leaned back against it.

My knees were still a little shaky and my heart pounded in my chest, but I couldn't stop the cheek-wide grin shooting across my face.

Lucas Alexander, the object of every one of my thoughts and fantasies for years, wanted me.

Me.

Holy Christmas.

As I slid into bed with a grin on my face I couldn't wash off, one thought popped into my head that gave me a moment's pause. My sisters and Nanny were going to go bat-shit crazy when they found out.

Chapter 9

When Eileen got sick and I found myself getting annoyed at something family related, or irritated about a problem concerning the inn, I'd try to remember to take a deep breath and ask myself, "In five years will this still be a concern, and am I going to even remember why I was angry?" Ninety-nine percent of time the answer was a resounding *no* on both counts. Helping my twin get through her chemo treatments, deal with the hair loss she experienced, and manage her perpetual pain became my new normal. Her plight was so much more devastating than any little aggravation that popped up.

Like when the contractor we'd hired to install new bathrooms in each of the suites suddenly ghosted us after cashing our check. I took a breath and left the legal stuff in Cathy's hands, told myself it was a lesson learned, and cared for Eileen.

On opening weekend when we had most rooms booked and the electricity decided to go out the day before our first guest arrived, I contacted every electrician listed in the telephone business directory while simultaneously driving Eileen to her treatment.

And when our parents moved away immediately after we buried my sister, claiming they couldn't bear to stay in the house she'd grown up in, I told myself the hurt of their abandonment would ebb away and be forgotten. They would come back again, or at least visit as soon as their grief was under control.

They hadn't, and now, more than three years later, they'd only returned once, for Colleen's wedding. They blew into town late Friday night, missing the rehearsal dinner. Saturday morning, Cathy, Nanny, and I were the ones who got Colleen ready while my mother pleaded a headache and said she'd meet us at the church. My father walked my sister down the aisle with a stoic expression on his face and then sat next to my mother who wore dark sunglasses throughout the ceremony.

The reception had taken place at the inn, thereafter. My parents had stayed for the first course, then claimed they'd been forced to book a late flight home due to airline scheduling concerns. Before the cake was served, they were on their way.

Slade had tried to joke Colleen out of her disappointment by telling her at least he didn't have to worry about meddling in-laws.

When Cathy set the date of her marriage to Mac, my mother emailed and stated they wanted me to save them a room for two nights again, which I'd done. The plan was they'd arrive Friday and leave Sunday morning.

When they hadn't arrived by Friday lunchtime, I texted my mother.

When I got no response, I texted my dad.

And when four o'clock rolled around and I was finishing up some last-minute decorating to Cathy's cake and giving Robert another piping lesson, my phone finally buzzed.

—*Call me*—my father had texted.

"Uh-oh," I said when I read it.

"What's uh-oh?" Lucas asked as he walked into the kitchen, his gaze immediately going to me.

"Maureen got a text," Robert said.

"What's wrong?" Lucas moved close to me but, mindful of his son, didn't touch me.

Since Saturday night when he'd made his astounding declaration of intent, I'd seen him every day, including Sunday morning when he came to have breakfast with my family, Robert in tow. He took great pains not to touch me, but the few times we'd accidently knocked fingers when I'd refilled his coffee cup, or when he'd taken the fruits of Robert's baking lessons home with him in the afternoon, the effect had been profound. My sisters, thankfully, hadn't noticed any change between us.

A few times I thought about what a horrible person I was because I wished the wedding was already over with. But I never said it out loud. I loved my sister beyond all measure, and I wanted her day to be perfect. My own happiness could wait a few more days.

But now with the ominous tone of my father's text, worry blew through me.

"My parents were supposed to be here by noon. I've been texting with no response until now." I showed him the phone screen so he could read my father's text.

His eyebrows lifted, and he cocked his head. "That doesn't sound good. Go call him."

I went into my office and did. Five minutes later when I returned to the kitchen, Robert and Lucas were seated at the kitchen table, the insomnia cookie jar open between them.

"They're not coming," I said, not bothering to hide my fury.

173

"Why the heck not? Their oldest daughter's getting married."

"My father said they were all set to leave this morning for the airport when my mother went to lift her suitcase into the car and threw her back out. To hear him tell it, she's practically paralyzed from the waist down." I shook my head and clicked my tongue in disgust. "He took her straight to the emergency room where they put her on muscle relaxers, sent her home, and told her to stay in bed for a minimum of four days. Dad was told to stay close to look after her." I plopped down at the table, my arms crossed over my chest. "This sucks. Cathy's gonna be so disappointed. Who's gonna walk her down the aisle tomorrow, now?"

"I will," Lucas said without a second of hesitation.

I gaped across the table at him. I swear, my heart flipped over inside my chest. If Robert hadn't been sitting between us, I would have jumped into Lucas's lap and kissed him silly.

He shrugged and said, "It make sense. Cathy's practically my sister, so if her own father can't do it, it seems right I slide into the role."

"Lucas." I shook my head, unable to put into words what I was feeling.

"I'm gonna be standing at the altar with Mac anyway. Might as well walk up with Cathy. You gonna call her now and tell her about your parents, or wait until the rehearsal to let her know?"

"I should tell her now, but I'm not going to call. News like this should be given in person."

"Come on, then." Lucas stood. "Let's go tell her together. Robert, you come, too."

Thankfully, Sarah hadn't left for the day yet, so I

put the inn in her capable hands for an hour.

Five minutes later, the three of us drove up Cathy's driveway. I knew she would be home because she'd started her two weeks of honeymoon vacation yesterday.

"Number Four," Nanny greeted us when we came in through the garage door linking to the kitchen. Her knowing gaze jumped to Lucas. "This is a surprise, and from the looks on your faces, not a good one. What's up?"

"Where's Cath?" I asked, bussing her cheek.

"Just got out of the shower and is gettin' ready for us to head over t' the church. Why is the law here?" she asked Lucas.

Before he could answer, Cathy came into the kitchen in her robe, her hair tied up in a bun and a happy grin on her face. The second she spotted the three of us her grin disappeared. "Something's happened." Her voice broke when she asked, "Colleen?"

"Fine," I told her, moving to give her a hug.

"Tell me," she ordered, barring me from doing so. "Just say it."

This was Cathy to a tee. Bad news always had to be delivered without any sugar coating.

"Mom and Dad aren't coming."

Her face went white, and a thin line popped up between her brows. I quickly explained why they weren't.

"*That woman.*" Nanny stood to her full four-foot-eleven height, fury spewing in her periwinkle eyes and anger slashed across her lips. "It's not surprised I am by this news," she spat. "Probably did it on purpose."

"Nanny." Cathy shook her head.

"Everything's always got to be about her," my grandmother continued, not heeding the warning in Cathy's tone at all. "Didn't even stay long enough to toast Colleen at her own wedding, did she? Just slithered away before the festivities were done with some cock-n-bull tale about airlines and such. It's a selfish woman your mother is, Cathleen Anne, to be sure. I've known it for forty years." The true indication of Nanny's anger was apparent because she'd referred to my sisters both by their Christian names and not the hated number nicknames.

"And don't you be saying I'm a mean old woman, Maureen Angela"—she pointed a gnarled index finger at me—"for sayin' so and speaking th'truth."

"I wasn't going to because I totally agree with you, Nanny." I rubbed my hands down Cathy's robed arms. "Daddy called and asked me to tell you, which is low in my book. He should have been the one to call, tell you, and then apologize."

"Don't be holdin' ya breath, lass," Nanny said. "Fintan's well and truly under that woman's thumb. Has been since the day she put her hooks into him, and it's only gotten worse since she spirited him away after Eileen's death."

"Nanny, you are talking about our mother, you know," Cathy chided.

"Poor excuse for one from where I'm standing," she mumbled. Nanny's sigh, honed from decades of practiced theatricality, rang loud in the kitchen. "Well, now, it looks like ya need someone to walk ya down the aisle, lass. Since I'm the relative closest to ya, 'twould be my pleasure to do it, seeing as me poor excuse for a son bailed."

Cathy's expression went blank. "Um…"

I flicked a glance at Lucas.

He cleared his throat and when all eyes were on him, he addressed Nanny first. "Fiona, while that is the most unselfish thing I've ever heard someone offer, I'm sure Cathy will agree with me when I say you shouldn't be forced to give up your role of *grand dame* tomorrow. I know you'll want all eyes on your granddaughter as she walks down the aisle, and it won't be possible if you're with her. You know everyone in the church will be looking at you and not the bride. You don't want to outshine her, not intentionally, do you?"

Nanny squinted at him, but I could see her lips twitch up while she did.

"I'll escort Cathy to meet Mac. If you're okay with that, I mean," he said to Cathy.

It was as if sunshine broke through a cloud-laden, stormy sky when she beamed across the room at him. In the next second she flew into his arms, hugging him so tightly you could hear the wind whoosh out from between his lips.

"I'm so okay with it I can't speak," she said, tears in her eyes. "Thank you, Lucas. Thank you so much."

She pulled back, dabbed at her eyes with her robe sleeve, and grinned up at him.

"That's what best friends are for," he told her, then kissed her forehead. "And don't worry." He cut his eyes to me, one side of his mouth lifting up, then back to Cathy. "I won't be wearing a blue velvet tux to the wedding. Maureen saw to that."

"Dad. Lame," Robert mumbled and shook his head.

Nanny's all-seeing eyes nailed me with their intensity. "Isn't that interestin'. When did this occur?"

I told her about the three of us going to Concord and added Robert had gotten a new suit as well. As a diversion tactic, it worked well.

"Did ya, lad?" she asked him, smiling. "Well, I'm sure you're gonna look dashing. Promise me you'll escort me down the aisle, ay? The best-looking lad in the church you'll be, and I'll be the envy of every female in the place."

Robert blushed to the roots of his hair, then grinned at my grandmother and nodded. "It'll be a pleasure, Mrs. Scallopini."

"Ach now, I think you can be calling me Nanny like the lasses do. You're one of the family, you are." She squinted over at Lucas and added, "Despite being the son of a lawman."

Lucas grinned at her, then bent to kiss her on the cheek. "You love me, and you know it, Fiona."

"I know no such t'ing."

"Yes, you do. Maureen assures me you do, and you know how truthful your youngest granddaughter is."

Once again, Nanny cut her eyes my way. "Ay, that's one word for her."

"Oh, my God," Cathy cried. "Look at the time. We have to go soon, and I need to get ready. Mac's meeting us at the church after he finishes up at the museum."

"Go on, then," Nanny said, making a shooing motion with her hands.

"See you in a bit," she called over her shoulder as she bounded back up the stairs.

"We've gotta go, too," I said, cocking my head at Lucas. "I need to get the rehearsal dinner started and make sure everything is set to go for tomorrow morning. See you in a bit, Nanny." I kissed her cheek again.

She grabbed my hand and pierced me with the intense glare we'd all squirmed under as kids.

"You and I need to have a little confab, darlin' girl." She snaked a glance over my shoulder to Lucas. My stomach flipped. "Seems there's t'ings goin' on I've no knowledge of, and you know how that makes me a bit…unsettled."

"Let's get Cathy married first, Nanny, okay? Then we can have a girl's night at the Arms. I'll bring the scones."

Once again, she narrowed her eyes at me. "Ay, I'm running low on me supply, 'tis true. Okay, after the weddin', then. But you and I are gonna have a talk, lass. A big one."

I kissed her again, happy to dodge a nanny-quisition bullet for the moment.

Three hours later, we were all back at the inn, including Slade and Colleen, who'd joined us at the church. Colleen's jaw clamped so tight when she heard the news about our parents I was afraid she was going to crack a molar. From a wedding-planner perspective, the bride's parents pulling a no-show was the equivalent of one of the seven deadly sins. From a daughter's viewpoint, it was just hurtful. And unforgiveable. Slade grabbed her hand and forced her to look at him. Without a word said, he managed to dissipate her anger. Her shoulders relaxed, and the pinched, sour look on her face dissolved. When Lucas told her not to worry because he'd be the one walking Cathy down the aisle, tears swelled in her eyes.

The rehearsal went off without a hitch, our parish priest, Father Duncan taking the news of my parents in stride. From her perch in the front pew, Colleen instructed us all in our duties, and within an hour, we were back at the inn for a final supper together before the morning's festivities.

"Are ya staying at the house tonight, Mac, darlin'?" Nanny asked as we dined on one of Cathy's favorite dishes, chicken Alfredo, that I'd made special for the event.

Mac slid a side eye toward his fiancé and with a tiny lift of his lips said, "I'd planned to, Fee, but your eldest granddaughter has proven to be something of a traditionalist where marriage is concerned." He took Cathy's hand and kissed it. "She doesn't want us to see each other until we meet at the altar."

"Not so much a traditionalist," Cathy countered, "as superstitious. I don't want to start this marriage off on the wrong foot or take the chance something will go wrong. There's a reason you're not supposed to see each other beforehand. I know it's considered to be bad luck, but I can't remember why. I want only good luck coming our way."

Nanny nodded, and her grin turned devilish. "The reason why you're not supposed to see your intended is because in the olden days, with arranged marriages and such, the bride and groom never laid eyes on one another until after the vows were spoken and the veil was lifted. By then, 'twas too late to run."

"What do you mean?" Robert asked her. His cheeks immediately pinked when all eyes landed on him.

"If your new spouse wasn't exactly pleasin' to the

eyes, lad, then too bad. Ya were legally wed, and there was no reneging on th' deal now that you'd gotten a gander at her. Or him."

Robert's mouth fell open. "You mean they never saw what they looked like before they got married?"

The horror in his tone was comical, and I had to cover my mouth to prevent a loud laugh from spewing forth.

"Think about it," Lucas told his son. He was having his own problems keeping his laughter contained. "You think you're getting a swimsuit model or an action hero, and you wind up with, well, neither of those."

"Your father's tryin' to be a diplomat, lad, and skirtin' around the truth, which is there was many an ugly duckling from diseases, birth problems, and poor nutrition back then. Daughters fathers couldn't marry off because they were homely as sin or covered in pock marks. Sons fathers worried weren't *manly* enough in the procreatin' department or unpleasing to the eyes. Their looks were kept a secret until after the vows were said and the license signed. No such thing as divorce back then. 'Twasn't legal or condoned, punishable by stonin' or even death."

Robert's face went from flushed to milky white. I couldn't tell if he was embarrassed at my grandmother's candor or her crack about divorce, but whichever it was, I didn't want him upset.

"To answer your question, Nanny," I said, trying to divert the conversation back to the original discussion, "Mac's staying here tonight in one of my empty rooms." I didn't mention it was the one I'd reserved for my parents. I'd assigned a different room to him

Peggy Jaeger

originally, but when my parents bailed, I switched him to the bigger suite. "That way Cathy gets her good omen wish, and Mac has a place where he can get ready in peace tomorrow morning."

Nanny smiled across the table at me and held up her wine glass in a salute. " 'Tis a good lass you are, darlin' girl."

I grinned back at her.

The evening wound down early. Colleen pleaded exhaustion, and with a big day tomorrow, she wanted to be well rested. Slade, the ever-hovering, always-comforting husband, whisked her home right after I served dessert. In all fairness, she did look done in.

Nanny was spending the night with Cathy, but before they packed up to leave, Mac pulled his intended away for a few moments of alone time. Robert and Lucas helped me clear the table, even though I told them both to leave everything and I'd get to it once everyone was gone.

"I'm kind of an expert at bussing now," Robert said while he helped me rinse and load the dishwasher.

I hip-bumped him and said, "Don't forget you're also an up-and-coming cake decorator."

His cheek-wide grin was so like his father's my heart sighed.

"Robert, you got this?" Lucas asked. "Cuz I need to talk to Maureen about something."

The boy nodded.

Lucas ticked his head toward my office. Once we were inside, he closed the door. When he flipped the lock, my eyebrows lifted.

"What's so important you have to lock the door to discuss?"

"This."

He pulled me into his arms with one smooth move and pressed his lips to mine. The only thought in my mind before I lost all capacity to think was I was glad he'd secured the lock.

I lifted up on my toes, my arms shooting up and around his neck to hold on tight, while his hands snaked around my waist and settled on my hips, pulling me as close as he could.

"All afternoon and evening long, I've been wanting to do this," he whispered against my cheek, then brought his lips back to mine. "I couldn't concentrate on a thing Father Duncan said." He trailed down my neck, captured my earlobe between his teeth and then bit down, hard enough for me to jump, but soft enough so the erotic sensation shot straight down to my toes. "Every time I looked your way, all I could think about was getting you alone. It's getting harder and harder not to touch you like I want to when there are people around, Maureen."

From the intimate way we were pressed up against one another, I could tell that wasn't the only thing getting hard.

He cupped my chin and swiped at my cheeks with his thumbs. Little blasts of electricity sparked throughout my system from his touch. It was a good thing he was keeping himself in check around the others because I don't know how I would have hidden how my body responded to his touch if he'd made good on his desires.

"The wedding is tomorrow, and then we can take a breath," I said, as I ran my finger across his lips. "With Cathy and Mac on their honeymoon and Colleen and

Slade staying close to home until the baby arrives, you and I can have some quiet time together. Okay? Let's just get through tomorrow."

One corner of his delicious lips tilted up. "I always thought Cathy was the rational, logical sister. Seems I've been wrong for years."

I rolled my eyes and hugged him. "Don't let her hear you say that. She'll have an anxiety attack. Come on." I pulled back and grabbed his hand. "I don't want to be gone too long. If we're missing, it'll lead to questions neither of us wants to answer right now, especially from my grandmother. I'm not in the mood to be raked over the coals by Nanny."

I unlocked the door, but before I could open it, Lucas tugged me back into his arms.

"Just one more to hold me over." He pressed his lips to mine in the sweetest kiss I think I've ever received. It was filled with such tenderness and intent, the notion to relock the door and simply feast on this man blew straight into the front of my mind.

That rational, logical trait Lucas mentioned beat it back.

I stared up at him and was in such danger of telling him how much he meant to me, I had to pull deep for control. It wouldn't do to tell him. Not now. Not ever. Quirking my lips and dropping my chin so I could look up at him through my lashes, I asked, "What are you, three? You need a kiss to hold you over like you need a cookie before dinner because you're starving?"

His eyes went to half-mast and he trailed his tongue along the seam of my lips.

"I'm starving, all right." His voice was soft and dark and dangerous. My thighs shook as it whispered over me. "But only for you, Maureen." He kissed me once, hard. "Only for you."

I had no defenses again this man, try though I might.

I swallowed, then said, "Hold that thought until after the wedding."

The grin he shot me was pure sexy male.

After dragging in a huge calming breath, I opened the door. Robert, Cathy, Mac, and Nanny were all in my kitchen. When Lucas and I came in, the three adults in the room all threw us questioning stares.

"Slade took Colleen home," Cathy said. "She was practically asleep at the table. Robert told us you two had something to discuss." She lifted an eyebrow. "In private." The implication of those two little words echoed through the room. I hadn't watched my older sisters deal with my parents and my grandmother my entire life without learning several lessons on how to worm my way out of hairy situations and avoid punishment for bad behavior.

Nonchalantly, I nodded. "We did. And if you make me tell you, it's gonna ruin tomorrow's surprise."

She peered at me across the room, indecision blowing across her face. Ask or don't ask; push me to confess, or let it go.

I stayed calm while Lucas got the hint and nodded at his son. "You ready to head out?"

"Yeah."

"We'll see you all at the church," Lucas said.

"Don't be late," Cathy told him.

"Have you ever known me to be late? For anything?"

"Always a first time," she mumbled.

Lucas stopped to kiss her cheek as he walked past, and said, "Not gonna happen, Counselor, so don't worry."

"I'd like to get on home, too, lass," Nanny said, rising from the kitchen chair. "It's worn out, I am."

Minutes later, after Mac kissed his fiancé, then Nanny, goodnight, they left.

"Need a wake-up call?" I asked my soon-to-be-brother-in-law.

He shook his head. "I'll be up and ready to go on time. No worries."

I hugged him. "I'm really happy you're marrying my sister."

"Not as much as I am," he said back, with a grin.

Later, just as I was about to snuggle down in bed, my cell phone pinged with an incoming text.

—*I'm still starving*— Lucas wrote.

I laughed out loud and texted back —*Have a cookie and go to sleep.*—

While three little waving dots undulated across the screen, I shut my bedside light.

—*I'd rather have you.*—

That thought was enough to make my heart flip over.

—*After Cathy and Mac are married we can have all the...cookies we want.*—

The line of laughing emojis he sent back went a long way in helping me fall asleep with a smile.

Chapter 10

When Cathleen married her first husband, she wore my mother's outdated, old-fashioned wedding dress as her something old and borrowed. Nanny had loaned her an ancient garter she'd already worn to two of her own weddings as her something blue, and Colleen, Eileen, and I combined all our allowance money for two months to buy her a beautiful gold cross she wore around her neck as her something new. She'd been barely eighteen years old and was marrying the only boy she'd ever kissed. The wedding had been the definition of a no-frills affair. Her bouquet was a sprig of bluebells and baby's breath from my grandmother's lake property. My father had elected to wear a suit instead of renting a tuxedo, and he'd driven the two of them to the church in our old family minivan.

Now, twenty plus years and a lifetime of growth later, her wedding dress was handmade from a designer shop in Concord (her something new), the lace veil she'd had commissioned by a local seamstress was made from the one Nanny wore to marry our grandfather (her something old), Colleen had loaned her the pair of three-carat diamond earrings Slade had gifted her on their wedding day (something borrowed), and I'd bought her an antique comb shot through with sapphires to wear in her hair as her something blue.

Since Colleen was in charge of all the wedding

details now, she'd decreed Cathy and Mac were going to have a wedding to remember.

She'd hired a white Rolls Royce complete with a liveried chauffeur to take Cathy and Nanny to the church. The church itself exploded with flowers. Arrangements of white and pink roses garnished the end of every pew, and the altar was chockablock with standing creations as tall as Lucas.

A trio of classical musicians sat to one side of the altar, hired to serenade the guests as they waited for the bride, and then to play her down the aisle to meet her groom. Colleen's trusted and talented photographer, Kolby, had volunteered to shoot the wedding as a gift to Cathy and Mac, and they were assured a magnificent photographic memory of the day.

All in all, her second marriage was completely different than her first, save for the church. Father Duncan had married her the first time and would again, something he told us during the rehearsal he was delighted about.

After making sure everything was set for the wedding brunch at the inn, I then got myself ready. The dress Cathy had picked out, with Colleen's veto approval, was a mid-length, pale green, and cap-sleeved chiffon creation cinched in at the waist and billowing downward. The color and cut were perfect, and if I had to be dressed in something other than jeans and a T-shirt, this was perfection. As my wedding-planner sister had instructed, I'd worn my hair down for once instead of up in a knot secured with a pencil and had pulled it back on the sides and away from my face. Convinced I was as good as I was going to get, I drove to our family church, appropriately named Heaven on Earth, and pulled past the sign on the lawn which read *God never takes a summer vacation. Remember to worship when you're away from home.*

I parked around the rear, grabbed my shoes, and slid into the back entrance. The sounds of a classical melody drifted in the air, accompanied by the quiet hum of lowered voices. I made my way to the setup room, commonly called the *bawl* room, in the back of the church where my sister was getting ready.

The forceful voice drifting from the room told me my middle sister was in command mode. With a headset and microphone secured around her head and her electronic clipboard in her hands, she was ensconced in a Queen Anne chair with her feet up on a stool, her eyes darting all over the place.

Cathy and Nanny were seated, plastic aprons covering them from neck to knees as individual hairdressers and makeup artists worked on them. I'd opted out when Colleen had asked me if I wanted my hair and makeup done, knowing I was in a time crunch with getting the brunch ready. This was Cathleen's day, and she should be the one pampered and fussed over. I considered it a major concession I'd agreed to wear a heeled shoe.

"Hey," I said to the room when I entered.

Colleen zeroed in on me while she spoke into a microphone, her gaze raking down from my head to my toes and zeroing in on my flip-flops. The rise of her left eyebrow when she saw them told me she was prepared to have a come-to-Jesus lecture with me about footwear, so I lifted the shoes in my hands into her line of sight. She bobbed her head and tapped at her earbud.

"You need blush," she said once she disconnected.

"You're gonna look like a ghost in pictures." She pointed to one of the makeup girls. "Make sure she gets some lipstick, too."

"I think you look pretty," Cathy told me with a smile.

"And I think Mac's gonna be drooling the entire ceremony once he gets a gander at you." I air-kissed her cheek so I wouldn't disturb her makeup. Cathy had elected to wear her hair in a loose chignon, the comb I'd gifted her holding it in place. Her beautiful, clear, and unlined skin, a DNA gift from our grandmother, radiated and glowed. Colleen only worked with the best professionals, and this was the proof. My sister was gorgeous without makeup, but the enhancements to her eyes and face were subtle and only served to heighten her beauty.

I repeated my air-kiss with Nanny.

"Did ya feed Mac a good breakfast, lass? Wouldn't want him peckish during the mass, now."

I laughed. "No worries, Nanny. He's all set."

"It's getting close to time, isn't it?" Cathy asked. "When is Lucas due?"

"He just got here," Colleen said, tapping her earpiece again. "Charity's bringing him back."

The workers removed the apron from around Cathleen, and I got to see her in her dress for the first time. I'd only viewed it once before on the day she'd ordered it, and the sample dress had been a few sizes too big when she'd decided it was *the one*.

Now, with the alterations completed to perfection, the dress was more beautiful than I remembered. Layers of white organza floated from her waist down to the floor and hid her just-showing baby bump completely.

You'd never know she was expecting. A silk bodice was covered with an intricate hand-stitched overlay in a pattern of roses winding on vines. The design extended down the sides of her torso and stopped at mid-hip. The sleeves had the same lace and pattern dropping down to just below her elbows and were attached to the bodice with illusion material covering her collarbones and décolletage.

With her porcelain skin and striking red hair, she looked like she'd stepped out of the pages of a book about fairy princesses and wood sprites.

As she stood before us, happiness radiating from her every pore, tears swelled in my eyes.

"You'd better not be wearing regular mascara," Colleen chided from her chair. "You know better."

I rolled my waterproof-mascaraed eyes at her and shook my head.

"Ah, now darlin' girl, 'tis a vision you are." Nanny beamed at Cathy, her voice shaking with emotion. "Mac Frayne's a lucky man, he is."

"I'm the lucky one, Nanny." Cathy took her hand. "I never thought I'd find a man I could love like this again."

"You're a wonderful woman, Cathleen Anne, and you're deserving of a wonderful man. I couldn't'a handpicked a better one than Mac for ya if I'd been given the task to. I can't tell ya how happy I am for ya both."

Nanny squeezed her long, gnarled fingers around Cathy's, and to say I was surprised to see tears start to build in my grandmother's eyes wasn't an exaggeration. Nanny reserved her tears—as she'd told us numerous times—for sad occasions like funerals and not happy ones like weddings and births.

"No crying," Colleen bellowed from her throne because, really, that's what it was.

"Okay, I won't cry."

All heads in the room turned to the male voice, lit with laughter, coming from the doorway. Since every head in the room was female, the looks tossed at Lucas Alexander were pure feminine appreciation, my own included. Even Nanny's eyes twinkled when she got a gander at him in his classic-style tuxedo.

"Oh, thank goodness." Cathy lifted her hand to her chest.

"I told you not to worry, Cath." Lucas shook his head and grinned at her. "I'm never late."

"There's a first time for everything," she said. "But you're here, and that's all that counts."

He moved to her and grabbed her hands. "You look beautiful," he told her. "I don't want to muss you, so I won't kiss you. Mac gets the honors today. BTW, he just pulled in alongside me."

"He's here? Thank God."

"You couldn't have been worried he wouldn't show up."

She tossed him her lawyer glare. "It can happen," she said, pulling a pout. In the next instant she asked, "How is he?" as worry slid across her face.

Lucas's grin lit the already bright room. "I'd like to tell you he's as calm as a clam, but he's not." When he laughed, the corners of his eyes crinkled. "I've never seen him anything but cool and collected, but his hands are shaking right now like a leaf during a windy peeping season. Told me he's never been so nervous or so excited at the same time in his life. It's not like this is the first time he's getting married and doesn't know what to expect."

Cathy's worried expression melted like an ice cube tossed into boiling water. A slow and serene smile wiped the pout away. "He's nervous?"

Lucas cocked his head. "Why does that make you happy?"

She imitated his head tilt. "I'm not gonna tell you, but thanks for letting me know. And for the record, this *is* the first time he's doing this"—she swiped her hand around the room—"because he got married at City Hall before. He's never experienced his own church wedding, and it's more different than he could possibly guess." She took a deep breath and glanced over his shoulder. "Where's Robert?"

"Bathroom. He'll be right in."

"Okay. I'm ready," she told my sitting sister. "Tell me what to do."

Lucas shook his head and then finally—*finally*—saw me. His eyes widened a fraction, and his gaze did a quick dip-and-return from my face down to my dress, a tiny, private grin pulling at one corner of his mouth.

"Hey," I said from my spot in the corner.

"Hey," he said back. "Um, you look...I mean...your hair...that color's...nice."

From her seat, Nanny shot him a look halfway between amused and pathetic. The amusement won. With a teasing grin and a twinkle in her eyes, she cocked her head at him. "You must have to fight the women off in droves when ya unleash that silver tongue on 'em," she told him. With a shake of her head, she muttered, "It's no wonder you're currently residing with your da."

Lucas, never one to hold back from a verbal tête-à-tête with Nanny, went to my grandmother and, with a grin that rivaled hers for devilment, said, "Mrs. Scallopini, you're a vision as always. You simply take my breath away." He laid one hand across his heart and closed his eyes for a second.

Nanny *harrumphed* and shot back, "What I should be doing is beating some sense inta that thick head o' yours."

Into this sparring match, Robert walked.

Colleen called for everyone's attention and said it was time to start.

"Okay," she said as Lucas helped hoist her from the chair. "Let's get everyone in position." She tapped at her earpiece and said, "Charity's signaled the musicians to finish up their selection and get ready. Let's roll."

With the timed precision of a general leading her troops into battle, Colleen managed to wrangle us all into place.

In the church foyer, a tuxedoed Slade stood with Charity, waiting to walk his wife down the aisle to their seats.

"Robert and Nanny will go first, then Slade and me," Colleen said. To Cathy she added, "Charity will get you three down the aisle last. You ready to meet your man at the altar?"

Cathy grinned, nodded, and blew her a kiss.

"Okay, then. There's the music change. Everyone set?"

Charity lined us all up. After counting to three, she opened one of the church doors and let Nanny and Robert go.

"Remember, step, stop, step," Charity said.

"Me memory's fine, young lady," Nanny said as she twined her arm in the crook of Robert's elbow. "I've gone down the aisle four times. I could teach a class on how it's done."

"No lie," Colleen mumbled.

As soon as they were through the door, Charity closed it over again.

"Kolby's in place?" Colleen asked her assistant as Slade took his wife's arm and held it.

"Shooting as we speak."

Colleen turned around to me. "Take your time. Let them wait for Cathy. Don't rush. I want them to all ooh and ahh over her."

"And me, too," Lucas said, a cocky grin spreading across his lips.

Colleen leveled a stare at him I imagined terrified people who didn't know her.

"You're just filler," she told him. "The bride is everything. Remember that."

Lucas saluted her. "Yes, ma'am."

"Ready?" Charity asked.

Colleen nodded and latched on to her husband. "Whatever happens, don't let go of me. I feel like the slightest move and I'm going to topple over like one of those inflatable clown punching bags."

"Not gonna happen because I'm never gonna let go of you, babe." To underscore the point, he kissed the hand he held.

For the first time all morning, I saw her smile.

"Let's get this show on the road," he said to Charity.

She opened one of the doors.

Once it was closed again, she turned to Cathleen and said, "I know Colleen has prepped the hell out of you, so I don't need to say anything, except congratulations and just enjoy this moment. Take it all in and remember to smile at your guests as you go down the aisle. You look amazing."

"You do," I echoed.

"Okay. Here we go. Take a breath, let it out."

The three of us did.

This time she flung open both doors, wide.

I waited until the guests all stood, then, with Charity murmuring from behind the door, "Step, stop, step," I set off.

****

"Your grandmother is in rare form," Lucas whispered to me as he popped another hors d'oeuvres in his mouth.

The woman in question was seated at a chair surrounded by a gaggle of men of all ages. Slade's brother-in-law, Cathy's godfather, Judge Asa Dupont, Father Duncan, one of the bailiffs from the courthouse, even a grinning Robert all stood or sat around her with a few others, as she flirted and batted her eyelashes at them.

"She kinda resembles Scarlett O'Hara in the opening scene of *Gone with the Wind*, doesn't she?"

Lucas swallowed and muffled his laughter. "She's a long way from seventeen and a virginal southern belle, but she's just as calculating and manipulative as Scarlett when she wants to be."

I hid my own smile behind one hand and flapped my other in the air. "Truer words…"

Slade's sister, Isabella, tapped me on the shoulder

and then pulled me into a hug. I'd hosted her wedding party and reception the previous year when Colleen had been her wedding planner and Slade had been footing the bill for the shindig.

"It's so good to see you," I said, meaning it. Isabella Rainier, née Harrington, was one of the loveliest people I'd ever met. She could have been a spoiled, demanding debutante due to her family's name and power, and her brother's bucks, but she was one of the most down-to-earth women I'd ever had the pleasure to know. And she was so thrilled her brother and Colleen had grown to love one another, when at first blush they'd been like two junkyard dogs thrown together in an arena, fighting to the death.

And I know that sounds dramatic, but…

We chatted for a few minutes until Sarah gave me a high sign from the doorway.

"We're ready to serve. Is Colleen going to announce?" she asked me.

I told her I would.

Since this was a brunch and less than fifty people had been invited and most of them Cathy's friends and co-workers, I was fine leaving Sarah in a leadership role so I could enjoy my sister's day without having to run to and from my kitchen like I usually did when I hosted an event.

I rang the dinner bell and asked everyone to find their seats so the first course could be served.

The way we'd set up the room, Cathy and Mac were at a private table in the center surrounded on both sides by everyone else. They'd wanted an intimate brunch and none of the typical wedding things like first dance or garter throw. Our parents' last-minute cancellation had me moving Lucas and Robert into the chairs I'd reserved for them, and now they sat with Nanny, Colleen, Slade, and me.

Brunch moved along at a relaxed pace, and Cathy and Mac took the time to visit with all their guests individually.

"How are you feeling?" I asked Colleen before the cake was served. She'd been keeping an eagle eye on everything going on in the room and had conferred with Charity a number of times.

"Like I've got two bowling balls in my belly," she said, rolling her eyes. The second she said it, her eyes went wide and she gaped at me open-mouthed. "Um, ignore me. I'm tired. I-I don't know what I'm saying."

Her eyes darted to her husband who dropped his chin as he regarded her. His mouth pulled into a tolerant grin, and he cocked his head as he reached over and took her hand with his. When he squeezed it, Colleen shook her head.

Slade turned to me, a question in his eyes.

My own had started to swell with tears. I'd long suspected Colleen was carrying around more than one little niece or nephew, but I'd been reluctant to ask her about it because I knew how sensitive and body-conscious she was. If I questioned if she was having twins and she wasn't, I knew her feelings would be hurt. I'd kept my suspicions to myself, but with each passing week they seemed more and more real. The fact they were able to keep the truth hidden for so long was a miracle in our tiny community where gossip is a reality of small town life we all suffer through every day.

"I think I'll go talk to Charity about getting the

cake ready to cut," I said, rising. The relief on both their faces was almost comical. Why they wanted the number of babies they were having kept a secret was a mystery, but I was going to respect their privacy.

It dawned on me as I helped Charity bring the cake out of my walk-in storage refrigerator that if I'd been the one having twins and Colleen knew about it, she'd have told the entire town.

I guess there's a reason my family calls me the quiet one.

When the cake was finally served and I'd received a number of compliments on its design and taste, Nanny dinged her champagne glass and called for everyone's attention.

With all eyes on her, she smiled at Mac and Cathy.

"There now, seeing as I'm the family matriarch, it's me duty to propose a toast to these two lovelies. But before I do, I'd like to say a few words."

Lucas leaned over and whispered in my ear, "Any chance it really will be just a few words?"

I bit down on my bottom lip to keep from laughing out loud.

Nanny slanted the both of us a look, and I felt exactly the way I had when I'd been a student in her Communion class and she'd caught me talking out of turn. After giving us both a blistering, periwinkle stink eye, she turned back to the newlyweds.

"From the moment I met ya, Mac, I knew you were the man for me darlin' Cathleen Anne. I knew down to me soul you were the one who could bring the happiness back into her eyes and the joy back into her heart. And ya have. I'll always love ya for it."

Mac smiled at her and then took Cathy's hand.

"Cathleen Anne, me darlin' girl. You're me oldest granddaughter. From the moment your da put ya in me arms, I've loved ya. It didn't hurt that ya were me own spitting image."

Scattered laughter filled the room. Cathleen's grin dipped down on one side, and she rolled her eyes good-naturedly.

"I've watched ya grow from an inquisitive, smart, responsible wee lass into an independent, beautiful woman who's a force to be reckoned with inside a courtroom and out. Blessed, ya are, with beauty, brains, and a soul made for lovin'. And now with a man who loves ya as much as me and your sisters do, you have everything I've always dreamed of for ya, darlin' girl, and I couldn't be happier."

Tears pooled in Cathy's eyes. She laid her head down on Mac's shoulder as he brought her hand to his lips.

"Well now, before ya all complain I'm getting too long in the tooth here"—she glared at Lucas and pursed her lips, to which he lifted his glass and saluted her—"stand and raise your glasses."

When everyone in the room stood, champagne flutes held high, Nanny told Mac and Cathy, "This is an old toast I learned when I was a young lass back in Ireland. 'May you have warm words on a cold evening, a full moon on a dark night, and the road downhill all the way to your door.' Congratulations, me darlin's. May love and happiness follow you all your days."

While everyone cheered and echoed Nanny's words, Cathy and Mac rose and hugged her.

"Short, sweet, and to the point," Lucas said, rubbing my shoulder while I swiped at my leaking eyes with a napkin. "The old girl did good."

"Good God, man, never let her hear you call her that," I said, choking on a laugh. "You won't live to say it again."

His cheeky grin knocked the wind from me and for a moment I got lost in the moisture in his deep eyes.

"I'm a big boy. I can defend myself," he said. "Don't worry."

The rest of the brunch went well, and by the time Cathy and Mac bid a heartfelt goodbye to each of their guests, it was midafternoon.

For once, I'd left my staff to clear and clean up from service while I sat with my family, Lucas and Robert included, in my private kitchen. Dressed in all our finery, we looked a funny bunch sitting there, drinking afternoon tea.

"It went well, it did," Nanny said to me while I refilled her cup. "The food, as usual, was marvelous, lass."

"Do you guys need a ride in the morning?" Lucas asked Cathy.

"We're good, but thanks," Cathy said. "We're gonna leave the car at the airport so we can get home right away when we land. Shelby's coming over in the morning to take Georgie, so we're all set."

Shelby Sinclair had been a friend of Cathy's since kindergarten and was now the town veterinarian. Mac had adopted their puppy, Georgie, from her vet practice.

After a few more minutes, I noticed Colleen's head bob. Slade, ever the vigilant husband, rubbed her arm and said, "I think your job here is done, babe. Let's get you home so you can rest and put those feet up."

A heavy and exhausted sigh blew from between her lips. "You won't get an argument from me," she said as he helped pull her up to stand.

"I'll come back for you, Fiona," Slade told Nanny. "Let me get Colleen settled first."

"I'll drop her back at the Arms," Lucas offered. "I need to get Robert home and then go check on a few things at the station." He glanced once at me, then my grandmother. "That okay with you?" he asked her.

"Depends." She slitted her eyes at him. "Are ya driving your police car today or your regular vehicle? 'Cuz I don't want to be seen by the community in all me elegance sittin' in the back of a squad car. The tongues'll be waggin' I'm being hauled in for some trumped-up malfeasance. If I'm gonna be arrested, I want it to be for a worthy cause."

Lucas assured her he'd taken his nonofficial car to the wedding.

"All right then. But I want to sit in the front for once and not the back."

Lucas grinned at her and nodded. "Done."

Hugs and kisses were given around as both my sisters and their husbands left. When Lucas and Robert went to get the car, Nanny pulled me into a body-crushing hug, her strength belying her age.

" 'Twas a beautiful affair, lass, everyone said so."

"Thanks, Nanny. I'm glad you had a good time."

She held me at arms' length and dragged a piercing eye-rake over my face.

I knew better than to ask, but curiosity got the better of me. "What?"

"You're the last one left, darlin' girl, and I'm not getting' any younger."

"Who are you kidding?" I asked, knowing full well what she was talking about. "You're going to outlive us all."

She grinned. " 'Twon't be for lack of tryin', that's for sure." She grew serious when she added, "But you need to find yourself someone like your sisters have. It's not good to be alone."

"I'm not alone. I've got all of you plus my staff."

"You know what I'm talkin' about, lass. You need a man in your life, who'll love ya, give ya babies, and take care o' ya in your dotage. It's a sad thing to get to a point in life and have no one by your side. 'Tis the reason I took four walks down the matrimonial aisle."

"I'm more than capable of taking care of myself, Nanny. I don't need a man."

"Not *need* in that sense, no. You're right. 'Tis a fine, strong, independent gal ya are. But you've got other needs, I'm sure, that could use some tendin' now, don'tcha?"

She opened her eyes wide and dropped her chin, the wicked glint in her eyes pointed and unmistakable.

Since everyone always says I'm the granddaughter most like her, I gave her lack of tact right back to her.

"And I can take care of those needs, too, *Nanny darlin'* "—I lifted my voice and mimicked her brogue to perfection, my hands on my hips—"without a man."

I opened my eyes as wide as hers and stared her down. This little spitfire could dish it out with the best of them and many before me had succumbed to one of her intense lectures. But, as mentioned, I'm the one who people say resembles her most in looks and personality. The difference between us is I tend to keep my words unspoken where Nanny says everything that pops into her head out loud.

A few beats passed where we just stared each other down. It was a testament to my age and willpower I outlasted her. With a shake of her head, she squinted those wide-open eyes at me and clicked her tongue.

"You grow more stubborn every day, Maureen Angela."

I cocked my head and pointed at her. "Okay, Mrs. Pot?" I turned my finger to myself. "Meet Miss Kettle."

A quick grin danced across her face. In a heartbeat, a belly laugh accompanied it. Her arms went around me again, and she squeezed with all her tiny might.

"I do love ya, darlin'. Stubborn thing though you may be, you've got me heart in your hands."

I kissed the top of her head as Lucas came back into the room.

"Everything okay?" he asked.

"Aye. Just saying goodbye to me girl." She stretched up and kissed my cheek. "Don't forget about me scones and the little gab fest we talked 'bout."

"I won't. Promise. I'll be by Tuesday."

With a final kiss, she accepted Lucas's outstretched arm. He tossed me a look over her shoulder and mouthed *I'll call you later* as he escorted her out.

Those four little words held such…promise.

Despite the wedding and my musings over Lucas, I still had an inn to run and Saturday afternoons were busy any time of the year, so I changed out of my maid of honor dress, wound my hair back up into its usual knot, and slipped into my flip-flops. I had work to do. Baking for tomorrow's breakfast service had to be done and the menu for lunch planned.

While Sarah and I decided on the best food to

serve, I rolled out pastry dough and started a batch of scones, muffins, and cinnamon rolls.

No rest for the wicked. Or New England bed and breakfast owners.

Chapter 11

By eleven, long after Sarah had left for the day and my cleaning and serving staff had all gone home, I sat down in my private kitchen and glanced at the text Cathy had just sent.

—I don't have the words to tell you how much what you did for me today means— she wrote. *—I'm blessed with sisters I love beyond all else. You and Colleen made this the best day of my life, and that's the plain truth. I don't know what I did in a former life to deserve the two of you but whatever it was, I'm thankful and I love you.—*

I swiped a tear from the corner of my eye and typed back *—I love you, too, and I adore your husband. Now, stop texting and go kiss the man. See you when you get back from Hawaii.—*

A string of kissing-face emojis blew up the screen.

After making sure everything was locked up for the night, I started up the stairs to my private quarters, tired, but smiling, when my phone pinged.

—Are you still up?— Lucas asked.

—Yeah, why?—

—I'm outside. Can I come in?—

Lucas? Here, at this time of night?

Worried, I typed *—Use my private entrance.—*

I hit send, then went where I directed him to meet me. I rarely used the private entrance located in the back of the inn and just down the staircase from my apartment. It was easier to come through the main part of the house. I opened the back door as Lucas pulled out of his vehicle and came toward me.

He'd changed from his tuxedo into a button-down shirt and jeans. He'd been magnificent in his formal wear, but I much preferred this casually dressed Lucas Alexander. He wore jeans as if they'd been hand tailored for him, the faded denim hugging him in all the right places. I knew if I touched the material it would be as soft as a sigh covering all that hard, toned muscle beneath.

"Is everything okay?" I asked as those long legs pounded up my porch steps.

"Fine, why?"

"I thought you were bringing me bad news or something."

He stopped in front of me, angled his head, and peered down at me, his brows pulled in. "I told you I was gonna call before I left with Fiona, remember?"

"*Call*, yes, not show up out of the blue."

"I show up out of the blue all the time, Maureen."

"Not when it's almost midnight."

A tiny grin tugged at one corner of his lips. "Well, that's true. You gonna let me in, or are we gonna stand out here all night?"

I stepped back so he could enter. Once he was in the little entryway leading up to my apartment, I shut the door behind me and asked, "Are you hungry?"

He nodded.

I started to walk back toward the kitchen when he grabbed my hand and spun me around. One look at his eyes and I knew his hunger wasn't for a few insomnia cookies. He stretched one arm around my waist and tugged me flat up against the hard length of him. I arched back so I could see his face, and when I did, I knew without a doubt those cookies were staying in their tin tonight.

"I thought you were hungry?"

That tiny grin twitched as he lowered his head to mine. With a gentle caress that sent every nerve fiber in my soul firing, he trailed a finger down and across my cheek, stopping at the corner of my lips. "I am." His low, deep voice melted my insides. "Ravenous, in fact. I may fall over in a faint if I don't get something to satisfy me. And soon."

When I grinned up at him, he traced the outline of my lips with the tip of his finger. Forget firing. My nerve endings were exploding like a raging, spewing volcano.

"You'd better not," I told him as I stretched up on my toes. "You're too big for me to catch. I'm strong, but I'm not hulk-catching strong."

His forehead creased as he cocked his head. "Hulk-catching?"

I nuzzled his chin, then kissed the hard edge of his jaw. "You know what I mean." I slid my arms up and around his neck and stretched up even further. "Now, let's get you something…nourishing."

Right before I touched my lips to his, he grinned.

I'd had fantasies for almost twenty years about this man's kiss. As a tween, when I hadn't known the mechanics of kissing, Eileen and I had pretend-kissed our pillows, trying to figure out where our heads should be, our hands, etc. We never did discover how to do it properly. I mean, who could? It was a pillow, for goodness' sake. I'd been given a firsthand—and nose—education about the aroma of my mother's fabric softener, but not much else in the way of useful knowledge.

My first real kiss had been behind the Heaven High bleachers after a student rally, and the boy had been even more unschooled than I was. After a gross session of tugging tongues and dripping spit, it would be another four years before I got any further training. My college boyfriend had been older, worldlier, and technically proficient; so much so, after college, we'd moved in together for two years with a thought toward marriage. The nuptials died a horrible death when Eileen asked me to co-partner in purchasing the inn and my not-quite-officially-engaged-yet boyfriend told me to choose my sister or him.

Needless to say, after we broke up I'd been too involved with running the inn, then caring for my sick sister, to worry about kissing a man.

But every time I had, I'd always wondered if Lucas's kiss would be different.

And now I knew it was.

Now I'd experienced firsthand—or mouth—what it truly meant to be seduced. Lucas kissed with his whole body, his entire being. From torso to touching torso and hipbone to hip, his body enveloped mine. While his lips did wicked and sinful things to my own, his hands caressed, stroked, and glided over me as if memorizing every curve and cranny. He slid his hands along my temples and reached up to the knot on top of my head. With a swift tug of the pencil securing it, my hair fell down over his hands and the pencil dropped to the floor.

"You always wear it up," he said, nuzzling my cheek.

"To keep it out of the way when I'm cooking and baking." *Good Lord.* Was that breathless voice mine? "No one wants to find a long, curly red hair in their soup or scone, you know."

"I like it better this way." He kissed my temple, then moved down to my neck. His breath fanned over the column of my throat sending heated flares straight through me. "When I saw you at the church, I lost my breath at how lovely you were. Are."

I grinned. "You said the same thing to Nanny."

His shoulders shook under my hands as his lips slid up, then down, my neck. "I had to say something 'cuz it seemed like she knew the effect seeing you all decked out was having on me. Watching Cathy use diversionary tactics on her for so many years helped me quick-think something to say. Your grandmother loves nothing better than a compliment tossed her way."

"No lie."

He pulled my earlobe between his lips and gently bit down, while his hands gripped my hips. "But saying it to you is the plain truth."

He pulled back and kissed the tip of my nose. "You did take my breath away, Maureen. You do every time I see you, whether your hair is tied up on your head and you're wearing one of your ten million aprons with something quirky written on them"—I smiled—"or you're dressed for a wedding." He laid his forehead against mine and sighed. "I could stare at you all day. Every day."

"I think you'd get bored fairly quick."

"Never."

I shook my head and dropped my gaze to his chest.

"Look at me," he commanded. When I did, he asked, "Why don't you believe me?"

"I don't *disbelieve* you."

"What, then?"

"It's just so...I don't know." I shook my head, making my hair tumble into my face. Lucas brushed it back and cupped my cheeks. I stared up into those hypnotic, gorgeous, verdant eyes and told him the truth. "I never imagined you considered me anything other than a friend."

"I've been thinking about you and me, like this, Maureen, for a long time. Just like I told you the other night. And we are friends. Good ones. The best relationships start when the two people in them know each other well, like you and I do."

That one word scared me to my bones.

"Is that what this is? A relationship?"

One of his shoulders hitched. "If you want to give it a label, then sure. I'm not with anyone else and don't want to be. Just you." He placed a light kiss on my mouth, then one corner of his mouth kicked up. "I'm pretty sure you're not dating anyone else, right?"

I nodded.

"And you want to be with me, correct?"

Another head bob.

"So we're both unattached, attracted to one another, and have been in and out of each other's lives forever. I'd say it's about time we got together, don't you?"

This time when he kissed me, I could taste the truth on his lips. I did want to be with him—had wanted to forever. I wasn't going to fool myself, though, into thinking what we'd started would last. We could enjoy one another for now—God knows I'd been dreaming about it for years—but there'd be no happily ever after for us. In my mind, I was still on borrowed time, and I didn't want Lucas to get hurt. We could enjoy and explore one another, though. There was no harm in that.

"Why are we standing here," I asked while he skimmed his lips across my jaw, "when we could be upstairs and much more comfortable?" I pulled back and took his hand in mine. "Come on."

Halfway up the staircase, my phone rang. Even though it was tucked in the back pocket of my jeans, the noise exploded in the quiet.

"*Holy Christmas.*" We stopped and I pulled the phone out. "It's Cathy. What the heck are you doing calling me on your wedding night?" I asked when I connected.

"Get to the hospital. Coll's in labor, and Slade said it's going fast."

"Oh, sweet Jesus. Is she okay?"

"Just get there."

"I'm on my way."

"I'll drive," Lucas said, tugging me back down the stairs.

One of the perks of living in a small town is it's easy to get anywhere within the city limits fast. The bonus of Lucas flashing his strobe light as we barreled down the roads to the hospital made the trip even quicker.

Holy Mother of God Hospital sat on the south edge of town surrounded by lush woods and quiet farmland. Lucas pulled up to the emergency room entrance and double-parked his car with the hazard lights engaged.

We sprinted up the stairs to the second-story maternity ward where we found a floor-pacing Cathy and a seated Mac.

"How is she?" I hugged Cathy, astounded to feel her shaking. My usually stalwart and calm sister was anything but right now. When she pulled away from me, her hands automatically went to the bulge at her belly.

"The nurse came out a minute ago to give us an update. She said things are going as expected. What the heck does that even mean?"

"Calm down, Counselor." Lucas pulled her into his arms when I let her go. "It means Coll is doing fine. Relax."

"You didn't hear Slade's voice when he called me, Lucas." She pulled back and glared up at him. "I've never heard a man's voice shake with such terror before. It scared me to my bones and—wait." Her eyes went to slits. "How did you even know? I only called…" She turned to me, her eyes now wide and her head tilted to an angle.

It took every ounce of courage I could muster to keep my face calm and expressionless. One single eye twitch or facial flush would signify something had been going on between Lucas and me, and she would have pounced.

"Did you two come together?"

Before either of us could answer, Slade burst through the maternity suite doors.

My brother-in-law, like my elder sister, is routinely a font of calm. Manners, good breeding, and a lifetime of living in the public eye have taught him to always maintain a controlled façade around others. But I guess having a wife in labor wasn't something the breeding and manners rulebook had a chapter devoted to, because Slade Harrington was a man unraveling.

"Oh, thank God, you're both here," he cried. I understood Cathy's statement about him sounding terrified now. His voice warbled and echoed in the empty hallway, and he must have dragged his hands through his hair a time or two because the ends stood straight up to the sky and not plastered down like they usually were. Faded sweatpants dropped down his long legs and the T-shirt covering him was ancient. He had two different shoes on, and I don't even think he knew it. His face was devoid of all its usual color and his eyes looked crazed. "She's screaming for you. Both. Now." He flew back through the door, stopped, and shouted over his shoulder, "*Come on.*"

Cathy grabbed my hand, her anticipated interrogation forgotten. Before leaving, she spun around and kissed her now standing husband on the lips. "Don't leave," she commanded.

"I hadn't intended to." A tiny tug yanked on a corner of his mouth.

I flicked a quick glance at Lucas, who nodded.

The last thing I heard him say before Cathy dragged me into Colleen's room was, "Don't worry. She's gonna be fine."

****

"You coulda told us you were having twins, lass. 'Twoulda made shoppin' much easier. At least they're both girls, so they can share for a bit until I can get out to a store."

Nanny sat in the only chair in the room, across from a sleepy, weary, and bedridden Colleen, and held her first great-grandchild. She was dressed for bed, her floor-length Irish linen robe covering her tiny body, her long hair braided and tossed over one shoulder.

At four o'clock in the morning, my sister's hospital room exploded with people.

While Colleen had been pushing her daughters into the world, with Cathy holding one hand, me the other, and Slade at her head, Lucas had driven to the Arms and collected Nanny. He knew she would have been sorely miffed if she'd missed the delivery. Plus, since he was the one to tell her Colleen was in labor and then escort her to the hospital, I knew Nanny would give him brownie points for his consideration, something I don't think slipped his mind.

Slade's sister Isabella and her pediatrician husband Jack had been notified by Mac and had arrived just after the first twin came into the world, a mere five minutes after Cathy and I got into the room.

"We wanted to keep one thing about this pregnancy a secret, Fiona," Slade told her, holding his other daughter. With a hip perched on the bed, he smiled down at his wife. "Plus, we knew you'd all worry more than you already were if we told you she was having two girls instead of one. And it wasn't a total secret." He eyed me. "Mo knew."

"I suspected," I corrected. "Colleen was too big to be having just one baby, and if she was it was a thirteen-pounder. And besides, you were the one, Coll, who let loose with the bowling ball comment. I knew then my suspicions were true."

"Why didn't you say anything?" Cathy asked. She reached out for the baby, and Slade put her into my sister's arms.

A quick bark of a laugh had all our attention turning to the window. "Maureen's like a vault," Lucas said from his perch there, arms crossed over his chest, a wry smile tugging on his lips. "She never tells a secret. You know that."

"Unlike Eileen who couldn't keep one if you paid her," Colleen said with a tired smile.

For a moment, the room grew silent, as, I imagined, we all thought about the sister who was absent.

"Well, now, I'm assumin' you've known for a bit about the two of 'em," Nanny said. "What have ya decided to call them, then? And please, don't be telling me you're gonna do what your pain-in-the-keister mother did with your names. I don't take kindly to having to think up nicknames at my age."

Colleen paled for a second, and I knew she was thinking about her dreaded Nanny-name of Number Two.

"Since they're girls," Slade said, "it was pretty easy to come up with names. You want to tell them?" he asked his wife.

She nodded.

"It's appropriate you're holding that little girl, Nanny, because we're calling her Fiona Mary after you and Slade's mom."

Nanny never cries in public. Ever. She always says she reserves her precious tears for sad times when she's alone. So to see her eyes fill and spill over was a once in a lifetime, if you were lucky enough to see it, occurrence.

"Ah, now, lass. Lad." She smiled up at Slade. "It's made this old woman's heart fill, it has, with the honor of being this little one's namesake."

The baby startled and let loose with a yowl loud enough to wake the dead. While she rocked and cooed and calmed her, Nanny grinned and swiped at her tears with one arthritic finger.

"She seems aptly named," Lucas said, his lip twitching.

The room erupted with laughter while Nanny side-eyed him, her mouth pursed. Lucas merely smiled back at her.

"What are you calling this little lovely?" Cathy asked as she handed the baby to me.

"Eileen Belle," Slade said. "I know how much you dreaded being called Isabella when you were little," he told his sister. "Belle seemed like a good alternative."

Like Nanny, tears had sprung to my eyes at the honor. Isabella darted to her brother and threw her arms around him. The sound of her sniffling told us just how pleased she was.

As I rocked my sister's namesake, I caught Lucas staring at me from across the room. Heat so scorching it could have melted metal filled his eyes. I can only imagine what was raging through his brain. If we hadn't gotten the call about Colleen, the two of us would have been in my bed right now, and I'd bet every insomnia cookie in my tin we wouldn't be sleeping.

A few minutes later, Colleen yawned, and Slade took it as his cue to ask us all to give mom and babies some quiet time. Kisses given, hugs performed, Isabella and Jack left first, followed by Cathy and Mac.

"We can sleep on the plane," Mac told his wife when she said she was too keyed up to go back to bed.

After wishing them safe travels—again—Lucas

helped Nanny into his car, me following.

"The lass is closer," Nanny told Lucas, hitching a thumb to where I sat in the back seat. "Makes sense to drop her first. Then you can take me back to the Arms. Breakfast'll be served in a bit, and I want to be dressed and present to tell everyone me news."

"It's really Colleen and Slade's news, Nanny, not yours."

She turned to me and even in the darkness of the cab I could see her steely-eyed glare. "It's me first great-grandchild, Number Four, and you can bet your last coin I'm gonna make sure everyone knows it. Happy news so rarely gets passed around in an old-folks home and a new baby is just about th' happiest news there is, so don't you be telling me it isn't my news to share."

I caught a quick flash of Lucas grinning in his rearview mirror reflection. For once, he wasn't the person being chastised by my grandmother.

It was still dark when he pulled up to the back of the inn.

"Mind your manners and walk her inside, boy," Nanny commanded.

"Yes, ma'am." Stifled laughter filled his voice as he held the car door for me.

I leaned into the passenger window and kissed Nanny's cheek.

"Take a nap today," I told her. "Or else you'll be exhausted come the afternoon."

"Aye, I'd planned on it. And I'm relying on you to take me shopping sometime this week for presents for me namesake and her sister."

I told her I'd call her later to set up a day.

"You really don't have to walk me in," I whispered to Lucas as he followed me up the three steps to my back entrance. "I'm a big girl now."

He laughed as he held the door and let me go in first.

"Yeah, but I was trying to figure out a way I could do this without Fiona becoming suspicious. This gave me a legitimate reason because no one says no to your grandmother when she issues a command."

The moment the door closed behind him I was in his arms, his lips covering mine, our bodies touching from chest to thighs. The promise of what could have happened had we not been interrupted earlier swirled around us.

Lucas shifted and pressed my head against his chest. "Is it wrong to say I wish you lived farther from the hospital?"

I laughed and shook my head.

His sigh was long and deep. "I wish I could come back here after I drop her off, but I've gotta get some sleep before I head to the station."

"I need some rest, too," I said through a yawn.

His lips were back on mine before the yawn ended.

My shoulders shook with laughter, as did his.

"I'd better get her home before she marches in here to find out what's taking so long." He kissed my forehead. "I'll call you later, okay?"

Nodding, I held the door for him and watched as he got back into the car. The last thing I saw before heading back upstairs was Nanny's face, a knowing smile gracing it, as she stared at me.

Chapter 12

Running an inn is, as I've said often, a twenty-four-hour, seven-day-a-week job.

The morning after Colleen's babies arrived, while Mac and Cathy were off to their honeymoon, I still had a full house of guests, half of whom were checking out. I usually serve a bigger than usual hot and cold breakfast for my guests on Sundays, so that those getting on the road won't have to stop along the way if they find themselves hungry, and those who are staying get a nourishing meal to last them the better part of the day.

I managed to get two solid hours of sleep once I laid my head down and before I had to get up, bake, and cook for the day. Around eleven, my phone pinged with an incoming text.

—*You get any sleep?*— Lucas asked.

—*A little. U?*—

—*Same.*—

The little floating dots indicating he was typing ran across the screen.

Then, a sad-faced emoji and —*I miss you*— popped up.

Grinning, I scrolled through the emoticons in my phone until I found a happy face with closed eyes and tongue lolling out of its mouth. I clicked on it and typed —*You miss my cooking*—

—Truth. But I miss u more. I'll try to stop by later if I can. Okay?—

Unfortunately, a domestic disturbance call took up much of his afternoon and evening.

The next morning, he dropped Robert off without coming in because he had to deal with a car accident.

Tuesday, I slipped away for a few hours and took Nanny to Concord to do some baby-present shopping. She was exceptionally quiet on the drive, something she rarely was, so I asked if anything was wrong.

"Tilly was hospitalized last night, and I'm worried about her."

Tilly Carlisle was Nanny's best friend and also a resident of the Arms.

"What's going on?"

"Losing weight, and she's a mite more distracted of late. They found her wandering about the grounds last week in nothing but her girdle. Had no idea where she was going when the staff asked. I suppose they're doing tests and such today."

I reached across the seat and grabbed her hand, gave it a squeeze.

"It's a carin' lass you are, darlin' girl," she told me, a half smile on her lips.

Nanny's spirits improved greatly with each baby store we frequented. After about two hours, though, she started to tire. Back in the car, she fell asleep almost instantly and only woke when we were back at the Arms.

"There now, lass, we still haven't had a proper gab fest, and you promised me we would."

"We will, Nanny." I stored the box of scones I brought for her every week into her bedside table as requested. "Things look light next week, schedule-wise, for me, so I'll see what evening works best. Okay?"

She agreed and then kissed my cheek before going into the residents' lounge for a visit with her friends.

For most of the week, Lucas and I kept having near misses, most often due to his job.

Even Robert claimed there were a few days he only saw Lucas when he dropped him off at the inn and then picked him up again, having to go right back out to work as soon as the teen was home.

He was helping me carry bags of food into Colleen and Slade's home when he confessed how busy his father was.

I wanted to get the place stocked so when they came home with the babies, neither of them would have to worry about feeding themselves.

"I've never seen so many casseroles," Robert said as he unpacked a few bags filled with plastic containers.

"They're fast, easy, and the way I make them, nutritious," I told him. "A new baby is a lot of work and exhausting. Double the number, and Colleen and Slade aren't gonna want to do anything like grocery shop and cook when they have any free time. They'll probably want to rest, themselves."

After I got everything put away, I left a note telling Slade where everything was and how to reheat the dishes.

Back at the inn, I found Lucas sitting in my kitchen, a cup of coffee and my insomnia cookie tin in front of him.

"Sarah said I could have some," he told me when he caught me eyeing him and the open box.

He looked worn out. Dark swatches colored the

skin under his eyes, and the corners of his lips were crevassed. Those little lines fanning out across his temples seemed deeper and more etched today.

"You don't need permission, Lucas." I picked up his cup and refilled it from the pot.

To his son, he asked, "You done for the day?"

The teen nodded.

"We were just at Colleen's, filling her fridge with food," I said. "The babies are coming home tomorrow, finally. Almost a week in the hospital seems long."

"It's because they're twins," Lucas said, stifling a yawn. "And Colleen's not nineteen anymore, so they probably kept the three of them to make sure no postpartum complications arose."

He lifted the refilled coffee mug to his lips, and the sigh that broke at the first sip told me just how tired he was.

"Robert told me how busy you've been the past few days," I said when the boy excused himself to go wash up. "You look like it's been a rough week."

He lifted a hand to me. "Come here."

When I was close, he gripped my hand and lifted it to his lips.

"It's better now." He placed a sweet kiss across my knuckles. My free hand snaked up and cupped his cheek. The way Lucas nuzzled into my palm and kissed it had my legs shaking.

"I need to see you," he whispered. His gaze bored straight into me, leaving no doubt about the intent behind those words.

"It's been hard to schedule time," I said. "We're both so busy."

"Do you have a wedding this weekend?"

"Just tomorrow night. It's small. Twenty for dinner. I've got nothing planned for the next two weeks." Grinning, I added, "Colleen wouldn't give up more than three weekends. Even if she needs to bring the babies with her, she's working again and not leaving it all up to Charity."

"Your entire family consists of workaholics," he said, kissing the hand he held again. "The normal forty-hour workweek doesn't exist for any of you."

I smiled at him because it was true.

"So, can I come by tomorrow, then? After?"

I was all set to say yes when he added, "I miss you."

Those last three words sealed the deal in stone.

"Any time after nine, I'll be free."

Robert's footsteps had Lucas releasing my hand.

"You all set?" he asked his son.

They left shortly after, a container of leftover chicken parmigiana and a few cupcakes with them I'd put in a go-bag.

"See you Monday," Robert said.

Lucas mouthed *I'll text you later* over his son's head. I nodded.

****

Never let anyone tell you a small wedding is easier than a large one. They'd be wrong.

By the time the dishes had been cleared and the happy couple had gone back to the room they'd share for the night before leaving on their honeymoon in the morning, I'd been on my feet for over sixteen hours. I was operating on sheer momentum and muscle memory to keep myself upright.

As I put the last dish in the dishwasher, my phone

pinged.

—*You free?*—

Lucas.

I typed back I was and to come on over when he could.

—*I'm at the back door.*—

Laughing, I all but ran through the hallway to let him in, my fatigue magically flown.

"That was fast," I said as I closed the door behind him.

"I've been sitting out there for twenty minutes, waiting for the damn car clock to read nine." He hauled me up against him. "Watching it take forever to tick the minutes by was as torturous as waiting for cement to harden."

I smiled against his quick, hard kiss.

"Well, you're here now," I said, nuzzling his jaw. "That's what matters."

"Are you done for the night?"

"Just let me lock the front door. Go on up." I pointed to the staircase.

After one last sweep through the rooms to make sure all was settled for the night with my guests, I bounded up the back stairs to my apartment and found him standing in the living room, hands on his hips, surveying the room.

"I don't think I've been up here since I helped you and Eileen move in," he said. "You've done a nice job fixing it up."

"Thanks. Eileen was in charge of decorating the inn, but this space was mine from the beginning."

"It looks like you, your taste. Your touch." A half smile warmed his lips. "Cozy and comfortable, welcoming and relaxed. Just like your inn, your private space feels like the best parts of home. Being able to create a space like that is a rare gift, Maureen."

Saying his compliment pleases me is too tame.

Unexpected nerves appeared. We were all alone in my apartment for the first time, and thoughts of where I wanted the time we were spending together to go sailed through me. I folded my hands together and asked, "Do you want anything to drink? Eat? Did you get a dinner break?"

"I'm good. Come here." Just as he had in my kitchen, he stretched out a hand to me. When I slipped mine through it, he tugged me close and wound his other around my waist. The green in his eyes was bright, and they glistened as he stared down at me.

His fingers trailed up my neck and across my chin, his thumb swiping at my bottom lip. Tingles of anticipation exploded within me.

Lucas rested his forehead against mine. On a long sigh, he whispered my name.

"What's wrong?"

He pulled back, a half grin playing at his lips again. "Nothing and everything."

I cocked my head. "Cryptic, much?"

His short bark of a laugh echoed around us. He slipped his hands into mine and tugged me toward the couch. "Let's sit down for a minute."

Once we were seated, Lucas tossed his arm around my shoulder and pulled me in close.

"Care to explain now?" I asked as I ran my nose down his neck and then back up, taking in his plain man-and-soap essence.

With his head tilted to give me better access—

which I dutifully took advantage of—Lucas grabbed my hand and brought it to his lips.

"Can I just tell you how much I adore when you do that?"

He smiled and kissed my palm.

"And that, too?" I said.

His smile grew, then softened. "That's one of the things I wanted to talk to about," he said.

"What? How much I enjoy when you kiss my hand?"

He chuckled. "I've been thinking, and I need to be clear about what I want if we're going to be together. What you want, too."

Those little nervous kicks started dancing in my stomach again. I swallowed. "Okay, like rules or something?"

He shook his head. "No, that's not what I mean. *Christ,* I'm no good at this." He took a breath, then squeezed the hand he held. Those tiny lines at the corners of his eyes deepened. If I didn't know better I'd think he was nervous. "I want to assure you I'm all in with whatever you want between us. We can take it slow and date, go out in public, or simply keep our relationship to ourselves for a bit. I don't care. What I do care about is you. Being with you. I want you. Just you. In any way. If that means we take a beat, get to know each other better on a personal, adult level, then fine. But make no mistake"—his eyes drilled into mine—"I want you. In every sense of the word."

I didn't need to be convinced. The way he'd kissed me proved the physical attraction between us was profound. That he was giving me a choice to take it further instead of simply accepting we'd wind up lovers was a huge insight to the kind of man he was.

"I won't push you," he continued, "into anything you're not ready for or don't want. You're too important to me, Maureen."

Cathleen has commented many times over the years about a gene for boldness running rampantly through Nanny. Since I'm the one who's the most like her in other ways, it stands to reason the genetic trait resides in me as well.

Lucas's words sparked it to fire up. Taking a deep breath and never breaking eye contact with him, I slid up over his thighs and straddled his lap. He shot his hands to my hips and held on to me as I gripped his shoulders.

"You're important to me, too, Lucas. More than you can ever know."

I bent, placed a hand across his cheek and kissed him, keeping the contact light. "And I think you should know what I want from this relationship, too." His eyebrows rose. "You. Simply you. In every sense of the word."

I kissed him again, this time with a smile blooming across his mouth.

"I don't need to be wined and dined or to show off we're together to the gossips in this town. I simply want to spend time with you. Without anyone else around. You."

The moment our lips touched, I knew there was no way I could keep the contact light again. One swipe of Lucas's tongue across my lips and I was a goner. He deepened the kiss, his hands sliding up my back to press me in closer. The throbbing of his lengthening erection against me was full proof of how much he wanted this…wanted me.

I pulled back and stared down at those lips, now swollen and wet, his eyes half closed and so damn hot it was a wonder smoke wasn't billowing from them.

"I'm not sixteen anymore, and neither are you." Confusion sailed across those hooded lids. "We don't have to be relegated to a couch make-out session when there's a perfectly good bed in the next room." I skimmed my mouth across his jaw, trailed my tongue across his bottom lip as he'd done to me. A rush of power washed through me when his hands flexed against my back.

"Maureen?"

"Come on." I hopped off his lap, then grabbed his hands and hauled him up. No easy feat since he was built like a tank. He used the leverage to pull me back down on top of him.

His eyes were intense and searching. "You're sure?"

"More than anything I've ever been sure of," I said.

I never knew such a big man could move so fast, but before I could take a full breath I was lifted up in his boulder-like arms.

"I think I like this as much as having my hand kissed," I said on a laugh as he carried me to my bedroom.

Lucas stopped short at the doorway.

"That's some bed." Laughter rang in his voice. "A man could get lost in it."

"You won't." I kissed his neck.

"Oh, I know I won't," Lucas said, dropping a knee to the mattress and still holding me. "And I'm stoked we'll have some room to roll around in."

He sat me down on the bed with my legs draped over the edge and kneeled between them. With his hands fisted next to me on the comforter, we were both eye level. Amusement ran across his face.

"What?"

"I'm trying to figure out why you need such a big bed, and I'm coming up blank."

I shrugged, then placed my hands on his shoulders. Lucas leaned in closer so I could wind them around his neck. He shifted so we were pressed together, intimately.

"The easy answer is I'd spent almost all my life sleeping in a twin single since Eileen and I shared a room from birth and our bedroom wasn't big enough for anything larger. It made turning over at night almost impossible without the danger of falling out of bed. Which I did. Often."

A quick grin shot out in front of me.

"When we bought this place knowing we'd each have our own room, I wanted the biggest bed I could find. Big enough so I could flip over, roll over, even sleep in it sideways if I wanted to without fear of waking up on a cold, hard floor at three a.m."

"I think you accomplished your goal. You could sleep four in this thing, and nobody would touch. I'm way taller than you, and even I don't have a bed this big."

"You can come over and sleep any time," I said. Then immediately blushed from head to toes. "I mean—"

"I know what you meant." He leaned in and pulled my bottom lip between his teeth. "And I'm gonna take you up on that offer right now."

Oh, goodie.

"Only, Maureen?"

"*Mm?*"

"I don't think I'm gonna be doing any sleeping tonight."

"Promises, promises," I said on a sigh.

I didn't have the opportunity to say much of anything else because Lucas silenced me with a kiss.

While his mouth sipped and nipped and lapped at mine, his hands went on a wild excursion, starting with yanking the pencil out of my topknot. My hair whooshed down my back, and in the next breath, my T-shirt was yanked over my head and tossed... somewhere.

Lucas shifted back and stared at me. I tried to remember which bra I had on: one of my nicer, lacier ones or an older, less feminine, and more serviceable one. I didn't have enough nerve to glance down and check.

I needn't have worried which kind I wore because the determination simmering in Lucas's eyes made it obvious I wasn't going to be wearing it for much longer.

And I was proven correct when he reached around and unfastened it, my breasts spilling into his waiting hands.

I gasped when his thumbs rubbed against my hardening nipples, threw my head back and planted my fists on the bed for support when he pulled one swollen tip into his mouth, sucked, then gave equal time to the other.

My vision blurred when he did it again.

"Your turn," I said when a moment of sanity broke

through. I tugged the shirt from his pants, then tried to open the buttons, but my hands were shaking with excitement. Frustration whirled through me when I couldn't get more than one undone.

"Take this off," I commanded, slapping at his arm. "And from now on, no more button-downs."

His deep laugh filled the room. In a smooth move I swear only a man can do, he tugged the shirt over his head with one hand—buttons still fastened. It joined my shirt and bra.

"Better. You're good at that." I took my hands on a happy journey, scraping up, then down his torso, weaving them through the thatch of hair covering him like a pelt. Hard and thick, his muscles flexed and contracted with each touch of my fingers. I didn't know if Lucas worked out or was simply gifted from God with this body, but either way, it was an absolute pleasure to see and run my hands over.

"You're built like a tank," I said as I dipped my head and played with his nipples the same way he'd done with mine. The air hissed from between his lips when my tongue swirled over a flattened disc, my ministrations causing it to pucker in a heartbeat.

While I was busy, Lucas was, too. Both hands snaked through the waistband of my slacks, downward, to cup my butt. His hands, big and warm, cradled me and then pulled me flat up against him.

"We both have too many clothes on," he whispered over my jaw and up my cheek. We pulled back just enough to shed what remained of our clothing.

I was done first.

I grew up sharing a bathroom with three sisters. Walking around half clad or naked was the norm, and

I'd never been shy about being so in front of them.

But being naked in front of Lucas was an entirely different experience. My sisters had never looked at me with hot lust in their eyes, causing me to erupt in a full body flush. They'd never dragged in deep, resounding breaths when I'd stood before them in nothing but skin and freckles. And they'd certainly never been struck speechless at the sight of me without clothes. Lucas had his fingers tucked into the band of his pants and was about to drag them down his long legs, when he stopped moving.

He was blatantly gaping at me, his eyes wide, his mouth open.

Nerves flittered through me again. I willed myself not to cover my nakedness with my hands.

"What's wrong?" I asked.

My voice shocked him out of his trance. He dragged his gaze back up to my face from where it had settled south, and blinked a few times. Then swallowed.

"Nothing. Why?"

I pointed to him. "One of us has stopped getting undressed, and if you'll notice, it's not me."

That panty-wetting half grin bloomed over his face. He sprang into motion, first toeing out of his shoes, then he pulled something out of one of his pockets, and then finally—finally—dropped his pants.

The only sound in the room was of me trying not to swallow my tongue at the sight of him. What's the old saying about reality never living up to the fantasy?

Well, in Lucas Alexander's case the reality was a gazillion times better than any fantasy I'd ever had about him without his clothes. And I'd had a lot of them.

As he'd done to me, I took my eyes on a slow, slow tour of his amazing body.

Hands on his hips—his naked hips—Lucas cocked his head, and it sounded like he was trying not to laugh when he said, "Maureen?"

"Um…y-yeah?" It took a supreme effort to drag my eyes back up to his face.

He lost the battle not to laugh. Shaking his head, he stalked to me, equal parts of determination and desire flying across his features, grabbed my hand, and drew me up against him.

Body to body, he'd felt wonderful when we were both fully clothed. But naked? What's better than wonderful? Mind-boggling? Life altering, maybe?

Whatever it was, I stopped trying to define it the moment Lucas shifted, lifted me in his arms again, and then up onto my massive bed.

Once we were stretched out on our sides facing one another, I threw a leg over his thighs and cuddled in close, nose to nose. With his eyes closed, Lucas ran a hand down my side, across my hips, and settled just north of my butt, where his fingers drifted back and forth. Divine tingles of pleasure slid up my spine.

"Your skin is the softest thing I've ever felt," he whispered, dropping a kiss on the tip of my nose.

"Good genes." I laid my hand over his cheek. "And religious use of moisturizer."

My hand shifted when he grinned and opened his eyes. The depth of emotions swirling within them was almost too much for me. Desire mixed with humor, kindness sifted with raw need. That this man could feel so much, and feel it for me, was dumbfounding.

And if I have to admit it, pretty damn fantastic, too.

He brought his lips to mine in a kiss going from gentle and sweet to poker hot in a heartbeat. Deep, guttural sighs moaned from each of us as our hands explored, tempted, and teased one another.

My skin may be soft, but his felt like velvet as I trailed along his broad shoulders and down his tight back. I'd always admired the view of Lucas walking away from me. With my hands now gripping his fabulous, toned, and tight ass, I knew why.

My toes flexed, then curled, when his hand slipped between my thighs and took a long swipe from front to back and front again. Instinctively, my hips rose from the bed and my legs opened, allowing him full access to whatever he wanted.

He got the hint pretty fast.

With his palm resting against my mound, his fingers began circling around my clit, pressing inward, then releasing in a rhythm that had me panting and writhing in record time. It had been a long, long time since a man had brought me to an orgasm. I hadn't been kidding when I'd told Nanny I didn't need a guy to take care of my *needs*. But the feel of this man's touch against my most sensitive area was better than anything mechanical could ever be.

That all-too-familiar tingling sensation firing in my pelvis signaled I was close to coming undone. "*Lucas.*"

His kiss absorbed the scream I let loose a moment later when everything inside me shattered.

I should have been mortified at the speed at which I'd come and the tears that formed behind my eyelids.

That I wasn't, was something I'd think about much later.

"Open your eyes," Lucas commanded when the

tremors inside me calmed.

When I did, I almost came again at the naked need facing me. Where I got the energy to lift my hand and cradle his cheek is a mystery. Every bone, nerve, muscle, and corpuscle in my body was drained.

He kissed my palm.

"You have no idea how beautiful you are, do you?" he asked. "Not only right now, but every day?"

Heat ran up my cheeks as those little tears slipped down my temples. Lucas captured one on his finger, then bent to kiss me.

"I want to make you come again," he whispered against my lips. "And then again after that, just so I can keep watching you fall apart and know it's because of me."

Oh, good Lord.

"Promises, promises," I managed to eke out between breaths that were still staggered.

His deep, resonant chuckle had all the hairs on my body standing at attention in anticipation of him doing exactly what he'd promised.

But first…a burst of energy blew through me, and I bucked my hips, lifted, and pushed him on his back so I could straddle him like I had on the couch. With my hands pressed into his shoulders to keep him in place, I swiped a quick, hard kiss across his smiling lips and said, "You're not the only one with plans."

I kissed his neck, then pulled his earlobe between my teeth and bit down. Lucas gasped.

I moved down his throat, sliding my tongue along the notch in his neck, then down farther to his pecs. While my mouth caressed his torso, my fingers moved south and threaded through the swirling hair beneath his flat belly. One small touch of his jutting erection and his hips bucked as mine had.

"I like this plan," he half laughed, half moaned. When I fisted my hand around the long and pulsing length of him, he added, "A lot."

I couldn't help but smile when I watched him swallow, the notch at his neck going concave when I tugged up and ran my thumb along his wet tip.

"A whole lot."

With a laugh bounding through me, I continued moving my hand, astounded when his erection grew even bigger. A sense of power I'd never experienced before filled me at the knowledge of what I could do to this wonderful man I'd been in love with for a lifetime.

"I want to be inside you," Lucas whispered, placing a hand over mine to stop me. "I want to feel you when I come. Sit on top of me."

Shifting, I spotted something on the bed, reflecting from the bedside lamp.

A condom.

At least one of us was acting responsibly. It had been so long since I'd had sex, I hadn't even given thought to needing one.

Lucas turned to my line of vision and reached out for it.

I beat him to it. "I want to."

He nodded, his eyes staying focused on me the entire time.

After rolling it down the long length of him—and being rewarded with another chance to hear him moan—I went up on my knees, positioned myself above him and slowly, slowly slid down until he was engulfed within me.

I think I blacked out for a moment from the sheer and overwhelming pleasure of having him fully inside me. I know we both went stock still when he was settled in all the way.

Eyes opened and focused on me, Lucas grabbed my hips and hauled me up, almost to the point he was out of me, then pulled me down again while he pushed up, deep. The force of the action made me cry out. This time, it echoed around the room.

He did it again and then again, quickening the pace with each plunge until I lost the capacity to see clearly. The bed shook, and I reached out to grip the headboard as Lucas thrust one last time, his voice breaking as he called out my name.

****

"You weren't kidding about being able to sleep sideways on this thing," Lucas whispered against my hair.

I opened my eyes to find we were, indeed, lying crossways on the bed, spooned.

The sheets were a mass of chaos, the comforter lying half on, half off the bed.

All in all, it had been a…vigorous night.

Lucas shifted, kissed my cheek, and then rose to go into the bathroom. I should have righted myself in the bed, but I was truly so exhausted, the thought of moving didn't even compute in my brain.

I must have fallen back to sleep because when Lucas dragged a finger down my cheek, I opened my eyes to see him dressed.

"I've gotta get home." He knelt beside the bed and pushed my hair off my face.

"What time is it?"

"A little before three. I wish I could stay, but with Robert and Dad at home…" He shrugged.

"It's okay." I pushed up. Lucas's breath caught when his gaze dropped to my breasts.

I should have pulled the sheet up over me, but the boldness gene reared its head again. I liked having this newfound power over Lucas, I wasn't gonna deny it.

"You're making it hard for me to leave, Maureen." He stretched and pressed his lips against mine.

"Sorry," I mumbled against his mouth, not sorry one whit.

He leaned his forehead against mine and sighed.

"I've got a full day ahead of me," he said, "but I'll try to stop by later on. Okay?"

I yawned. "Don't worry. I know you're busy keeping the citizens of Heaven safe. It's okay."

I finally sat upright fully and shimmied back toward the top of the bed.

"Go back to sleep for a bit," Lucas said as he readjusted the sheets and comforter over me. "I know you have to be up soon, but try to get some rest, okay?"

"I'm good." I snuggled down on my side and burrowed into the pillow. "I survive on less than two hours of sleep most nights."

I have no memory after that until I woke, two hours later.

Without a Saturday wedding, the inn was quiet, and I didn't have the usual crowd of workers to help serve, cook, and wait on people I usually did on a wedding weekend. The relative quiet was a gift, and I was able to take a little time in the afternoon to get some work done I'd been putting off, like getting all my quarterly tax receipts ready for the accountant and planning staff for the fall. Leaf peeping season in New Hampshire usually runs from September until the beginning of November, and my inn is routinely filled every single day. Colleen had at least one wedding per weekend booked already, and that meant limiting the amount of rooms I could offer to tourists. I wished I'd made the decision to add on the bungalows earlier.

I called Slade to make sure Mom and babies had arrived home and was thanked effusively for all the food I'd stored in their fridge. I made a promise to visit and bring Nanny with me once they were all settled and up for visitors.

Just when I started a batch of scones to add to Nanny's dwindling supply, footsteps turned my attention to the breezeway separating my personal kitchen from my professional one.

"Why are you here?" I asked Lucas as he strode into the room.

And strode is the correct description because the focused and intense glare in his eyes as he moved toward me reminded me so much of a hungry panther stalking his lunch there really was no other way to describe it.

He held my gaze prisoner on his trek from the doorway, stopped directly in front of me, took the mixing spoon from my hand and tossed it into the sink.

"Hey, I was using that."

It was as if I hadn't spoken. With one quick flick of his wrist, I was wound into his arms and pressed flat up against his hard-as-stone torso.

"When did you turn into such a caveman?" I asked, a grin twitching across my lips. What I didn't say was how much I liked it. He shook his head, his own lips lifting, a laugh floating in his eyes as he bent and kissed me once, softly.

A sigh shuddered through my entire body.

"Do you have any idea how hard it was for me to leave you this morning?" Lucas whispered against my cheek on his way to nuzzle my chin. "To know you were cuddled under the covers, warm"—he kissed my temple—"and naked and sleepy from our lovemaking…" His mouth dragged across my ear, pulled the fleshy part between his lips.

I gasped and tightened my hold against him.

"I wanted to stay more than I've ever wanted to do anything. Spend the day with you, in your ridiculously big bed, and make you come again and again."

It was a good thing he was holding me because I lost the capacity to feel anything south of my knees at that statement.

"Promises, promises." I yelped when he bit down on my neck, laughter shaking through his chest.

He pulled back, and the sight of him smiling, his eyes clear and bright and no longer shadowed with exhaustion, filled me with such profound joy I couldn't think straight.

"Maureen." He kissed me again. "I can't tell you what last night meant to me."

"You don't have to." I cupped his cheek.

"I do. I need you to know this isn't just some…passing thing with me. I've been imagining us together for so damn long." He hauled in another breath as he held me tighter. "I…care about you. Really care. Deeply. And I want to be with you. All in, just like I said last night."

My heart stuttered at the words. I knew what *all in*

meant to me, but I wasn't certain it meant the same thing to him. Was he telling me he wanted a future with me? A commitment of some sort? I knew there couldn't be, and I should have told him so. I should have said it was okay for us to live in the here and now and not think of anything other than today.

I don't know why I didn't. Fear, maybe? What we had was so new to both of us, I didn't want to say anything to jeopardize any time we could have together, because for as long as he'd been thinking of us together, I had been imagining it for much, much longer. Instead of saying it out loud though, I told him the truth of what was in my heart.

"I feel the same way, Lucas."

He laid his forehead against mine, nuzzled my nose, and closed his eyes.

"I can't stay. I wish I could, but I've got to head back to the station. I've got about a dozen reports I have to file by Monday morning. But I needed to see you, Maureen, hold you, even for just a few minutes."

Good Lord. Was it any wonder this man had claimed my heart?

Lucas's pager beeped loud and harsh.

"I've gotta go." He reattached it to his belt after reading the screen. "Pete's got a situation and needs some help." He hauled me back into his arms, squeezed, then planted a swift, hard kiss on my mouth. "I'll call later when I'm free, okay?"

"You don't have to ask, Lucas. I'll see you when I see you, hear from you when you have the time. Don't worry. I know and understand how busy you are."

He cupped my jaw, ran his thumb over my mouth one last, final time, then left.

Alone again, I took a moment to center myself. The depth of Lucas's words and the emotion he'd shown me was thought-provoking because their intensity was something I'd never seen from him before. He was a passionate, thoughtful lover, and discovering it had been a top-five event in my life. But his words hinted he wanted more than I could ultimately give him, and I wondered if, by not being honest up front and telling him, this would somehow come back and bite me in the ass at a future date.

I shook my head and pulled the discarded spoon from the sink. Too many what-ifs about things I couldn't control would give me a headache, so I went back to making Nanny's scones and worrying about the fifteen different things I needed to get done before tomorrow came.

Lucas wasn't the only one who was busy in this town.

Chapter 13

Despite not having any weekend weddings, the next two weeks flew by. I had a full house every day with most of the guests staying a night or two before they were off and another guest checked in. The turnover was akin to what I usually saw during peeping season.

Lucas had been tied up with police work and was busy as well. It seemed August was a month for kids to get into trouble as the summer wound down and the school year approached. He spent most of his days dealing with recalcitrant, button-pushing teenagers looking for a little trouble and his nights working accidents and dealing with his father who was growing more stubborn and grumpy every day. Our shared time together had consisted of Lucas showing up late at night, spending a few hours in my bed, and then having to leave before dawn to get home and make sure everything was okay before he started his day.

It was harder to see him go every single time he left, something he commented on, too. But with Robert staying with him, he wanted to spend as much time at home with him as he could, something I understood completely.

Boyd had come by with the preliminary plans for the bungalows and was all set to start construction at the end of the month. As usual he flirted outrageously with Sarah and me, but I'd finally realized his flirting was as harmless and habitual as my grandmother's was.

Speaking of Nanny, I'd taken her to Colleen's to visit and drop off her baby presents one afternoon when I'd found an hour to take off from the inn. My sister, despite telling us the babies routinely only slept two hours at a clip, looked refreshed and much less tired than she had before their birth. Even Nanny commented on it.

"For someone with two babes up at all hours, lass, you're lookin' almost back to yor normal self. You've a bloom in your cheeks and those smudges under your eyes have faded."

"From you, Nanny dear..." Colleen laughed. "That's a huge compliment."

Nanny wasn't wrong. In the span of two short weeks, Colleen's body had deflated from its pregnancy bloat to the point she was wearing one of her old college sweatshirts. She'd pulled her hair back into a long ponytail and didn't have a smidge of her usual full-face of makeup on, and still managed to look beautiful.

"It's the hormones." She laughed when I commented on her skin. "A postpartum glow I wish I could bottle. We'd make a boatload of money with it on the open market."

I'd brought another supply of food with me, so while I stocked her fridge and pantry, Colleen visited with Nanny, passing the babies back and forth between them.

"Cathy's due back tomorrow," Colleen said as she gave baby Eileen Belle to me.

"She hasn't seen the babies since the night they

were born," I said, cradling my niece. "They look so different even in these two weeks."

"No lie. Sometimes when I look down at them in their cribs, I think they've changed since I put them down an hour ago."

"The first year's a bundle o' change." Nanny cuddled her namesake as she sat in Colleen's rocking chair. "Your father was different from one minute to the next."

"Speaking of Daddy"—Colleen lifted her eyebrows at me—"he called the other day to tell me Mom's doing a bit better, but they're still not sure when they'll be able to come and meet their grandchildren. He wanted to know if Slade and I would travel to them instead of them coming here."

Nanny mumbled something that sounded remarkably like a curse.

"You'd think he'd leave her alone for five minutes to come up and see his only grandchildren," she chided, "but no. You'll be lucky, lass, if the babes aren't in college by the time your parents get 'round to coming back here. And I don't want to hear anything about ya traveling anywhere when the babes are this young. They need stability and constancy, not traipsing hither an' yon."

Colleen nodded. "You, Slade, and I all agree. But it is what it is," she said, "about Mom and Dad. At least the babies have you around, Nanny, like we did. Cathy and I are blessed you'll be involved in their lives even if their grandparents won't."

"Ach, lass, that's a sweet thing to say." Nanny slanted a sly look my way. "Remind your younger sister, there, I'm not getting any younger though, would ya. I'd like to be around to see her babies, too, but from the looks a things, I'm not holdin' me breath it's gonna happen soon."

"Sorry to be such a disappointment, Nanny dear," I said, grinning at her. "You'll have to make do with only three great-grandchildren."

My grandmother is nothing if not devious when the mood strikes her, and from the way she squinted slyly at me from across the room, the corners of her lips lifting into a crooked, wicked smirk, I knew she was up to some devilment. What it was, though, I hadn't a clue, and because I didn't, a tiny bit of unease bounced around inside me.

I was busy kneading bread a few days later when my oldest sister sauntered into my kitchen. It was the first time I'd seen her since she'd come home from her honeymoon.

"It smells great in here," she said as she kissed my cheek.

"You look wonderful," I told her, taking in the golden tan she sported. "Married life agrees with you."

She grinned and poured a cup of tea from the pot I had ready on the stove. With the tin of insomnia cookies in front of her, she filled me in on her two weeks away. My heart sighed at how happy she sounded and how the free and easy smile on her face lit her eyes. If any of us deserved a happily-ever-after ending it was Cathy. With a new husband, a baby on the way, and a rambunctious puppy filling her days and life, she truthfully never seemed better, more relaxed, or content.

"If you ever take a vacation," she finished, as she sipped her tea, "you should go to Hawaii. It's a different world."

I laughed. "If I ever take a vacation, I'm gonna spend it upstairs in bed, sleeping. That's my idea of the perfect vacay."

With a shake of her head she said, "You're too young to be such a fuddy-duddy."

"Why is Mo a fuddy-duddy?" Lucas asked, sauntering into the kitchen.

Like it did every time I saw him now, my heart quickened and my mouth pulled up into happy smile. "Because my idea of the perfect vacation is to spend it in bed and not traipsing all over the place playing tourist."

"I didn't traipse," my sister said. "I just didn't spend my entire honeymoon in bed."

When we both grinned at her, Lucas's eyebrows wiggling suggestively, she blushed, waved a hand in the air, and said, "You know what I mean. Maureen thinks sleeping is the perfect way to spend any free time she gets."

"Since she doesn't sleep more than two hours a night, I can't fault her for thinking that way," Lucas said while he reached into a cabinet and pulled out a cup.

"I just made a fresh pot," I told him as I formed the bread into the shape I wanted. Then, his statement flittered through me, and a ball of worry sank into my stomach. I sent up a quick prayer Cathy didn't read anything into his words. We still hadn't gone public with our *relationship,* and I didn't want to give my sister any reason to suspect something was going on between us.

Cathy accepted the kiss he planted on her cheek,

her eyes slitting. "And how do you know Maureen only gets two hours of sleep a night?"

And here was the reason for my prayer. Thank God Lucas is quick thinking because my mind went blank and I couldn't conjure an answer fast enough I knew would satisfy her curiosity.

"You know she doesn't," he said, then took a sip of his coffee, his entire demeanor calm and composed as he leaned a hip against my counter. "She's commented on it more times than I can remember and in your presence, Counselor. Now, how was Hawaii?"

Cathy is like the proverbial dog with a bone you can't make let go. "Why are you here? Robert's not working today. I know because I just saw him downtown as he was going into the library. He told me he's doing some SAT prep."

"Look at you." Lucas pulled a cookie from the open tin and took a bite, a grin tugging at his mouth. "Heaven's own lady detective. Maybe I should hire you to ferret out crime in our fair city."

Her eyes narrowed even more. Nobody is better at diversionary warfare than Cathy, and even I recognized Lucas was trying to steer her attention away from her own question.

"You do a fair enough job of it all by yourself. Now, answer me."

Lucas took another bite. "If you must know, Miss Nosy—"

"Mrs., now," I said.

His cocky, quick grin made my toes curl in my flip-flops, and I was afraid Cathy would notice.

"Robert's the reason I'm here." To me he said, "I need to discuss a few things about his schedule this week."

I placed a towel over the bread and then slid it into the warming tray in my oven to let it rise.

"Nora called last night, and they're coming back earlier than planned. Seems her new husband got a job offer, and he needs to start a week from Monday, so since they're coming home ahead of time, she wants Robert home sooner."

"He okay with that?"

Lucas cupped the back of his neck as he sipped his coffee. "Not really. He told her he wants to stay out the summer, keep working, and stay with me. She wasn't too happy about it."

"Not surprising," Cathy said as she bit a cookie. "Nora's not the type who likes when people don't agree with what she wants. Just saying."

"Truth." Lucas sighed as he sipped his coffee. Dealing with his ex-wife wasn't a picnic on any day of the year.

"What's he going to do?" I leaned back against my counter and crossed my arms in front of me. Lucas's gaze dropped to the bodice of my apron which today read *All this and I can cook, too* across the front flap. His lips lifted, and when the smile reached his eyes, it took everything in me not to reach out, grab him, and kiss him silly. The only reason I didn't was because my older sister would have had heart failure if I had.

"He convinced Nora to let him stay. But first she's gonna pick him up Thursday afternoon, take him home for the weekend so they can"—he lifted his fingers in air quotes—"reconnect, then she's gonna bring him back Sunday so he can finish up his commitment to you. I wanted to let you know in case you need to readjust your worker schedules."

"Thanks for giving me a heads-up."

He nodded again, and I got the distinct impression from the hungry look in his eyes if Cathy hadn't been there he would have hauled me into his arms. At least, that was my fantasy.

He asked my sister about her new husband while he finished his coffee, then glanced down at his pager.

"Gotta go. Say hey to Mac," he told Cathy. To me, he reached out and squeezed my shoulder. "Thanks for the coffee. I'll…see ya." When he squeezed it again, I knew he'd left unsaid he'd see me later.

Silence filled the room in his absence. I shot a look at my sister and knew from the concentrated way she was staring at me she was assessing what she'd just seen. Lucas was her best friend, and she knew him better than anyone else. The way he'd tried to divert her away from asking questions, the subtle glances he'd shot my way—glances filled with what I recognized as desire and wondered if she did too—were characteristics uncommon to him. If I knew it, she did as well.

Standing there in my kitchen, prepared for a barrage of questions about the man I was hopelessly in love with, Nanny's voice sounded loud and long in my ear. Whenever one of us had to face something unpleasant in life, she would remind us to *gird our loins*. Even as a child, I'd known it meant prepare yourself for the worst.

Heeding her sage advice, I swallowed a deep breath and clamped down on the need to run.

Cathy sat, her face perfectly composed and her expression blanked. This was the reason opposing counsel in a courtroom was intimidated whenever up against her. They never knew what she thinking; could never guess what would come out of her mouth.

But I'd grown up with her, and I knew Cathy was never as deadly as when she adopted an air of calm serenity. She was an awful lot like her best friend in that regard.

And so, I girded my loins.

"Lucas looks…well," she said.

I nodded. Staying silent was always a good tactic with my stealthy sister.

She mimicked my nod. "Having Robert around is good for him. I know he misses him since they moved."

"That's the truth. He's smiled more in the past few weeks than in a long, long time, and I know it's because of his son. He's such a great kid. It's sad he doesn't see Lucas as much anymore. And speaking of—" I clued her in on what Colleen had said about our own parents.

"Mac and I were talking about maybe taking a long weekend and flying down to see them sometime soon. I want to wait until after the twins are christened, though."

"Don't wait too long, or Nanny will be after you about flying. You know her views on pregnancy and travel."

She nodded. "She made them more than clear when I suggested we might go see Mom and Dad. Her exact words were 'ya don't want to be poppin' the babe out on a runway surrounded by strangers lookin' at your girlie parts, do ya, Number One?' "

Her perfect imitation of our grandmother's lyrical lilt had me snorting.

"Colleen does that well," I said, swiping at my

eyes, "but you've got her down cold."

"A lifetime of listening," she said. "Well, I've gotta get going, too. I haven't been to the office since I've been back, and I can guess what my desk must look like. I've no doubt it's exploding with messages."

She stood, her empty teacup in her hand, and walked it to the sink. I let out the breath I'd been holding since Lucas exited, thrilled she hadn't cornered or grilled me on what—if anything—was going on between us.

While she rinsed her cup, I slid a few aluminum foil packets of leftovers into a bag for her. "Here. You won't have to cook later, just reheat."

Accepting the bag, she pulled me into a hug. "I'll thank you on Mac's behalf since he loves your cooking and on my own since I'm still on vacation mode."

I walked her to the front door. Halfway down the steps she turned, grinned at me, and said, "Oh, and Mo?"

"Yeah?"

"I don't think Robert visiting is the reason for the smile on Lucas's face."

When the import of her meaning broke through, I went stone still, my mouth dropping open. Before I could think of a response, she was in her car and pulling down the driveway.

Damn.

For the first time in years, I'd been blindsided. Just because Cathy hadn't commented on the interaction between Lucas and me didn't mean she hadn't noticed it. Since I had personal knowledge of what a cunning tactician she was, I should have realized her silence was meant to throw me off track.

It had.

As I closed the front door behind me, my mind flew to different scenarios where I could counter her assumptions.

It's been said war is hell.

That's a mild way of describing it when it involves family.

Chapter 14

Despite my claim I'd spend any vacation time catching up on the missed sleep my chronic insomnia robbed me of, I was actually sleeping better than I had in years, and I had Lucas to thank for it.

Most nights he managed to come by the inn, routinely between nine and ten p.m. I'd make him something quick to eat, since he always *conveniently* missed his dinner break, then I'd lock up the inn and we'd go up to my apartment. We'd snuggle together on the couch and talk about our day, watch the late news, and then find our way to my bed where we'd spend a few hours absorbed in pleasuring one another. Sometime during the night I'd fall asleep, Lucas would dress and leave after kissing me awake, and I'd tumble back into a contented sleep for several hours and not the customary two I'd been plagued with for years.

While sex with Lucas was physically draining, not to mention wildly satisfying, I didn't think it was the sole cause of my ability to sleep better. In truth, it was because I was happy. Truly happy, for the first time in years. Yes, I still worried about my financial responsibilities for the inn, my sisters' welfare, and Nanny's health, but they no longer occupied the top spaces in my subconscious.

Now, Lucas did. Just having him hold me while we watched television filled me with such a wealth of peace and contentment, my mind was able to calm and relax and therefore sleep better and longer. Gone were the previous one a.m. marathon baking sessions because my mind wouldn't settle down. Having Lucas as a part of my personal life had cured my insomnia.

Too bad I couldn't bottle the feeling and offer it to insomniacs everywhere. As Colleen is fond of saying, we'd make gazillions.

My current state of serenity was put into perspective the day Robert was due to be picked up by his mother, when Sarah commented I hadn't baked any extra cookies or cupcakes for over a week.

Robert glanced up from where he was practicing his decorating piping skills on a parchment paper and agreed. "Granddad asked last night why I hadn't brought home stuff from you this week. I told him you'd been too busy to bake." He shrugged. "He kinda grumbled and said something under his breath I didn't catch."

Guilt ran through me at the thought that I'd been busy but not with the inn. I promised him I'd make something over the weekend. A little while later, Sarah left for the day and I told Robert to go wash up since I knew Lucas would be by soon to pick him up.

I was rinsing the pastry bags when I felt a pair of familiar tree-trunk arms slide around my waist. I hadn't heard him come into my kitchen. Of course, the fact I'd been daydreaming about the night we'd spent together could have had something to do with my nonattentive state.

"You smell good enough to eat." Lucas's lips trailed down my temple.

"That's buttercream frosting," I said, cocking my

head to give him better access.

His deep chuckle reverberated down my spine. He kissed my cheek, then spun me around.

Laughter filled his eyes. "Whatever it is, it's making me...hungry," he declared right before his lips clamped down on mine.

We were in my kitchen in broad daylight where any of my workers could see us if they happened by, and I never even considered pulling away from him. I should have, goodness knows. But I simply couldn't. The contentment of being held by him, the taste of his kiss, uniquely flavored and intoxicating, and the undeniable wave of love flowing through me were powerful motivators in dismissing everything else but this moment with this man.

His hands skimmed down my back, cupped my butt, and lifted me up on my toes.

"You're a walking ball of hunger," I managed to say between kisses. "Nothing satisfies you."

"You do." He pressed his forehead against mine, kissed my nose. His sigh drifted over me and sailed right to my soul. If ever there was a moment to tell him what was in my heart, what had been in it for years, it was now.

Fear kept me silent. It didn't, though, prevent me from sliding my arms around his neck and pressing myself against him in what Nanny would have termed a wanton display.

Lucas didn't seem to mind my overt action at all, evidenced by the way his eyes narrowed and focused. His lips crashed down on mine, and one of his knees parted my thighs and rubbed across the front of my jeans.

Talk about wanton displays.

Instant lust bounded through me when his tongue slipped between my lips and claimed mine as a reward.

How had I survived thirty-two years without this man's touch? His kiss? His attention?

His fingers drifted up my back and untied my apron. Then, he slipped his hands under my T-shirt and skimmed them up along my ribs to find the cups of my bra. His fingers glided over the material covering my nipples.

"Have I told you how much I love how soft your underwear is?" he said between nibbling my lips. "It's almost as soft as what's underneath it." I gasped when one of his fingers slid beneath the edge and scraped along the now bullet-hard area.

"*Dad.*"

The shock exploding in the room shot me straight out of Lucas's arms so fast it was a miracle I didn't slam into the sink behind me. Robert stood in my kitchen, his face devoid of color save for the two cherry-red spots flashing over his cheeks. Eyes wide, mouth twisted into a scowl, his hands were fisted at his sides primed to hit something. Anger slashed across his face as his gaze darted between his father and me. A silent accusation seeped from every pore as he stared his father down.

I can only imagine how we'd looked, standing there, groping one another like horny teenagers. There could be no mistake about our intentions.

"Robert." Lucas's voice shook with emotion as he walked toward his son, hands up, palms out in a pleading hold. His neck bobbed as he swallowed. "Son."

"How could you?" he yelled. I wasn't sure his question was only for his father.

"Robert, listen. You don't understand—"

"I'm not an idiot, *Dad*. I *know* what you were doing with Maureen and it's…it's—" He threw up his fisted hands and glared at me. In that moment, I recognized another emotion flowing through him: hurt.

Shame bounded through me, hit up against sorrow, and warred with regret.

"Son, let me explain. It's not what you think," Lucas said reaching out a hand to the teen.

The boy recoiled and stepped past him. "Seriously, Dad? That's what you have to say to me; it's not what I think? So, what I saw wasn't you feeling Maureen up? Wasn't you practically on top of her where anyone could see you?" He shot by me, slicing me with a look so cutting I was afraid if I looked down I'd see my skin pumping blood.

"Robert—"

"I can't believe you." He stopped and turned back to his father. "You preach all that garbage about how to act with girls, about the consequences of stuff I do and taking responsibility with how I treat people, and I find you dry humping in a kitchen? You're no better than some dirty old man."

My cheeks were on fire, and from the shock burning in Lucas's eyes, he was just as embarrassed at his son's words.

"I'm outta here," he declared shrugging off his father's second attempt to grab him.

"Bobby—"

"Don't," he spat at me. "Just…don't." Tears choked his voice and shimmered in his eyes. On a sob, he bolted from the room.

"*Fuck.*" Lucas dragged his hands through his temples and chugged in a quart of air. "I'm sorry, Maureen. I'll make him understand how it is between us." He reached out and grabbed my upper arms.

"He's hurt—"

"He's not hurt; he's surprised. And acting like a hothead, exactly like my old man. He shouldn't have spoken to you like that. To me, either."

I pulled out of his hold and wrapped my arms around my midsection, suddenly chilled. "I'd be surprised too if I found my father like…" I flipped my hand in the air. I shook my head again, then ticked it in the direction Robert had fled. "Go on. Go take him home. Nora's probably waiting for him."

"Maureen—" He took a step toward me with his hands stretched out. When I stepped backward and shook my head, he flinched.

"No, Lucas. Go. Please. Just go. It's…it's better this way."

He stopped right in front of me, cupped my chin, and forced me to look up at him. "What the hell does that mean?"

Tears cascaded down my cheeks. I'd gone into this relationship with Lucas knowing there was an end date. There had to be. Robert's reaction pushed the end date closer than I wanted, but it only served to remind me Lucas and I had no future together.

I repeated my plea.

His lips pressed together in a line so tight they blanched. "I'm coming back here, later, Maureen. We're gonna talk about this."

Too tired to argue, I dropped my chin to my chest.

With another oath splitting from between his lips, Lucas sprinted after his son.

After Eileen died, my body went numb and the emotional part of my mind shut down.

Not exactly a surprising reaction.

I operated on autopilot, my subconscious taking control of my life. It allowed me to concentrate on running the day-to-day operations of the inn, helped me get through each day upright and not dissolve in a puddle of anguish. Having the inn to see to, Cathy had commented, helped focus me, helped guide me through the grief of losing my twin. Gave me a purpose.

She wasn't wrong. If I hadn't promised Eileen I'd do everything I could to make the inn a success, I don't know how I would have coped. So I conceded to the logical, nonemotional part of my brain and let it guide me through the daily motions. Doing mundane things like buying paint and laying carpet, picking out china patterns, deciding on menus, all helped pass the time.

Until the day my brain finally decided I was ready to deal with my loss.

By then, Eileen had been gone three months. Ninety days without her next to me as she'd been every day since the moment we'd been conceived. My heart was still broken, yes, but keeping busy kept me from falling apart.

When Lucas walked out of the inn to chase after his son, once again my subconscious took over.

I had a business to run, food to prepare, guests to see to. I couldn't let the hurt from Robert's reaction prevent me from doing so. I had responsibilities.

Luckily, none of my workers had been a witness to the scene. My fingers instinctively rolled out dough to make the next morning's pastries. Soup stock for tomorrow's lunch simmered in a pot on my stove as I cut and tossed in vegetables without thought.

I worked through the rest of the afternoon, late into the evening, never stopping. When I did, I had enough food prepped for the next week.

Just as I settled the inn for the night and started walking up to my apartment, Lucas knocked on my back door.

I wanted to ignore him but knew that would solve nothing.

"Lucas, what—"

He grabbed me into a hug so fierce it stopped the words from being expelled. His entire body engulfed me. It took me a moment to notice he was shaking. A cavernous breath broke from him as he laid his head on top of mine.

After a few moments, he asked, "Can we go upstairs and talk. Please?"

Resigned, I nodded.

"You want something to drink? Eat?" I asked once he was seated on my couch.

He shook his head and patted the seat next to him. "Come sit next to me."

I wasn't sure I could say what I needed to say if I did, so I shook my head and planted my butt across from him in my lounge chair.

"I think it's better if I don't," I said.

Lucas leaned forward, his elbows balanced on his knees. "Talk to me, please. Tell me what you're feeling. I know Robert upset you."

"I think it's truthful to say seeing us…like that…upset him, more."

"He'll get over it. It was just a shock."

It was more and I said so. "He sounded angry, Lucas, but the expression on his face, in his eyes…he looked…shattered. Like he did when he found out you and Nora were divorcing."

Lucas swatted his hand in the air. "That was different. Plus he was younger. A kid never wants to see their parents break up, that's normal."

"Still—"

"He didn't know we were together, Maureen. We'd decided to keep it from everyone for a while, remember? He was simply surprised to find me kissing you. I think he'd be shocked to see me kissing anyone, but he'll get used to the idea of you and me together. He adores you. Give him a few days to cool off, spend time with his mother. When he comes back and sees how it is between us now that we won't be keeping it hidden anymore, he'll be fine. I know he will."

"No."

"*Yes.* Trust me, I know my son. He's a typical teenager. Runs hot and emotional, acts like the world is ending, then calms down."

"No, Lucas."

Something in my tone must have filtered through because his face paled and his eyes narrowed as he stared across at me.

"What do you mean, no?"

"Robert won't have to get used to seeing us together."

If possible, his color blanched even more. Knowing what I was about to say was going to hurt him, and hating that I had to do it, I stood and moved into my apartment kitchen. Diversionary tactics weren't only for

Nanny's benefit.

Lucas followed me.

"Why not?"

I filled the teapot and placed it on the stove. My hands were trembling so much it took me two tries before I could fill it without splashing water over the sides.

"I knew when we started this...*thing*, between us, it would eventually have to end. I imagined we'd have a little more time together before it did, though. I didn't count on it being so soon, but Robert's reaction forced me to see the inevitable."

That beautiful mouth I'd lost myself in kissing was flat, his forehead trenched as he squinted at me. His hands were fisted at his sides like his son's had been, prepared to do battle.

"What do you mean the inevitable? You're talking like it's over between us."

"It is. It has to be."

Shock exploded across his face. "Why?"

"Because it does!" The thin tether on my emotions finally snapped.

Lucas slid his hand around my arm. "You're arguing like a two-year-old."

I wiggled to be set free, but he wasn't having any of it.

"Tell me why you think we have to break up, because from where I'm standing, that's not an option. It can't be because you don't feel anything for me, Maureen. I know you. You would never have gone into this with me if you didn't."

"So what if I do?" I yelled. "It doesn't change anything." I gulped in a huge chug of air and pulled for calm. "It's better this ends now before emotions get the better of us and we start saying things we have no business saying to one another, or thinking about things we can't have, like a future together."

"Too late."

My entire body stilled. "What do you mean, too late?"

"All I can think about, all I've been able to think about for years is a future with you." He slid his other hand around my waist and held me close, his eyes so filled with emotion I was mesmerized, unable to turn away from them. "I've been in love with you for so damn long." He shook his head. "I don't even know when I started feeling this way. It seems like forever. But I love you, Maureen, and I've been waiting to tell you because like I said, I know you. I knew you wouldn't believe me."

He was right, I wouldn't have. Didn't, now.

"You can't be."

"You know me better than that. I never say anything unless I'm absolutely, one hundred percent sure. I've been going slow with our relationship, letting you dictate the terms because I knew, if I told you, you'd have run scared. But I'm not waiting any longer. I love you, and I believe we do have a future together, so much so I'm gonna say this right now because you need to hear it."

He pushed away from me but kept me at arms' length. When he took a deep breath, his gaze fixed on me, so intense, so powerful, I swear I would have slid to the floor had he not been holding me.

"This isn't exactly the way I pictured telling you this, asking you, but this craziness about us breaking up is forcing my hand. I want us to be together, all the way together, for the rest of our lives, Maureen." He chugged in another breath. "I want you to marry me."

For a moment, I didn't comprehend his words. He wanted to marry me? Me?

When the full import sank in of what he was saying, my entire body began to shake. The banging clatter of my knees knocking together was audible in the quiet room.

"The day we went tuxedo shopping? In the restaurant when the waitress said what a nice family we were? All I wanted was for it to be real. That we be a family. You, me, my emotion-laden teenaged son. And any other kids you and I make together. I want all that. With you. Only with you."

"No," I said, shaking my head. "That's not what this is supposed to be. This wasn't supposed to happen."

"No? What was it supposed to be then? What did you expect was gonna happen? We'd keep on sleeping together without anyone knowing, like it was something dirty and tawdry? That we'd be fuck-buddies until we'd had our fill of one another?"

I slammed my eyes shut at the harsh words. "Don't. Don't degrade it, Lucas."

"I'm not the one degrading it." With his head tilted, he asked, "You don't believe I love you, do you? That I want to marry you and make a life with you?"

The teapot whistled, jarring me so much I jumped. Lucas reached over with one hand and casually moved it to the back burner, flicked the knob to the off position. His other continued to hold my arm.

"Answer me," he commanded, in that calm voice I

knew was anything but.

"I-I don't...I can't marry you," I said. His eyes went flat. "I can't marry anyone," I added, quickly. "Ever. It's not...not in the cards for me."

That head tilt got more pronounced. "Why not?"

"I just...can't. Please, Lucas, don't push me on this."

"Too bad. You owe me an explanation. I've just laid my heart bare to you, said things I've never said to any other woman, including my ex-wife who I only married because she was pregnant. I deserve to be told why you can't bring yourself to marry me, to accept that I love you."

"It's not you," I said, then winced at how lame it sounded. "It really isn't. It's one hundred percent me. I can't...commit to a future. With anyone."

"Again, why not? You're not living a secret life are you? Not already married to someone else and none of us know it?"

"Of course not."

"You're not planning to run away, then, are you? Disappear from Heaven for some undisclosed reason?"

I shook my head.

"You're not dying of some horrible disease, are you?"

I gasped, then dropped my gaze to the floor, my shoulders sagging. In a heartbeat, Lucas gripped both my arms again.

"Jesus, Maureen, you're not...sick...are you? Like Eileen? Jesus, you're twins, everything is alike, your DNA, everything. You don't have...cancer, do you? Please tell me you're not sick."

The anguish in his voice was exactly what I'd

hoped to avoid ever hearing, ever causing.

"I'm...I...."

His grip tightened.

"I don't know for sure," I finally said.

"What do you mean?"

"I can't give you an answer because I don't know."

"I don't understand. Didn't you all get tested after Eileen was diagnosed? Wait. I know you did. Cathy told me you all had, just to be sure you weren't carriers of that"—he shook his head—"*whatever* gene. Even Fiona got tested. You were all in the clear."

And here I was now, faced with the truth and consequences of my inactions. I couldn't lie to him, but the truth would be no balm.

"Aren't you?"

"I...never...got tested." I huffed out a huge breath, my stomach quaking. "I never went to the clinic and had it done.

The expression in his eyes went flat and hard. "Why the hell not?"

I shook my head again. I couldn't look at him, couldn't bear to see the anger and disappointment in his eyes.

"You lied to everyone? Your sisters? Fiona? You let them believe everything was okay with you when you really have no idea if it is? You don't know if you carry the gene mutation that killed your sister?"

I nodded. "Now you understand why I can't marry you. Why I knew there was an end date for us. I can't—*won't*—allow you to think we could have anything permanent. I won't put you through that. I can't stand the hurt it would cause if I get sick."

"You are one of the most intelligent individuals

I've ever known," he said, his voice as hard as marble, "but that's the stupidest thing you've ever said."

My spine stiffened, and once again I tried to pull out of his hold. His grip was like cement.

"That's insulting.

"It's the truth. You don't even know if there's anything wrong with you, but based on the fact there *could* be, you're gonna deny yourself any kind of a future? That's stupid in my book and would be to anyone else who heard it. Why the hell don't you go get tested? It's an easy enough thing to do. Cathy said one tube of blood and you're done."

"Easy for you, maybe. You're not the one who has to live with the results; the one who may be given a death sentence."

"You're scared of the results? That's the reason you won't get tested?"

"*Terrified.*"

"My God, Maureen, do you hear how ridiculous you sound? A simple blood test could erase your terror."

"Or enhance it if I'm positive."

"I don't think you are—"

"You have no way of knowing that, Lucas. You're not a psychic."

"No, but what I am is rational, something you're not being right now."

"Again," I spat, "insulting."

"Call it whatever you want, but you're not thinking about this the right way. You need to get tested. If you're sick, then we'll deal with it."

"No, Lucas, *I'll* have to deal with it. And I'll have to watch my sisters and grandmother and even my absent parents go through the horror of another death of someone they love. I won't do that to them."

"So it's better if they just watch you wither away and die with no explanation? Or find you one day dead in your bed? That's what you want to happen?"

I winced, again.

"That's too dumb for words, Maureen. Look. Get tested to prove you're okay. I may not be psychic, but I'd think since you're an identical twin, if you were a carrier, you'd have been sick already. Which makes sense. What doesn't is never finding out for sure. If you have the gene, then we'll deal with it. And if you're not a carrier but never find out, then you're denying yourself a chance at a future with a man who loves you beyond all reason. And as I said before, that's just stupid."

"You don't understand."

"You're right." He finally released my arms and took a few steps backward. "I don't understand why you think it's a better option to live in ignorance. If it was me, I'd move heaven and hell to know the answer. And I can't understand why, if you love me like I suspect you do—even though you haven't told me in clear, uncertain terms you do—you wouldn't do me the courtesy to find out for certain."

I shook my head again and repeated my statement.

"One thing I do know, Maureen, is this. I love you, and I won't stop loving you. Gene mutation or no. The vows say in sickness and in health. You don't stop loving someone when things get tough. Think about that."

Without another word or move toward me, he left. The sound of his boots clanged on the carpeted stairs as he shot down my staircase and out the door. The last thing I remember hearing before collapsing in sobs on the kitchen floor was the sound of his truck as it rumbled over my gravel driveway.

Chapter 15

"You're not sleeping much, lass."

Since it wasn't a question, I didn't bother to give Nanny an answer as I refilled her mug.

"You do look tired," Cathy added as she rocked baby Eileen Belle.

"What's going on with you?" Colleen asked. Of the three of us she was the one who cut to the chase the quickest.

"I've been busy. Running the inn, starting the renovations out back." I shrugged as I put the kettle back on the stove. "Sleep's a commodity I don't trade in."

Even though I was facing away from them, I knew they were all looking at one another with raised eyebrows and questions tugging on their lips, so I girded my loins and waited.

It didn't take long.

"I saw Lucas yesterday," Cathy said. "He told me about Robert."

If I'd gotten the sleep I so desperately needed and had been thinking strategically like I knew I had to around my lawyer-sister, I would have responded in a much different way than by turning around and asking, "Is he still upset?"

The moment the words left my lips, I knew I'd made a tactical error. Three sets of eyes peered at me across the kitchen. Two of my sisters held newborns, and my grandmother had a teacup in one hand, a scone in the other. None of them were what anyone would consider swift moving on an average day, despite Colleen's history as a high school track runner. I calculated how fast I could bolt up the stairs to my apartment and lock myself away, knowing they'd never be able to catch me.

Cowardly? Yup. Not gonna deny it.

"Upset about...what?" Cathy asked.

I tried to think of a quick response, but my hesitation before saying, "About Nora coming back early," proved my answer wasn't truthful. "And him not wanting to come back and work anymore," I added in the hope it would sound more honest. It was, after all, the truth. Lucas had texted me Sunday evening Robert wanted to spend the rest of his vacation at home so he could practice for his driver's test.

All three pair of eyes narrowed at me.

Colleen repeated her question.

"Lass? Is there somethin' you should be tellin' us?"

I couldn't blame brain drain and lack of sleep on what happened next. The pain I'd been carrying around in my chest since Lucas walked out of my apartment over a week ago finally became too much to keep hidden.

A deep, guttural, and heartbroken sob rose up from the depths of my core. All three women instantly rose and came to engulf me in their arms. My sisters wrangled the babies one handed, while their free arms went around my shoulders and Nanny slid both her gnarly hands around my waist and pulled me to her. At five seven, I towered above her barely five foot frame.

The sobs went on for a few minutes, and while they did, I was led to a chair and pushed into it. Cathy's voice calling out to Sarah to take care of *things* was a distant echo as I laid my head down on the table and cried until I had no tears left.

A cup of tea was shoved into my hands with a command to drink it. The fact it was laced with the Irish whiskey I kept stocked for Nanny's winter hot toddies proved she'd been the one to make it.

"There now, darlin' girl," Nanny cooed once my bawling eased. "Drink the rest and tell us all about it. You'll feel better once ya do."

So I did. Despite being the sister who keeps everything so close to the vest you need to pry info from me, I told them about Lucas and how we'd begun a relationship, but it was over now. The one thing I didn't divulge—couldn't—was his offer of marriage.

"I knew it," Colleen said with a self-satisfied grin gracing her face. "The man can't look anywhere but at you whenever you're in the same room. Slade even said at Cathy's wedding he had to ask Lucas something three times before he responded. He'd been watching you the entire time."

"Lass, I feel like you're omittin' something. What caused the two o' ya to call it a day if you've been gettin' along so well?"

Admitting to Lucas I'd never been tested had been a million times easier than having to tell these three women I hadn't. It took me a few tries to get the words out, fear doing its darndest to keep the secret hidden.

When I finally did, silence rang around the room, scaring me so much more than yelling ever could.

Their faces were masks of differing emotions. Cathy wore shock across her widened eyes and open mouth; Colleen's scowling brow and pursed lips told me how angry she was at my behavior. But it was Nanny's face, rife with disappointment, which tore at me the most.

"Lass, aside from lying to us about taking the test—which is a bad enough sin in me book to begin with—why in the name of all that's holy, haven't ya?"

"I was afraid of the results. Eileen was my genetic double, Nanny. Getting tested and knowing for sure I was positive felt, well, like a death sentence. Not getting tested gave me—I don't know." I shrugged. "A little sense of hope, maybe? What I don't know can't hurt me?"

"That's just stupid," Colleen said, shaking her head.

"Lucas said the same thing." With my elbows propped on the table, I dropped my head into my hands.

"He's right," my oldest sister asserted. She sat down next to me and dragged one of my hands into her own. When I lifted my head she said, "You need to get tested. As soon as possible. No"—she pointed her index finger right in my face when I start to speak—"let me finish."

I slammed my lips together.

Cathleen took a beat, and from the concentrated, thoughtful look in her eyes, she was weighing her words, just as she did in court when she was preparing to argue a point.

Forget about a *come to Jesus* moment. This was gonna be much worse.

"You're the one who always pushes us to take care

of ourselves. The one who trolls Google and on-line medical sites for cures and research on problems."

"Truth," Colleen interjected. "When I was suffering with morning sickness, you were the one who found the right combo of foods and fluids to get me through it."

Cathy nodded.

"And when me hands were aching so with this arthritis and nothing was helpin'," Nanny said, lifting a hand to my face, "you were the one who discovered me vitamins were preventing the pain pills from being absorbed."

With another nod, Cathy added, "And I don't need to mention what you did for George when he was dying, do I?"

I shook my head, not liking where this conversation was leading.

"You take the time to make sure we're all informed, nourished, and fed appropriately, and you take measures to ensure we stay healthy. That's what you do, Mo. You're a born caregiver."

I shrugged.

"So I have to ask you." She stopped and squeezed my hand, forcing me to look at her. "If one of us did what you did, or didn't do as the case is, how would you feel? And more importantly, what would you do about it?"

Having sisters who knew you better than you did yourself is, at times, wonderful. At others, it's wicked annoying, like right now.

If we'd been in a courtroom and she'd been pleading a case with that kind of logic, the jury would have voted in her favor one hundred out of one hundred times.

I sighed, pulled my hand from her grip and rose.

"I'd tell you that you were being ridiculous, and then I'd bring you to get tested myself so you couldn't weasel out of it." I refilled my teacup and brought the kettle to the table.

Nanny beamed and nodded when I held it to her. "There you go, lass. No one ever accused ya of being stupid, now."

"Colleen just did," I said as I refilled her cup.

"No, I said not getting tested for the reason you gave us was stupid." She shot me an eyebrow-lifting glare. "You're one of the smartest people we know, Maureen."

Lucas had said that, as well.

"But not getting tested is dumb," she added. "And one thing you never are is dumb."

"I feel like it right now," I admitted.

Colleen grabbed her phone and began typing one handed while Cathy took my hand again.

"I need to ask you this, and I want you to be honest."

"I'm always honest."

She stared, hard, at me.

"Most of the time," I amended.

She nodded. "Are you in love with Lucas? I know you love him. We all do. He's been in our lives forever. But do you love *love* him, all the way to heaven and back and everywhere in between?"

To hear her quote our grandmother when the woman was sitting at the same table was almost comical. Nanny must have thought so too, because she sniggered.

I didn't even have to think. "Yes."

"And do you know how he feels about you? Really feels?"

"Yes."

She cocked her head as if waiting for me to say more. She really was a good lawyer.

"And you know this because..." She pierced me with another of those glares that made people squirm.

Oh, well. I'd told them everything else, I might as well get everything out.

"He asked me to marry him."

Once again the table went silent. Even Colleen's tapping on her phone quieted.

"I'm gonna take an educated guess that's when you told him about not getting tested, right? When he asked you to marry him?"

I nodded.

"And I'm also gonna guess," Cathy continued, "something you know I never do, you told him you couldn't because of this crazy notion you may die."

I shrugged again and took a sip of tea.

"What did he say?" Colleen asked, then resumed typing.

"That he didn't think I had the gene mutation, but we'd deal with it if I did."

"So, he still wants to marry you, regardless."

It wasn't a question, but I nodded anyway.

"Well, now, it seems I've misjudged the lad all these years," Nanny said. The three of us simultaneously gaped at her. One thing our beloved grandmother never did was admit she was wrong—even when she blatantly was.

"Okay." Colleen broke through our shock. "You're

all scheduled to have your blood drawn. Tomorrow at ten. You can get through the morning rush and be back in time for lunch."

Cathy reached into her bag and pulled out her phone.

"You made me an appointment? How can you even do that? What about privacy laws and stuff?"

She waved her phone at me. "It's done."

"I'm free," Cathy said as she typed on the keyboard. "And I'm your ride."

"Pick me up as well, lass," Nanny told her. "Might as well make it an outing."

"Wait a minute—"

"No," Cathy said. "No more waiting. This gets resolved once and for all."

"You're not the boss of me." As an adult it was a pretty piss-poor retort, but I couldn't come up with anything better.

"No, but I am," Nanny said, steel in her tone. "And you're going, Maureen Angela. No arguments. Have I made m'self clear?"

"Crystal," I mumbled, pouting.

"Now, about Lucas," Cathy said.

"One t'ing at a time, Number One. Let 'er get tested before we start plannin' her weddin'."

"Who said anything about a wedding?"

"You leave it all to Colleen," Nanny said as she patted my hand. "Now, I'd like another scone, if you would, please, lass."

I don't know what surprised me more: the fact Nanny had called Colleen by her Christian name, or the way I'd let myself be railroaded into doing something I'd vowed never to do.

Some days it really doesn't pay to get out of bed.

Chapter 16

The lab technician informed me my results would be available within a week.

"There now." Nanny sighed as she settled herself in the front seat of Cathy's car. " 'Twasn't so bad, was it? Now ya can have peace o' mind you'll be living a long, happy life, lass."

I wasn't certain on either point, but I nodded, knowing arguing with her wouldn't serve anything.

"I'm starving," Cathy said as she maneuvered onto the county road. "Let's go to the Last Supper and get something to eat."

"Ya won't get an argument from me," Nanny said.

"I should get back. Lunch service starts soon."

"Sarah can manage," my sister told me. "The inn won't go into foreclosure if you're not there to supervise a meal." Her phone pinged with an incoming message as she stopped at a light.

"*Oh, shit.*"

"Cathleen Anne."

"Sorry, Nanny," Cathy said at the same time I asked, "What's wrong?"

"Martha just texted me there's been a shooting at the courthouse." She flicked her gaze at the rearview mirror and connected with mine.

"Oh, my God. Did she say who was shot?"

"No names have been released, just that a police

officer and a bailiff are on the way to the hospital in serious condition. Lucas was due in court today," she said, tapping her fingers on the steering wheel. "And Asa was scheduled to preside."

I stopped breathing. I think my heart went silent for a few beats as well.

"Cathy—"

"Hang on, sis. Take a breath. Come on, breathe."

I did, all the air in my body whooshing from me in one long exhale.

"We don't know that it's Lucas who's been shot."

"But what if it is him? What if he….Oh, God! I need to know…I need to see him…tell him…"

I think I may have wailed that last part.

"Calm down, Maureen." She turned around to face me, a stern Nanny-worthy expression on her face.

My entire body shook with fear as my vision tunneled.

"Don't you dare pass out in my car, Maureen Angela O'Dowd. Breathe, damn it. *Breathe*."

Something in her tone pinged through, and I bent at the waist, my forehead hitting my knees as I dropped my hands down to the floor of the car.

"That's a good lass." Nanny's hand swung back to rub the back of my head.

"Sorry, Nanny, but lunch is gonna have to wait," Cathy said. From the movement of the car, I realized she was making a U-turn.

Nanny kept her hand on my head as she told my sister, "Floor it, darlin'."

The emergency bay was riddled with cars as Cathy sped into the circular drive.

"I can't leave the car here. I need to park."

"Let me out."

"No. From the amount of police and state cars in the bay, you'll have no pull in there to find out anything, assuming they even let you in."

She pulled into the first available spot.

"You two run ahead," Nanny said when Cathy opened the door for her. "I'll get there in me own time. Go." She shooed us with her hands.

Cathy and I bolted through the glass doors when they swung open.

The waiting area was as crowded as the drop-off bay had been, the noise level at a loud roar. We tried to push through a sea of uniform brown toward the reception desk, and were barred by several state troopers, just as Cathy predicted.

"I'm sorry, ladies. This is a restricted zone."

I was about to rail someone I loved may have been shot when Cathy, ever the calm and logical-thinking sister, pulled her wallet out and showed her license and county courthouse pass to the trooper.

"We're trying to find the name of the officer who was shot."

"I'm sorry, ma'am, but you know I can't give you any information. First, because I don't have any. But even if I did, this is an active investigation, and I can't let any civilians through right now."

"I realize that," Cathy said, "but is there anything you can tell us? Or anyone you can refer us to who can?"

I came as close as I've ever come in my life to screaming at a complete stranger when he continued to stonewall us. I was just about to push past him and suffer the consequences later when I spotted a familiar shock of black hair when the emergency room hallway doors opened.

"*Lucas.*"

He spotted me right before the doors closed again. I tried to sprint past the trooper, but he was fast and grabbed my arm in a grip of steel.

"Take your hands off me." I slapped against his hold and writhed, trying to break free.

"Maureen, calm down. This isn't helping," Cathy said in her best older sister you'd-better-listen-to-me voice.

I ignored her.

By now, a small crowd of state police had gathered around us. Cathy telling me I was going to be arrested if I didn't calm down never even penetrated through my need to get to Lucas.

I was released when a firm, loud voice commanded the trooper to let me go.

"Lucas," I cried.

"Let her go," he repeated.

"But Chief—"

"Now."

That simple word had enough threat and intent to do bodily harm woven into it to terrify even the bravest of souls.

Once I was free I bounded toward Lucas, stopping short before I could throw my arms around him.

"Oh my, God, Lucas. You're bleeding," I screeched. Bright, red bloodstains, wet and shimmering, covered his shirt and pants in a hopscotched pattern of gore. The sickening odor of metallic copper surrounded my senses and made my stomach churn.

Like it had in the car, my vision tunneled, and all

the noise blaring around me softened and muffled until it silenced to a dull thrum. Every movement around me decelerated, as if the speed had been changed from fast to slow motion.

Strong and able arms gathered me close and lifted me before everything around me faded, then went inky black.

****

"Her eyes are startin' t' flutter a bit. I think she's comin' 'round."

Nanny.

"Maureen? Can you hear me?" Cathy asked, dangerously close to my face, so close I could feel her concerned breath spraying over my cheeks. "Open your eyes if you can hear me."

"So bossy," I whispered. My tongue felt like sandpaper as I dragged it along the roof of my mouth. I did as commanded and opened my eyes, only to slam them shut again.

"It's too bright." I lifted a hand to shield the glare. When the intensity softened a moment later, I hazarded another eyewink.

"Better?" Cathy asked.

"What happened?" I was on my back on top of something soft and squishy. Cathy helped me to a sitting position.

"You passed out in the emergency room."

"You'd a hit the floor hard, too, lass, if Lucas hadn't a caught ya."

It all came back to me in a rush.

"Lucas." I gripped Cathy's arm. "He was hurt, covered in blood. I—"

"The blood wasn't his. It was Pete Bergeron's."

"Pete?"

"Yeah. He was one of the people shot in the courtroom, not Lucas. Got hit in the arm. Lucas tried to stanch the blood until the ambulance arrived. That's why he was covered."

"It wasn't his?"

"No. Pete's in surgery right now. Lucas is upstairs with Pete's parents and girlfriend. He's fine, Maureen. Lucas is fine."

I nodded. "He's fine?"

"Aside from being worried sick about Pete and you, yeah, he's fine. I've never seen him move so fast as when you started to go out."

"Oh, Lord." I buried my face in my hands. I can only imagine how I'd looked, what he'd thought.

"He hauled you in the first empty cubicle but then had to go up to surgery with Pete," Cathy said.

"But he's okay? You're not lying to me, right?"

She pulled her mouth into a puckered pout, then said, "You know better than to ever ask me a question like that. I don't lie."

"Sorry. I'm sorry."

I closed my eyes again, only to have them bolt right back open. "Asa?"

"Is fine, too. He wasn't hit, thank God. The minute the shooting started he ducked down behind the bench. Rusty, his bailiff, got hit in the knee while he tried to join Asa."

"I can't believe this happened in Heaven." Nausea engulfed me.

"Lass, I think ya should be getting on home since you're awake again. Maybe get somethin' to eat. I know how much ya hate hospitals."

"I'm okay, Nanny." I shook my head and shifted so my legs were dangling over the side of what I realized was a gurney. "I was just shocked at seeing Lucas covered with blood. I'm okay. Really."

She peered at me, her head tilted to one side, her periwinkle eyes squinting. "Ya still look a mite pale."

"I'm always pale," I said as I came to a standing position.

"Take it easy." Cathy reached out a hand to catch me if I went down.

"I'm fine. Don't worry."

"Like tellin' us not to breathe, lass."

I was able to convince them I was better, and when they finally believed me, Cathy asked if I wanted to go up to the surgical waiting room to see Lucas.

"No. No, let him be with the Bergerons. I don't want to bother him. As long as I know he wasn't the one shot, I'm okay."

We dropped Nanny off first and got her settled back into her room. Cathy spoke with the nursing supervisor about getting our grandmother a luncheon tray sent to her room since she missed the communal luncheon she usually attended.

We left her with hugs and kisses and promises to call later on.

The two of us were silent on the drive back to the inn. I didn't know about my sister, but I was drained. Emotionally, physically, hell, even spiritually. A hot cup of tea and a nap called my name. Unfortunately, I knew the nap would have to wait.

When Cathy pulled up to the back entrance of the inn, she put the car in park but didn't kill the engine.

"Go make yourself something to eat," she ordered.

I wasn't hungry, but she didn't need to know that, so I nodded.

"And do me a favor?"

"What?"

"Never faint again." She laid a hand over her belly. "Nothing good ever happens when someone in this family faints. My heart can't take it, and neither can Junior, here. Okay?"

I grabbed her across the console and held on tight.

"And call me as soon as you hear your results."

I nodded.

"No. Say it, Mo. Speak the words. I need you to promise me, out loud, you'll call me no matter what the test says. Good or bad. Understand?"

The concern wafting from her was humbling. I was already feeling guilty about not getting the test initially, and I didn't want to add any more anxiety to her pregnant state.

"I promise, no matter what the result, I'll call you when I've heard. Colleen, too."

She dragged in a breath and let me go. "Okay. Better. No more secrets. We're all in this together, understand?"

With another nod and hug, I told her I did.

Back in my kitchen, I received a status report from Sarah after telling her what happened at the courthouse and hospital. Thankfully, I had no fires I needed to extinguish, but when she pointed out I had blood smears on my shirt, I figured I should change before I got back to work.

After starting the pork I was serving for tomorrow's luncheon, I sat down at my office desk and pulled up my calendar. Colleen's first wedding since the birth of the twins was this weekend, and although Charity was in charge, I knew my sister would be around nitpicking the details. I'd been commissioned to do the wedding cake and called up the file of what the bride wanted.

An easy enough design, and the desired red velvet cake interior I could put together in my sleep. I decided I'd start on the cake layers after my day workers went home. When I closed out the file, I glanced at the desktop calendar and noted the date.

How had I forgotten the anniversary of Eileen's death was next week?

Easy, I countered. One sister's wedding, the birth of another's twins, and the emotional upheaval I'd been going through between worrying about this damn blood test and my relationship with Lucas, and it was no wonder I'd forgotten.

My sisters and I had briefly discussed a way to honor the day but hadn't put any definitive plans together. I took a moment and sent them each a quick text about it.

—*Let's give it some thought*— Cathy texted back.

—*We can discuss options this weekend at the wedding*— from Colleen. Multitasking is my middle sister's middle name.

The rest of the afternoon passed uneventfully. Once the inn quieted, I set about making the cake for the weekend wedding. While the layers baked, I made the dough for three-dozen cookies to replenish my insomnia cookie tin. It had stood empty since the last time Robert and Lucas had been in my kitchen. At the time, I'd promised Robert I'd send him home with a box for his grandfather. I'd never fulfilled my promise due to unforeseen circumstances.

My heart ached at the thought Robert was still upset at what he'd seen between his father and me. When Lucas had texted Robert wasn't coming back to work but was staying home to concentrate on passing his driver's test, I knew it was just a handy excuse for the boy to avoid any further drama.

Since his son wasn't coming to the inn every day, Lucas had avoided stopping in as well. I hadn't seen him since the night he walked out of my apartment until today in the hospital, and I missed him. Terribly.

Before I knew he hadn't been the one shot at the courthouse, my mind had dragged through an excess of twisted thoughts and dire scenarios. The one recurring reality was that I'd spoiled what there had been between us by admitting I hadn't gotten tested. With him potentially dying from a gunshot, I'd never get the chance to apologize. Or tell him no matter what the test result showed, I wanted to be with him, to make any kind of future I could with him. But mostly, I wanted to tell him how much I loved him—had always loved him—and wanted to be with him no matter what came our way.

By the time the cakes had cooled and the cookies were stored in the tin, it was after ten and I was running on empty.

I locked the front door, shut the kitchen lights, and was about to head up to my bed when I spotted headlights light up my back parking lot.

The moment Lucas pulled himself from the car's interior, I threw open my door and bolted down the steps.

Right before I flung myself into his outstretched

arms, he said my name.

We stood there, with the moonlight shining down on us, just holding one another. In truth, I never wanted to let go. The strong and steady beat of Lucas's heart against my ear, the rise and fall of his chest with every breath he took, even the way his hands felt around me—familiar and secure—solidified how much I needed this man in my life.

"You changed clothes," I managed to say when I could find my voice.

"One of the ER nurses gave me these scrubs after Pete's mom lost it when she saw his blood all over me."

I hugged him tighter and bit back tears.

After a few moments, Lucas blew out a breath heavy with exhaustion and asked, "Can I come in for a bit?"

I wanted to tell him he could come in and stay forever. Instead, I took his hand and silently led him up to my apartment.

"Have you eaten anything?" I asked once he was settled on my couch.

"Not since breakfast, but don't make anything, Maureen. I'm not hungry."

"You still need to eat. Give me a minute."

I left him, sprawled on the couch, fatigue clouding every pore on his face, while I made him what I knew was his favorite: a peanut butter and jelly sandwich. I brought it to him along with a glass of milk.

His eyes were closed, his hands cupping the back of his neck.

He opened them when I said, "Here. Eat this."

Glancing down at the plate and glass I'd put on the cocktail table, one corner of his mouth tilted up. "You always know exactly what to make me. But what? No cookies?"

"I'll run downstairs and get some."

Lucas stretched out his hand and caught mine. "I was kidding. Come on, sit down with me so I don't fall asleep. We need to talk."

He tugged me down on the couch next to him.

"Eat," I ordered.

"Yes, ma'am."

"How is Pete?" I asked after he took a bite.

"He's been better. The bullet went clear through his upper arm and nicked his brachial artery when it passed. That's why I was covered in blood. Before the paramedics arrived, I slipped my belt around his arm as a tourniquet and it squirted all over me."

I shuddered while he drank some milk.

"The surgeon says he won't know how much damage there is for a while, but he's hopeful whatever it is will be minimal." He shook his head.

"Is it his dominant hand?"

"No, thank God. Getting shot sucks to begin with. Having your shooting arm possibly damaged beyond repair is a career killer. Luckily, if you can call it that, it was his left arm."

I watched him finish the sandwich and then the milk.

"I guess I was hungry after all. Thanks. Leave them," he ordered when I stood to clear the table. He grabbed my hand again and cocooned it between both of his. "Sit down with me, Maureen. Please. I need…."

A deep, guttural sound pushed from within him. This strong, always calm man was hanging on to his emotions by the thinnest of threads. My heart simply flipped over.

I laid a hand across his cheek. He burrowed into it and kissed my palm.

"Do you want to talk about what happened? Can you tell me, or is it"—I shrugged—"classified, or something?"

He sighed again. "What happened should never have. The staties are conducting an investigation right now into how Harley Reacher was able to get a gun past the security machine."

"Oh, my goodness. Harley was the shooter? He's the mildest, meekest man I've ever known."

"One thing being a cop has taught me, it's you never really know a person or what's going on inside their heads."

"Why was he in court?"

"Harley and his neighbor, Earl Sharrod, were involved in a dispute about Earl's dogs barking at all hours. Pete and I have been out there three times this past month alone when Harley called with noise complaints. Earl filed a harassment lawsuit and wanted a restraining order served, so that's how they wound up in court today."

"And Harley brought a gun with him? Why?"

Lucas yawned. "Who knows. That's gonna be for the investigators to figure out. For now, my thoughts are on Pete." He turned and focused on me. "And you."

"M-me?"

He shifted so he was facing me, tucked one leg under the other, and reached for my other hand. When he held both, he squeezed them. "When I saw you through the emergency bay doors, Maureen, looking scared out of your wits, it gave me something I've been a little short on these past few days—hope."

"What do you mean?"

"When I walked out on you last week, I figured you'd call or text me in a day or two, once it got through to you I wasn't joking around when I said I loved you and would no matter what any damn test said. You never did, so I figured you didn't believe me after all."

"I thought you were mad at me about…everything. When Robert decided not to come back and you stopped coming around every day, I knew I'd hurt you, something I never wanted to do."

He squeezed my hands again.

"More discouraged than hurt," he said. "I thought giving you time and leaving you alone was the way to handle this. I was, obviously, wrong. Like I've said before, I suck at relationships. Ninety-nine percent of the reason Nora and I got divorced is because she claimed I never talked to her about anything, never let her know what I was feeling, thinking." He shook his head.

"Why did you say seeing me in the hospital gave you hope?"

"Because I know you. You hate hospitals with a passion and have since you were a kid. But it got ten times worse when Eileen got sick. You avoid them when you can and only go when there's no other alternative, like when Fiona drove into that parked car and broke her arm."

I shuddered again. "When I heard about the shooting and Cathy said you were scheduled to be in court this morning, I had to find out if you were okay. Cathy didn't even think, she just aimed her car for the hospital. Lucas, I was so scared—" My voice broke, and he tugged on my hands and brought me closer.

"I'm fine, sweetheart. Well, maybe a little shaken because I almost lost one of my men, but physically I'm okay. I wasn't close to Harley. Pete, unfortunately, was."

"I feel so awful I'm relieved it wasn't you. I don't know what I would have done if…" I shook my head and stared down at our joined hands.

"Right there's the reason why seeing you gave me hope. The fact you'd come to the emergency room and screamed my name when you saw me told me maybe, just maybe, you were ready to believe I love you."

Tears built in my eyes. When I blinked, they cascaded down my cheeks.

"And you were ready to admit you loved me, too," he added. "Because I've got this feeling you do, Maureen. Like I said, I know you. You'd never have let us be together if you didn't feel something for me. That thought's the only thing that's been keeping me sane this past week."

I swallowed the emotion clogging my throat and confessed what I should have given a voice to years ago. "I've loved you since I was eight years old," I whispered after a few moments.

He gripped my hands even tighter.

"I've never *not* loved you. Even when I was involved with Parker and you were married to Nora, I loved you."

"Why didn't you ever say anything?"

I shrugged and slid one of my hands free to swipe at my tears. "So many reasons. The age difference between us was a big one for years. Then, you were married and had a baby by the time I was a teenager."

"But what about after Nora and I split up?"

"By then, Eileen was sick, and I was terrified I was going to be too. Telling you I loved you, hoping we could be together wasn't fair to either of us if I was going to wind up dead."

He shook his head.

"And I know how stupid you think that sounds. My sisters and Nanny agree with you."

"They knew you never got tested?"

"No, they were in the dark about it, too. I told them after, well…" I swiped at my face again. "I guess they noticed something was going on with me, so they asked. Pressed, really. It all came out in a rush."

"I can't imagine they were happy about it, especially Fiona."

"Happy isn't the word I'd use, no."

For the first time his mouth lifted in a full smile.

"They made me promise to get tested. In fact, that's where I was when Cathy got the call about the shooting. She and Nanny went with me to the lab this morning to ensure I went through with it."

"And?"

"The results take a few days. One way or the other, I'll have a definitive answer soon. I either have the gene mutation, or I don't. There's no in between."

His eyes flickered for a second, then calmed again.

"I told them about…us, too."

His smile dimmed a bit. "How'd they take the news?"

"None of them were what I'd call surprised. Colleen even gloated, claiming she knew all along. She can be so annoying." I rolled my eyes and swiped at my now-drying cheeks. The moment I was done, he pulled my hand back into his.

"I have to tell you I'm glad they know. Keeping my hands off you whenever they were around was getting harder and harder. The night Robert walked in on us in the kitchen I was at my breaking point."

"Speaking of," I said, "how is he? Have you spoken with him since he went back home?"

"Every day. He feels awful about reacting the way he did, about being so rude to you."

"In his mind, he had cause to."

Lucas shifted until his leg bumped up against mine. He brought one of my hands up to his mouth and raked his lips against my knuckles. Every nerve in my body fired. That damn battalion of butterflies came to full-flap mode again in my stomach.

"After he calmed down, which took a few days, he started asking questions. A lot of them." He kissed my knuckles again, then drew my hand across his cheek. "I was honest and answered every one of them including the one where he asked if I loved you."

I swallowed when his eyes dilated and glistened in the dimmed lighting of my living room.

"When I told him I did, he asked me two things I didn't have an answer for."

"What?"

"First he wanted to know if you loved me back."

My heart was thumping so hard against my chest and those butterflies were beating nonstop, it was a wonder I didn't levitate off the couch from all the turbulence going on inside my body.

I swallowed again before I asked, "What did you tell him?"

"The truth. I thought you loved me, but since you hadn't said it yet, I wasn't sure." A smile pushed across his mouth.

"Why are you grinning?"

This time when he shifted it was to yank me up on his lap and keep me there by sliding his arms around my hips. My hands instinctively lifted to his shoulders.

"Because his response was to tell me how pathetic and lame I was for a guy of my age and experience. To quote my son, 'Geez, Dad, even I know when a girl likes me.' "

For the first time all evening, I smiled.

"There's nothing as humbling as being called out by a teenager." His sigh floated over me.

"What was the second thing you couldn't answer?"

His hands pressed against my lower back and pushed me in closer. I slid my hands around his neck.

"What I was gonna do about it if you did love me."

"What did you tell him?"

"Again, the truth is always best. I told him what I told you the other night. I want to marry you." He kissed my jaw. "Make a life with you." He moved up to the corner of my mouth, then worked his way down my neck.

It was difficult to take a full breath by the time his lips dragged across my collarbone.

"What-what did he say? Was he...angry or upset?"

"Just the opposite." He pulled back and lifted his hands to cup my cheeks. "His exact words were 'Go for it, Dad.' "

Tears built again and when one of them skidded free, Lucas caught it with his thumb.

"He loves you, Maureen. He considers you part of

our family already."

Humbled, I shook my head.

"Look at me." He ticked my chin up so I could. "Again, his exact words were 'She's the coolest person I know, and the nicest.' High praise from a fifteen-year-old."

"He's a wonderful boy, Lucas."

He laid his forehead against mine and let out a breath. "Despite having Nora and me for parents, he is." His hands slid up the sides of my hair and tugged the pencil holding my hair in place. It drifted down around us like a waterfall cascading down the side of a cliff.

Lucas clutched handfuls of it.

"Everything I told him was the truth, Maureen. I do love you. So much. When I was in the surgical waiting room, my mind kept drifting to you so I'd keep sane with the insanity all around me. How you look when you smile, the color of your eyes when you laugh, even how you look wearing nothing at all but all this hair splayed across a pillow."

Heat rushed up my cheeks.

"I simply can't imagine what my life would be like without you in it. If this past week has taught me anything, it's that I don't care if you and I have one more minute together or one hundred more years. As long as you're with me, nothing else matters. When it's real and right, you can't walk away. The results of the blood test won't change what I feel for you."

I placed my hand across his cheek.

"I know you're scared about what it's gonna say."

"Terrified."

He nodded. "But it makes no difference what the end result is, the one thing that *absolutely* will not change is how much I love you and want to be with you. Please believe me."

Nodding, I said, "I do. I really do. And I love you, too. More than I can ever describe."

I pressed my torso fully against his and kissed him with every emotion churning within me. I'd missed this man so much, missed his taste, his smile, missed…him.

"I missed you, too," he said with a grin, making me realize I'd said the words aloud. He pushed my hair back from my face again and hauled me in close for another kiss that left no doubt of the truth of his words.

Pretty soon just kissing him wasn't cutting it for me. I needed to see him naked.

In my bed.

In me.

"Come on." I slid off his lap, grabbed his hands, and tugged. The moment he was upright, he shifted our positions and the next thing I saw was his back from my upside down position over his shoulder. He had one hand on my butt, the other across the back of my knees to secure me in place.

"*Hey.*"

"My way's faster." He proved himself correct. In no time, he tossed me down on my bed and climbed in over me, both of us laughing like kids.

"I love this bed," Lucas said between kisses while we wriggled out of our clothes. "There's so much room to roll around in." The borrowed scrub top hit the floor by the doorway, my T-shirt and jeans following it. The bottom of the scrubs went next.

"Commando?" I asked as I raked a nail across his naked ass.

"The hospital could only provide so much." He

pushed me down flat on the bed, then dragged me to the edge by my ankles. With my legs draped over his shoulders, he slid his hands under my hips, lifted, and put his mouth on me.

"*Lucas.*"

"Have I ever told you how much hearing you scream my name turns me on?"

I was going to keep screaming it all night long if he kept doing what he was doing. His shoulders shook from laughter, once again proving I'd said the words out loud.

It didn't take long, though, before I lost the capacity to speak at all.

Or think.

All I could do was...feel, until a kaleidoscope of bright colors and shapes exploded behind my closed eyes as Lucas brought me to two back-to-back orgasms. Before the shockwaves ebbed, he sheathed himself and was inside me.

"Open your eyes, sweetheart," he whispered.

When I did, I almost came undone again from the wealth of love flying across his features. His moss-at-midnight eyes were almost black, and I swear smoke billowed from them as he stared down at me. One corner of his mouth was ticked up on lips kiss-slicked and swollen.

"I love you, Maureen." He rocked back and forth within me, each movement tender and yet so powerful. "I love you."

"I love you more."

Chapter 17

"There now, those sunflowers look grand, they do," Nanny said when she spied the bouquet on my counter. "Eileen did love her flowers."

"She loved the seeds more," both Cathy and Colleen said together.

My kitchen erupted in laughter.

" 'Tis a good day for a picnic," Nanny declared as she sipped her tea. "Have ya got everything ya need, lass?" she asked me.

"Almost. Lucas and Robert are bringing dessert."

"Are they, now? Well, I'm sure 'twill be delightful."

Something in her tone and the cagey way her eyes sparkled riled up my suspicion-senses.

My kitchen exploded with my family. Both sisters and their husbands, the babies, Nanny, and even Georgie were all packed around my table. The twins were asleep in their carriers, and Mac held his excited puppy to try and keep her from running around the room.

After much thought, my sisters and I had planned a family picnic out at the cemetery to honor Eileen. Commemorating the day of her death seemed wrong, so we'd decided to honor her life, instead.

Of course, I'd planned the food.

Cathleen had been in charge of bringing the

flowers.

Colleen had a bouquet of balloons in her car we were going to let go into the air once we were all at Eileen's plot.

The Alexander men were the only ones needed, and then we would caravan off to the cemetery.

"The mail's here." Sarah handed it all to me. "You all have a wonderful picnic," she said, smiling. To me she added, "I'll hold down the fort, no worries."

"Never had one," I said as I flipped through each letter. Halfway through I stopped. You know the feeling you get when you're about to faint? Noises around you become dim and you start to hear faint echoes? Your sight zeros in on everything right in front of you, cutting off your peripheral vision? Smells become potent, and you can feel your heart and breath quickening?

Holding the envelope with my name typed across it and the return address of the lab made all those things happen to me.

"Lass? What's wrong? You've gone bone-white, ya have."

Leave it to Nanny to be the most astute one in any room.

Cathy and Colleen echoed her question with each of them coming to grab one of my arms.

"What happened?" Colleen asked. "Nanny's right. You've lost all your color. Mo?"

"Your entire body's shaking." Cathy ran a soothing hand down my back.

Lucas and his son walked into this scene.

"Hey," Lucas greeted from the doorway. The sound of his voice, deep and calm, washed over me and allowed me to take a full breath.

"What's going on?" Lucas marched straight to me and when my sisters stood back, he handed a box off to Cathy, then wound his now-free hands around my arms. "Maureen?"

Eyebrows almost kissing over eyes drenched with concern, he pulled me against him. The mail slid from my hands, all except the letter from the lab.

"What happened?" He repeated his question to the room.

"We don't know," from Slade. His words were echoed by everyone else in my family, all except Nanny, who—as proven true so many times—was the most aware and perceptive person in any room.

"I think the letter she's clutchin' in her hands like a starving man holdin' on to the last scrap of bone is the reason."

Lucas pushed me away from him, his gaze dropping to the now-crumpled piece of mail I held, then back up to my face. "Are those your test results?"

I was able to give him one spastic nod.

Lucas did the same. He glanced over his shoulder at his son. I'd forgotten he was even in the room. It was the first time I'd seen him since he'd stormed out of my kitchen two weeks ago. He was holding a large white box, and when Lucas ticked his head at him, Robert returned the gesture.

Turning back to me, Lucas laid one of his hands over the letter I had clasped against my chest.

"Do me a favor and wait a few minutes to open it, okay? I've got something I need to do first."

I didn't bother telling him I had no intention of opening the letter. Fear wouldn't allow me to.

"I was going to do this out at the cemetery. It seemed fitting since your entire family was present, but I think I need to do it now before you read those results."

Confusion doused me. "Do what?"

Lucas took a breath and swallowed.

"Lucas?"

"Just give me a sec." He shook his head and swiped at the subtle sweat that had sprouted over his eyes.

"Dad. Don't be lame."

Robert's teenaged rebuke had one corner of Lucas's mouth tripping up.

He huffed in another breath. "Like I said, I wanted to wait until we were all out visiting Eileen so she could hear this, too, but…"

From the corner of my eye, I spotted Robert handing something from the box to everyone in the room.

"Maureen," Lucas said, "it's no secret how I feel about you. I love you with everything in me. Not a day has gone by in too long to remember where I didn't wake up with you as my first thought or go to sleep with your face as my last. You center me, calm me, make me feel as if I can do anything and face any challenge. There simply is no me without you."

Colleen's sigh drifted around the kitchen as tears pushed their way down my cheeks.

"I told you I wanted to marry you and then just assumed you would. My intelligent son"—he slid the boy a side glance—"is the one who pointed out I needed to ask you, not tell you."

"Lucas." I was barely able to whisper his name.

"Now, I could get down on one knee and do this the old-fashioned way if you want," he said, pained laughter pulling on his face, "but I know you'd probably scream at me to get up off the floor."

"No lie, there," Cathy mumbled with a sniff.

"So…" He reached out, and she handed him back the box he'd given to her. He opened it with the interior first facing him. Then he turned the box around so I could see inside it.

My gasp was the only sound in the room.

Nestled together were five white frosted cupcakes. Each had one word written in script across the top of it in green icing.

Marry. Me. Yes. Yes. No.

"You can thank Robert for the decorating. He paid attention to everything you taught him and helped me put this together."

The boy stood next to Nanny, a cupcake in his hand. In fact, everyone in the room held one.

"Maureen Angela O'Dowd, you have my heart, my soul, and every part of me that you want. Will you have my name, too? Will you—and just so we're all clear on this"—he glanced around the room—"I'm asking, not telling—marry me? Make a life and a home with me? Be mine just like I'm yours? Forever?"

As the tears continued their freefall down my face, I asked, "Why are there two *Yes* cupcakes?"

Lucas nodded at the group across from us, who all raised what they held in their hands: six identical *Yes* cakes.

"That one"—Lucas thrust his chin at the box—"is how I figure Eileen would have voted."

"You all knew he was going to do this?"

Before they could answer, Lucas did it for them. "I was leveraging the yes votes so you couldn't say no. And speaking of, I still haven't heard an answer."

Those rare nerves broadcast themselves again. Head tilted to one side, eyes slightly narrowed, and with the corner of his mouth clamped between his teeth, he truly was concerned about my response.

But I still held that damn envelope in my hands.

As if reading my mind, Lucas said, "I want your answer before you open it, Maureen."

"But we don't know what it says—"

"And I've told you I don't care. Nothing in there is going to change anything. I want you to be mine. If it's for the next hundred years or the next five minutes, I don't care. And those results don't matter to me."

This time it was Nanny's sigh echoing around us.

"I've misjudged you so much, lad," she said. She swiped one of her arthritic fingers under her eyes. "Seal the deal, now, darlin' boy. Me old heart can't take much more of this suspense."

"What does she mean?" I asked.

He palmed the box in one hand, then slipped the other into his pocket. When he brought it back out, it was clenched. "Just as a point of record and because I know you so well, I asked your grandmother's permission before I put this all together."

If it was possible for a heart to swell with love, mine grew right then and there.

"Knowing how she feels about me—"

"Felt, lad. Past tense. You've proven your worth, ya have."

Lucas smiled and shook his head. "Okay, *felt* about me, I wanted her to understand just how much you mean to me and how I wanted us to be together for the rest of our lives. She gave me this, hoping to influence your decision in my favor. Her exact words were 'Just in case she's on the fence about ya.' " He rolled his eyes. Then he opened his hand.

I gasped.

"*Nanny.*"

"Of the four o' ya," she said, "you were the one who always loved that ring, lass. When you were a wee one, you'd ask me if ya could wear it around the house. Ya held it up on your finger, modelin' it for all to see. Thought ya were the Queen o' Sheba, ya did."

"And you always let me." I had to swipe my hand across my wet eyes so I could see the ring clearly. "This was the engagement ring Grandpa gave you. The one you had blessed by the Pope."

A sigh broke from her. "The man had good taste in jewelry, to be sure."

"Women, too," Mac said, winking at her.

"You're still me favorite," she stage-whispered at him.

Lucas rolled his eyes again, then held the ring up in one hand by the band, the box of cupcakes still in the other. "So before your grandmother expires from suspense or I stress-sweat to an early death, I need an answer, Maureen. What do you say?" He took a step closer, and I tipped my head back so I could still look him in the eyes. "Will you join your heart to mine, walk hand in hand with me through the good and the bad? Will you marry me?"

He'd tilted his head again, his gaze intense and piercing. Then, he tossed me the cocky, slightly wicked grin that made the butterflies in my stomach come to attention. With a quick head cock to the people around the room, he said, "If it's any consideration, they all think you should."

He'd leveraged his bets, all right. Lucas knew just how to play to a person's weak spot. For me it was, and always had been, my family.

My sisters stared me down with expectant expressions on their faces from across the room, each holding their cupcake up to me so I could read their response, their husbands doing the same. Robert stood next to Nanny's chair, his cupcake pointed at me, too.

Nanny herself, eyes twinkling from the afternoon sun shining through the windows, held her cupcake up to her lips and, with one eyebrow raised toward me and a devilish smirk crossing her face, licked a bit of the frosting from the side.

"Maureen?"

The smile was still on his face, but Lucas really was sweating. The fact the man who was always the calmest, most controlled and focused of anyone in a room or a situation, was anxious about my answer sent such a surge of power through me, I shuddered.

"Answer the man, lass. And answer from your heart, not that overthinking brain o' yours."

There's a blessing having someone who always speaks their mind and who knows you inside and out, in your corner.

With my gaze glued to his, I reached into the box of cupcakes and pulled one out. I held it up to show him, then did the same to my family.

The room erupted, the noise jarring the babies in their sleep and making Georgie bark and squirm against Mac's hold.

Robert took the box from his father as Lucas grabbed my hand and slid the ring on it while I took a big bite of the *Yes* cupcake. Lucas yanked me against him and kissed my frosting-covered mouth, the both of us laughing.

Whoops, cheers, puppy barks, and one moaned, "Geez, Dad, let her breathe," surrounded us.

When we came up for air, Lucas hugged me so hard that when he lifted me I fell out of my flip-flops.

"So there's no argument or discussion about this in the future," Cathy said, the first to hug and congratulate us, "I'm marrying you."

"And I'm planning everything," Colleen added, wrapping her arms around both of us. "You won't have to do anything. Not even cook. We'll get it catered."

"I'll play for your wedding, lass," Nanny added, not to be outdone. "Anything ya want, as long as it's romantic."

I looked at each of these three women who had tears in their eyes and joy on their faces.

"Do I have any say at all?" I asked, then fisted my hands on my hips. It was then I realized I was still holding the lab letter.

"Let's wait until after we visit Eileen," Lucas said, taking the letter from my hand.

"No." I took it back. "I want to know now. I…need…to know. Now."

For a long moment, he held my gaze. Then, he nodded. "We do it together, then. You're not opening that without me."

"Or me," my sisters each echoed.

When Nanny stayed silent, we all shifted our attention to her. She was calmly nibbling on her cupcake, looking as if she didn't have a care in the world.

"I don't give a fiddler's fart when you open it, lass, or who's present when ya do. I already know what it says."

"How?"

"Nanny, what have you done?" Colleen asked.

"Or who have you bribed?" Cathy added.

She tossed them a stink eye, then turned to me.

With pursed lips and an eye roll I was a little jealous of because it was much more expressive than mine could ever be, she said, "I'll answer your question, lass, since you seem to be the only one of me granddaughters who trusts me."

"That's open for interpretation," I said.

She clicked her tongue and finished off her cupcake. "I've done nothing, bribed no one," she said once she'd swallowed. "And for the record, I don't know *exactly* what's in the envelope. But I have faith, a whole lotta faith, something you all should have more of, by the by, that the results are negative." Her striking blue eyes settled on me and softened. "You're not leaving this earth anytime soon, darlin' girl. I feel it, here." She pressed a fist to her heart.

"I wish I had your conviction, Nanny," I told her.

"Ah, well, lass. If it's wishes we're sharing, I'd like to be thirty again, touring the world, and flirtin' with the likes of royalty. But if I were, I wouldn't have you three in me life. So, let's not be wasting our time with wishes and find out for sure, eh?"

"Maureen?" Lucas wound a hand around my arm and squeezed. "What do you want to do?"

After a moment spent getting lost in the love in his

eyes, I tore the letter open. The room went silent as I read down to the first paragraph. The first line was all I got through, though. The word *negative* jumped out at me, and I dropped the paper to the ground and flung myself into Lucas's waiting arms.

****

Two months later

"You know, your cookie jar's empty again," Lucas declared as sat back on the couch and nestled me under his arm. "Robert made mention of it when he was here over the weekend. I realized he was right. What gives? That thing always used to be full."

I snuggled in closer and draped one of my legs over his thigh. "I've been sleeping better," I said, nuzzling the space under his ear I loved so much. "I'm not up at all hours baking, anymore. Baking used to be my insomnia cure."

"And what? Now I am?"

"Yup."

In truth, I'd slept through every night since Lucas had all but moved in with me a week after his proposal.

With the test results no longer looming over my head like a noose waiting to choke the life from me, we'd all caravanned to the cemetery and celebrated Eileen. Afterward, Lucas had driven Robert home and then spent the night—and every other night—in my bed. The news he was getting remarried had sparked his grouchy father to reluctantly agree to move into Angelica Arms. Currently, Nanny was helping Hogan get adjusted to his new life. Lucas's house was on the market, and his clothes now hung in my closet.

I figured I'd get some pushback from Nanny about the two of us *living in sin*, but to the astonishment of us all, she hadn't said boo about it. Lucas hadn't wanted a long engagement, telling everyone since he'd finally gotten me to say yes, he wanted to sign the license before I chickened out.

As if.

The wedding was a week away, and as promised, I hadn't done a thing except give an opinion here and there. Colleen, despite having two colicky newborns, had planned everything with the military precision her brides had come to depend on. Since now I could count myself as one of that elite group, I understood why she was so popular and booked solid for fifty weeks a year.

"I cured your insomnia?" Lucas said, tugging me up onto his lap, his hands settled over my hips.

"If I could bottle you as a sleep aid, we'd be gazillionaires." I splayed my hands over his shoulders. The diamond sitting on my finger winked back at me. "Honestly, I haven't slept this well in forever. Knowing you're next to me every night helps my brain to quiet down and allows me to sleep."

"So all the *exercise* we've been getting in that bed isn't what's cured you?"

I laughed. "While it's true all the *exercise* has exhausted my body, it's my brain that has never been able to shut down or calm before now." I lifted a shoulder. "I was up most nights worrying about the inn, paying bills, my family. Having you right there next to me must subconsciously let me realize everything is okay. Or will be. I'm safe and protected. Loved."

"Loved, you are." He pressed a gentle kiss on my mouth, then nuzzled my nose.

"You've got a look on your face that means you're thinking about something." Lucas trailed his lips down the column of my neck. "Care to share?"

Little frissons of pleasure shot down my spine from the sensation of his evening scruff rasping across my skin. I tilted my head to give him even better access, and God bless the man, he took it.

"It's just amazing to me how much my life has changed in the past few months. All of our lives, actually. Cathy and Colleen are married to men I adore because they love my sisters so much. One has twins, the other is due to pop soon. Nanny is staying put in the Arms, and now your dad is there, too."

I slid down and rested my head against his shoulder.

"The construction's started on the expansion; it's going well and moving fast. Come the spring, I'll be able to offer the bungalows for stays. I finally got tested after wasting so much time worrying about the results. Robert is doing well, and we're getting married in a week. So much change in so short a time."

Lucas was silent for a moment. I felt his neck shift as he swallowed, the tiny pulse of air blowing from him loud against my ear. "Is it too much change for you?"

The concern in his tone made me sit back up so I could look at him. Eyebrows beetled, the groove between his eyes deep, the worry I'd heard was evident.

"I mean, I realize I'm the major cause of your life turning upside down," he said, the corners of his lips pressing tightly together. "I moved in here as soon as you said yes to getting married. I didn't really give you any time to process what was happening or going to happen in our lives. I just steamrolled right in. Is it…too much for you? Too quick?"

I didn't think it was possible to love this man any

more than I already did, but I was wrong.

I kissed the tip of his nose, as he was wont to do to me, and smiled. "Lucas, nothing has been too much for me to take in," I added. "I love that you've decided to live here instead of keeping your house. It makes running the inn easier if I'm on site all the time. That you'd give up your home, the one you were raised in, to be here with me is simply mind-boggling. And heartwarming. I'm grateful you're being so considerate."

"Consideration's got nothing to do with it. The house was just a house, filled with some good memories but mostly bad ones. Your life is here, and I want to be where you are." He shrugged. "It was no hardship at all to leave it, believe me."

"Still, it was your home for most of your life."

"My home is wherever you are."

Honestly, I loved him more minute to minute.

"Just so we're clear," I said, clearing my throat of the emotion backing up in it, "I wasn't complaining, and I'm not worried about anything. Well"—I rolled my eyes—"I'm a little concerned about Colleen's *vision* for the wedding since she won't let me know what, exactly, it is. But aside from that, I'm worry-free."

"Really?"

I squinted at him. "Where's this…uncertainty coming from? Your life has changed, too, you know. You're basically working two jobs since Pete is still in recovery mode. Your hours are longer, and I know you've been worried about your dad adjusting to the nursing home life. Plus the upcoming wedding. Has it all been too much for you, maybe? Are *you* having second thoughts?"

His face cleared when he shook his head. "I've never been so certain of anything in my life, than I am of marrying you." He kissed me, hard and quick. "Yes, my life has changed, but it's only been for the better. Dad's gonna be unhappy no matter where he is, but at least at the Arms, I know he's got three hots and a cot every day and is safe in case anything happens to him, medically. As soon as Pete gets off desk duty and is out in the field again, things will lighten up a bit, I can take a break, and we can get away for a while. Just the two of us."

In one easy move, he rose with my butt cradled in his arms.

"The only second thought I've ever had is why I waited so long to tell you how much I love you. We could have cured your insomnia years ago if I'd moved sooner."

Both of us laughing, we fell onto my bed.

Resting side by side, Lucas trailed a finger from my temple down to my chin, tipped it up, then kissed me.

"I love you, Maureen."

"I love you, too. So much."

"That's all I need, then. You're all I need. Now and forever."

Yup, it was true: my love for him continued to grow, now, second by second.

"So whadda ya say we"—he shifted until he was nestled on top of me—"make sure you get a good night's sleep tonight? I'd feel awful if your insomnia came back." He wiggled his eyebrows and grinned at me like *the devil himself*, to quote Nanny.

"Even if it meant you still wouldn't have any fresh cookies tomorrow?"

"Well, a man can't live by cookies, alone." His mouth crushed down on my laughing lips.

I slept really well that night.

And every night thereafter…

Maureen's Insomnia Sugar Cookies
Makes 24 cookies

Ingredients:
   2 3/4 cups all-purpose white flour
   1 tsp baking soda
   1/2 tsp baking powder
   1/2 tsp salt
   1 cup unsalted butter, room temp, cut into squares
   1 cup + 2 Tbsp white granulated sugar
   2 Tbsp light brown sugar
   1 large egg
   2 tsp pure vanilla extract
   1/4 cup white granulated sugar (for rolling)

Directions:
   Preheat oven to 350°F. Line baking sheets with parchment paper.

   Sift dry ingredients, flour, baking soda, baking powder, and salt, into a medium-sized bowl and set aside.

   Cream the butter and both sugars together in a large mixing bowl on medium speed until light in color and fluffy.

   Add the egg and mix until well combined.

   Add the vanilla extract and mix until well combined.

   Add the dry ingredients 1 cup at a time and mix until the dough is well formed. Do not overmix.

   Using a tablespoon-sized scoop, scoop cookie dough into individual pieces. Gently roll each into a ball with your hands, then roll each ball in white sugar to coat.

Put the balls on the baking sheet 2 inches apart. Cookies will spread once they heat, and you want them to have room to do so without touching one another.

Bake cookies for 7-10 minutes, but do not overbake. Remove just before the edges begin to turn golden.

Remove from the oven and allow to cool on a baking rack for at least 10 minutes.

Enjoy!

A word about the author...

Peggy Jaeger writes about strong women, the families who support them, and the men who can't live without them. When she isn't writing, you can find her cooking or reading.

She loves to hear from readers on her website:
PeggyJaeger.com
and on her Facebook page:
https://www.facebook.com/pages/
Peggy-Jaeger-Author/825914814095072?
ref=bookmarks http://peggyjaeger.com

CPSIA information can be obtained
at www.ICGtesting.com
Printed in the USA
LVHW080009220721
693377LV00013B/746